WESTLEY JAMES

Loverboy Butch

Cover art by Sabira Langevin

First edition

ISBN: 979-8-9993858-0-2

This book was professionally typeset on Reedsy.
Find out more at reedsy.com

For all the people who told me stories. Each one stuck close to my heart and proved that a million more were waiting to be let out.

And for a past version of me, the one that really needed an escape. You got it eventually.

Contents

'She would have made such a lovely bride. What a shame she's fucked in the head.'
- Taylor Swift, Champagne Problems

A Note on the Text

This book is written in British English, so please anticipate the odd u, s or e where you might not expect it! Some words might look incorrect, but I swear to you that they aren't. Please do not report them as such. There are also several words specific to the region the story is set in, which I have attempted to make clear through context clues. Thank you!

I have chosen to mention a protagonist's dead name in the text on a few occasions. There is no transphobic rhetoric; rather, it is meant to reflect the reality of being in the midst of socially transitioning. If this will trigger or upset you in any way, please be wary when reading chapters nineteen and twenty-eight.

Chapter One

Dex

I am trained to lean into the fall.

It's second nature, survival instinct.

I close my eyes, breathe, and let go.

The glass tiles crunch under the weight of my wheels, rough and stickier than the other pools I've dropped into. It's a steep curve, sending me rushing toward the bottom, gravity taking control. I do what I'm best at. I lean into the fall, go with the flow of gravity and all but run off my board to avoid smashing into the other side of the empty swimming pool.

Above me, cheers go up. People I barely know applauding my reckless bravery from the safety of the patio.

I grin at them, squinting up into the bright afternoon sun and tossing a careless wink at Amber before turning back to watch Hawa.

She rides, as always, like a pro. Taking the fall with all the grace of a ballerina and emerging dignified and still on her board at the base. I sweep her up into a hug, sharing the waves of freedom radiating off us like steam from a frying pan.

It's the sort of feeling that can't be distilled down into

1

words. An ecstatic, ineffable human stupidity that cannot be replicated on command. The closest I've ever come to manufacturing it is falling in love. That effervescent, smile-inducing high you get when you're in the moment with someone. The thrum of energy beneath your skin as they brush their hand against yours or make eye contact across a room. It might sound ridiculous to say, but dropping in and falling in love are remarkably similar—a passing fullness that leaves you winded and giddy with your heart racing.

Maybe that's the common factor—the rush of the fall.

I'm good at falling, be it off a skateboard or in love. It's pretty much my area of expertise.

Hawa pats me on the back. A feeling so familiar to me that I know it means both, *get the fuck off me* and *nice one* wrapped into one succinct non-verbal message. Our impromptu display is over; no more showboating for this trip.

I am incredibly flattered to be brought along, as a connection twice removed from the initial invitee, my free Hamptons holiday has been miraculous. It ending with a suspiciously convenient drained pool and a captive audience in Amber's house is just the tip of my lucky iceberg.

It has been kind of beautiful in its own way. A bunch of veritable strangers dragged along to fill out spare rooms in a house twice the size of anything built in my home town.

I sort of stumbled into my invite. I've been crashing with Hawa in Bed-Sty for the last month, waiting for inspiration to hit me, and one of her partner's friends is dating a child star. We were all invited to a very fancy picnic with a bunch of very famous people, all of whom I was too starstruck to speak to, and, before I knew it, Hawa and I were being offered spare beds in a Hamptons house.

Since arriving, it's been clear that the incredibly generous woman who owns the house was just trying to set me up with her partner's daughter. A very sweet, very pretty and incredibly hyper-sexual girl named Amber. If I'm being honest, that last part freaks me out as much as it has benefited me.

Overall, it's been a good three weeks.

I can feel it coming to a close, though. I'm getting that familiar fidgety hunger for something else. I've seen sandy beaches, drunk rich people's wine and lounged in teal water too clear to be real.

So, as I follow Hawa up the steps and pick up my phone from the table where it's been baking in the sun, the email that greets me feels like a sign. A beacon summoning me home, back to the life I fled from.

When brides run away in media, they're always galloping at top speed astride a dappled grey horse, a storm of two beautiful manes whipping in the wind. Or they hop into a taxi and ask the cabby to take them as far away from the city as possible, bartering their unwanted ring for the price of the fare.

I wasn't like that. For starters, I was probably more of a groom than a bride, and my white dress was caked in mud from the spring weather.

It rained that morning, but it stopped drizzling right as I got my hair and makeup done. In fact, after that brief shower, the whole day was brilliant sunshine and inclining temperatures. Supposedly, that's also an auspicious sign if you ask my maternal grandmother. I can't say I agree, given that I never made it down the aisle.

Nothing felt auspicious at the time. I was too focused on

my laboured breathing, breaths coming in short and sharp. The delicate clasps at my back were pulling too tightly on my spine, the deeper I tried to inhale. The arched waist of the satin cut into the soft skin of my ribs. The pins in my hair put pressure on an already fragile skull. Being a bride was the opposite of that wild freedom I feel on a skateboard when I drop-in. It was a cage.

I was going to die there, red-painted lips parted, perfectly styled locks tumbling gently toward the floor like a modern Snow White. I was sure of it.

I would die in that dress, and the only thing anyone would remark on would be how beautiful I looked as I did it. A lovely, broken bride.

I had been told my whole life that I was meant to want this. That it ought to be my special day. It didn't matter that every stage of wedding preparation inched me closer to flinging myself off the end of the pier, that dresses made my limbs awkward or that the word bride gave me acid reflux. I knew this was how I made things easier for everyone else.

A miserable woman is better than a happy trans person. At least, that's the message you receive subliminally. I knew I wasn't a man, so I had always been told my discomfort with femininity was just unprocessed internalised misogyny. I pushed it down, slapped some more makeup on the problem and waited for the dread to abate.

If I killed myself to be beautiful, they could all process their grief the proper way. People would mourn the little girl they'd lost and look back on me fondly. But if I opted to be me, I would become both victim and killer. Every time people wanted to cry about their lost baby girl, they'd be forced to confront the newer, happier me, still alive and inhabiting her body. If I wanted to do the right thing for myself, I'd have to accept both roles and hope my family forgave me.

That left me with two options: I could stick around and suffer through my family coming to terms with the new me, or I could give them space to grieve the bride I might have been.

Outside, the sky shifted, rain and sun creating the subtle start of a rainbow.

I knew what I had to do. I would go away, give people time to process this without me around to remind them of the daughter I'd robbed them of.

I just had to get away from my wedding first.

Usually, the runaway bride has a friend, someone who offers them an out. An accomplice. I didn't have any of those anymore. The person waiting for me on the other side of the altar made sure of that. All my friends were *our* friends. My whole life, my opinions, my clothes, my home; we shared it all. She called my parents mum and dad. She once cried when I referred to my brother's daughter as my niece rather than our niece. I gave her my heart, and she'd used it to take ownership of my very existence. Worse still, I let her.

Around me, bridesmaids fussed. Mutual university friends that I wasn't sure even knew my middle name, toasting to my supposed happiness while I silently fell to pieces.

Only one person remained immune to the wedding buzz.

In the corner of the room, failing to mingle or assimilate, Dean sat rigid. Her discomfort was more than fair; when I picked her, I thought things would be awkward, and they were. I was told she was a bad influence, someone who didn't care about me. Like an idiot, I listened and cut her out...until I was one bridesmaid short.

There was no fight when our friendship died. We just let it fade away like it wasn't the lynchpin of our worlds for years. The only time we even vaguely touched on the topic, Dean told me it would be nice if I gained an ounce of autonomy. I laughed like it stung rather than branded me.

But, miserable in a beautiful dress, I regained my autonomy.

Staring out the window, holding back from a full-scale panic attack, I surpassed an ounce and went for a motherfucking ton.

I wasn't half of someone else. I was me, a whole, unhappy person. Capable of joy without anyone else's involvement. That couldn't be signed away so carelessly.

It was as if Dean felt me coming back. She stood, her eyes locking with mine for just a fraction of a second before she used that eldest daughter's voice to clear the room. She told them something I don't remember, maybe that I needed the bathroom or a moment of girl talk before the big walk, and helped me pop the sash window wide enough to get my hips through before I bolted away from her, the grand manor someone else picked out, and the home town I didn't know how to be me in.

I told you, I'm good at falling in love. I'm not very good at staying in it.

Chapter Two

Dean

My mum has the kind of friendship women dream of—Sitcom-level best friend experience.

Sabina and Serena. Matching names. Birthdays exactly nine months apart. Perfectly paired in every way.

They met at a uni orientation day, idly wandering around the Exeter campus, each dissected from their respective groups. Serena had bailed, already bored with the regimented itinerary of the day, while my mother got herself lost, head in the clouds unable to keep up. I'd love to know what she was focusing on, probably the certain slant of light as it glimmered through the trees or a deep philosophical take on age that she'd eventually craft into some painstakingly beautiful modern-day parable. As it is, I just know that they ran headfirst into each other. Serena probably swore a lot; she says she did anyway, and I'm inclined to agree with those chances. Mum apologised profusely, and all was forgiven. Serena's like that, easy to anger, easy to forgive. Mum offered her a hand up, Serena accepted, and in turn, offered her an accomplice for the day. The rest is pretty much history.

They were inseparable, even with Mum in the English department and Serena in History. They went on to live together in their second and third year, and both moved to London after they graduated, got a shitty little bedsit somewhere outside Richmond and took drunken walks in the deer park. By all accounts, my mum was easy to find love, and Serena was far too busy for it. When Mum moved out every six months with a new bloke, Serena kept her name on the lease for when it inevitably fell apart. Which it always did.

They stayed that way, in their Sex and the City years, as Serena calls it, dating, drinking, giggling together, and sharing a bed with each other more often than any man. Living in this perfect little feminist bubble, blissfully man-free.

Until Serena found someone she did care about more than her studies and followed him down to the south coast, a shitty little seaside city, with stunning views.

Kyle was a widower with a house, three sons and a whole life that didn't include girls' nights. Serena could just slot right in. But there was no room for a clingy, flighty best friend of the step-mum.

Mum says this was her dark night of the soul, lost and alone in London. I don't have any interest in hearing about the men she slept with or the drugs she took, so I pretty much always tune this part out until she gave up the bedsit. I know she spent a while in Donegal, somewhere in Greece, and then a handful of random European countries; I don't remember the names. Although Mum tells this story like she lived in squalor, I've been told that my grandparents funded the whole thing, under one condition: she visited her grandparents back in Dhaka. And, because she's not a fucking moron, she agreed.

If you ask her, there was an identity crisis moment here,

where she considered getting married to some family friend because settling down sounded nice. She panicked about it for a while until she called Serena, who told her she would support whatever she did, but she should come home first and feel like her best self before she made that decision. Pretty solid advice, ironically.

Back in the UK, sleeping in Serena and Kyle's guest bedroom, Mum weighed up her options. She listened to the couple talk ad nauseam, saw how in love they were and felt terrified where that would leave her. One fateful night, they went for dinner with his best friend, a big fancy thing that ended in a beautiful beach walk. Kyle popped the question, the one mum claims everyone else saw coming, and she got so wasted in the resulting celebration that she slept with his best friend. It must have been alright because they kept it up for a few months, right up until the time she realised she'd missed her period. Now, in typical, perfect girl friend fashion, Sabina and Serena had always been perfectly periodically in sync. So she'd never had to worry before because there had always been someone else there to remind her if it was delayed. Not that day and not for the next nine months.

Because, of course. Two perfectly in sync periods for the two perfect girls.

A shock firstborn for my parents, who thought they ought to give the relationship thing a whirl and a surprise youngest baby for the couple who thought their family was already big enough.

I can skip some chapters here because I'm sure you see where it's going. Dex and I were born a month apart, me the youngest of my year, them the oldest of theirs. We spent every spare second together at weekends, holidays, and after-school activities. They stayed outside and held my hand for the birth of my younger sisters, helped me babysit, and offered to do my chores in exchange for 'help' with their homework.

They were perfectly positioned to be my Serena. My perfect match.

I remember the way they cried when I finished year six and prepared to head up to high school, thick snotty sobs onto my summer dress at the thought of being left behind. Honestly, I can't remember if I cried, but I know I wanted to.

Being without Dex felt like being without a limb; I reached for them so easily and read their reactions when I needed to reel in my anger. We survived, though, and then they joined my side in big school, right up until university. I was leaving them again, excited to head off in our parents' footsteps. We had it all planned out, I'd go to Exeter, just like our mums and then in my second year, Dex would join me there. We'd live together. Except they never came, never even applied as far as I can tell.

Dex met a girl. Dex was always meeting girls, but Khloe was different. I fucking hated Khloe. But they loved her, fell in love and followed her right into the local Uni. They sort of stopped visiting then. I sort of stopped texting. And that looked like it was it. I only ever heard about them through Serena and Mum, apparently both oblivious to the gut-wrenching way our friendship had died out.

No one told me about the engagement. I saw the pictures on Instagram later and tried to be happy for them.

Not that it matters now, I guess.

I don't know what I expected; maybe that things would go back to the way they were after the incident. Or that I'd get some recognition for stepping in and rescuing them from a terrible marriage. In my head, I was a hero, doing what needed to be done, popping that sash window wide and saving them from an impending panic attack. I still feel like a hero for that, actually.

Offering Dex another future. Like Serena had done for my mum all those years ago. It was the right thing to do.

But not everyone saw it that way. In actuality, the wedding attendees were pretty pissed. There were a lot of details I hadn't considered, like the wasted money on the venue and the party, or the second bride who had to be told there would be no more wedding.

I took so much shit for that day, and Dex never came back to share it. Now they jet off all over the globe, sending the parents postcards like nothing happened, and I still get death glares whenever it's mentioned. Like I didn't free them from potential hell.

That's on my mind as I send the e-vite.

Dex and their stupid fucking trips. Dex and their responsibility-free life. Dex and their total lack of family loyalty.

Dex, always somewhere in the back of my brain.

I've been planning it for a few weeks now. Secretly scheming, a subtle revenge against them as a way to soothe myself on sleepless nights. Maybe that makes me sound bonkers, but I deserve an outlet for the resentment I've been holding onto. While Dex has been flown across the globe on expenses-paid trips by skateboarding sponsors, I've been stuck here, supporting our families, working a real job, watching our parents get older and preparing for the future. Just once, I want them to feel the repercussions of their running away. I wanted people to admit that they are a coward.

So, I send an e-vite to fuck them off. So they can't say they moved and never got it, so there is a digital trail, breadcrumbs back to their inevitable no. Just so I can point and say *See, I told you they don't care about us*, when they turn down attending their own mother's sixtieth birthday trip.

It's all meticulously planned out, my little victory dance, the smooth way I will hand over tissues as Serena cries about her precious baby never coming home, the praise I will lap up from my parents at my generosity. Oh, the sweet, sweet feeling of vindication. *They never cared about us.* Soon, everyone will see it. Oh, I can't wait to be proven right. At this point, the idea is a bright spot in my otherwise mundane month. The highlight of my sodding year.

Even as I click away from my spreadsheet and into the email, I can feel it; the oncoming waves of joy radiating over me like-

Fuck.

There, with no capitalised letters, 'sent from my iPhone' still attached underneath, are the words: *see ya there.*

Chapter Three

Dex

Do I have a plan? No. Do I know what I'll do when I get home? Nope. Have I thought through any of the details? Nah, not really.

All of this is abundantly clear as I wheedle past the airport crowds, through slow-moving security lines, towards the bathroom. The flight was eight hours, with an added two hours taxiing on the tarmac, which means I've long since missed the train I was planning to get. If I'm gonna be stuck in an airport, Heathrow's not a bad one, all things considered, but it's eleven on a Tuesday morning, I have next-to-no money and no route home.

It was supposed to be a surprise, my arrival back at the house. I thought it might ease the blow that I returned without a physical present for Mum's birthday, but it's looking more like I might end up unceremoniously calling her for a lift.

Less a triumphant return and more the stumbled entrance of the family fool.

Way to stay consistent, Dexy.

I wish I could say that my ineptitude is surprising, but

honestly, it's pretty in keeping with my brain at the moment. So, as I rummage in my hand luggage for another t-shirt to wriggle into, I resign myself to a less-than-stellar plan B.

Parker picks up on the third ring, the unmistakable sound of guns and yelling in the distance telling me he's not at work.

'Didn't expect to hear from you,' is all the answer I get.

I probably deserve it, given I haven't seen him in person since the almost-wedding and only call on special occasions. I've sent gifts and random mementoes that remind me of my siblings, picked up in each new city or country, and always something bigger for a birthday or holiday, but even I know that's not exactly quality sibling behaviour.

I called Parker because, of my three elder siblings, he's most likely to have the time in his day to pick me up. Archer and Liam both have full-time jobs and kids, and the general responsibilities that come with life around forty. Parker, on the other hand, well, he's a different kind of adult. He works for Archer and Dad but opts to take the evening shifts. For the best part of the last decade, Park has spent his days waking up at twelve, playing video games until four and heading to work late.

'I kinda need a favour,' I push on, hoping not to sound like a complete pillock.

'If you need money, Poppy and Liam are probably better-'

'I need a lift.'

'A lift?'

'From Heathrow.'

'You're back home?'

'Not quite.'

'So, how long do we have you for?' He says, his tone needling.

14

'I got stuck, missed my train, I've got no way to get home.' And then I add, for good measure. 'I don't know how long I'm staying.'

There's a noise on the other end of the line, a gruff hum of acknowledgement and then the unmistakable grumblings of a man over thirty turning off the TV and begrudgingly getting off the sofa.

'You owe me the best of whatever American crap you brought home, got it?'

I say a silent prayer to a god I've never believed in and drop my bags on the ground. 'First pick goes to you before any of the nieces or nephews. Pop Tarts and pickle crisps are all yours so long as you pick me up before it gets dark.'

'Too bloody right it does.' He mumbles. 'Hang tight, I'll be there in a couple of hours.'

'You're a fucking lifesaver.' I smile, hoping it's audible enough to ease the tension through the phone. Historically, I've always been a very good smiler; it's gotten me out of trouble and also into it. 'And Park, don't tell Mum yet, okay?'

* * *

By the time my brother's beaten-up car rolls into town, the back squealing unpleasantly with each turn, my phone is dead, and our conversation has mellowed out to basic life questions.

Neither Parker nor I have ever been the most attentive siblings, we work on the basis that we'll tell each other something if it's important or interesting. We've both respectively come out a handful of times and never bothered to tell the other person with particular haste. That said, I've dropped the ball in the past couple of years. His face has more wrinkles than I

15

remember, worn in around his eyes and cheeks from smiling. He's chipped one of his front teeth, breaking up a bar fight, he tells me somewhere along the A27 and never bothered to go to the dentist. He looks happy, his hair is longer, his general demeanour calmer, and I wonder what's responsible for it. Is it age, is it a new partner, did he move, did his job get better, did he finally get medication for his ADHD?

I should have asked all this a long time ago. Sure, I was in other countries, but I wasn't incapable of calling. I mean, I carry that thing on me twenty-four-seven, sleep curled up beside it, letting the ambient noise of whatever TikTok I just watched lull me to sleep. You'd think I could pick it up and do something useful with it occasionally. I'm not very capable of that, though, if the last two years are anything to go by.

I used to care intensely about every tiny minutia of things. I always wanted people to be happy with me, to feel proud of me, to think I was making the right life choices. Between the ages of seventeen and twenty-four, I fixated on being the perfect daughter, the perfect girlfriend. People pleaser extreme, to the point that I forgot how to value my wants. I had three older siblings, each one with their own life quirks and failings. When people talked about me, I was not just the golden child but the hopeful one.

When Parker dropped out of Uni, everyone swore I'd graduate, when Archer got a one-night-stand pregnant by accident at twenty, they all laughed that at least I was gay and it couldn't happen to me. When Liam struggled to make ends meet as an artist and eventually gave up, everyone told me not to be like him, to keep pushing until I made it big. For years of my life, I lived as someone else's failed wishes. I was so concerned about what everyone else would think and feel if I came out that I failed to put any stock in my actual happiness, my want to survive.

And now all I do is survive. I live recklessly. Value my life above everything else. I kinda feel like I'm owed it, and yet, here, faced with everything I've missed while I was focused on myself, it's hard not to feel guilty about it.

I care about these people, though I might have forgotten how to show it. It's not their fault that their hopes were handed down to me.

'So,' Parker says, throwing a rescue rope down into my pit of guilt. 'What kind of board are you riding these days?'

Ah, the common ground. The one universal safe place between my brothers and me: skateboarding. It's hard to remember a time before skateboards ruled my life. Seriously, one of my very first memories is Archer holding my hands as my chubby legs shook on a penny board, Liam behind me pushing away furiously because I was too small to push myself along. It's all on film somewhere. Park behind the camera, laughing maniacally in only the way an eight-year-old can. It might not be my memory if I'm being honest; there's a very good chance that I've pieced every part of it together from other people's recollections, but there's a hell of a lot more like it.

I remember butt-scooting on a board when the others got tired of pushing me and went off to do their own thing. The way they all grimaced as I screamed when Mum tried to return that little penny board to Liam and how happy I was when he just shrugged and said I could keep it.

Liam was always unphased.

I was small, he was big. The ever-cool middle teen brother, ready to ditch you or drag you along for the ride. It didn't make any difference to him. I still think of him like that, but now he's laden down with kids that he lets climb all over him and a beard thicker than a sailor's.

A quick huff escapes me before I can control it. I know the reaction I'm about to get over my skateboard. I'm fully prepared to have the shit ripped out of me when my brothers spy the sparkly pink deck and the image underneath. 'It's a collab between Welcome and Britney Spears.'

'Nice. The pink or the purple one?' My brother responds instead.

My legs halt their restless jiggling and fail to curtail the shock in my voice. 'The pink.'

Parker rolls his eyes as if to say *well, duh* and suddenly I am ten years old again, trying to show him something cool that he's already learnt how to do. Telling him about Paramore like they saved my life, only to find they saved his first.

'We might not be LA or Toronto, or wherever the hell you've been, but it's not exactly like Portsmouth's skate shop is stuck in the 90s Dexy. We do get new shit.'

And there comes that wave of guilt again, ready to wipe me out. Of course, they do. Of course, he's seen it. And of course, he knows exactly which deck would appeal to me.

Board Now is a beacon to Portsmouth kids. I've been staring at shit on their walls that I can't afford since before I could talk. I should have known Parker would see the collection. Honestly, I'm pretty sure my first Britney Spears tape was an old one of his that I stole.

'I thought of you when it came. Wondered if you were gonna get it wherever you were.'

I think back to how hard it was to get it delivered to a stranger's house in the Hamptons and how weird I felt asking to receive post at home I barely stayed more than three weeks in and curse myself for not checking all my options. But then again, there was no guarantee I would be returning home any time soon. I wasn't even sure myself until two weeks ago.

'It was a bit of a bitch to get the board shipped here, honestly. If I'd known Board Now had it, I probably wouldn't have used all my luggage space on it.'

'Christ, Dex, what else did you even get in there?' he jerks his head back at the boot, where my suitcase is tipped on its side.'

'Not much if I'm being honest.'

For the last two years, I've lived every day of my life out of that battered old suitcase. It's blue, with black piping, and it might have been my grandmother's from the 90s when she went on one of her big retirement trips to stay with her cousins in Auckland. It comes up to mid-thigh and houses a surprising amount of crap. Namely, all my worldly possessions.

I've made do with two pairs of trousers, one pair of shorts, a six-pack of men's tank tops, three cut-up work shirts and whatever weird t-shirts I picked up along the way. I have exactly two pairs of shoes, one pair of Chucks and black and blue Vans that I've taped together more than once, and never any more than seven pairs of socks or pants at any one time.

I am good at keeping my life small and making shit fit in a space it shouldn't. It's a strange life, but it's mine, which is not something I can say about the way I lived before.

'You got room for all your fancy pants books?' Park asks with a wide grin.

We have the same smile, different faces, but the same smile. I've always been weirdly proud of it. Big teeth, small mouth, smile lines on the side.

'Nah, man. I'm a Kindle person now. Got about forty different library cards though.'

His eyebrows pop up, but he doesn't say anything, a sure sign he's thinking something, though.

I don't care what. For the first time in years, I'm home. I can see his expressions. I don't care if they're good, bad or a little judgmental. I get to see them with my eyeballs.

It's fucking brilliant.

Chapter Four

Dean

The girls are practically buzzing when they get home.

Apparently, Parker called Liam, and Liam called Mum. Mum didn't answer, but Dad did, and Dad called the girls. They were like, 'Oh my days, Dex is coming home.'

These are direct quotes, by the way. Or at least, that's how it was relayed to me.

Priti and Pomona enter in their usual whirlwind. A storm of fast speech and squeals as they sit beside me at the kitchen table, Pom reaching her hand out and slamming my laptop closed as if I'm not currently in the middle of work. Sure, it's a remote day, but I still have to bend backwards to ensure these reports go out without a hitch.

'Excuse you.' The eyebrow arch I give them would have scared my sisters once upon a time, but now it doesn't even cause hesitation. 'I was in the middle of something.'

'I know,' the cheeky bugger replies. 'And we were in the middle of telling you some breaking news.'

Dragging my palm across my forehead to hide the rolling of my eyes, I let them go on.

'Dex is coming home.' They say in unison. It's never a good sign when the twin speech kicks in; it means their over-excited.

I blink, unsure what they expect of me.

'And?'

'Ugh, come on, that's like piping family tea, and you know it.' Priti watches my face intently, examining me for signs of intrigue or upset. 'They haven't been home in like-'

Two years, two months, and about eight days—Not that I've been keeping track.

Seriously, I haven't. I'm just good with numbers and dates.

'I already know.'

'You already know?'

'They replied yes to the e-vite I sent about Serena's birthday.'

'Bitch, when?' Pom smacks my arm, her perfectly mani-cured nails stinging my skin as they make contact.

'First of all, don't call me bitch. Secondly, they replied two weeks ago, so I assumed they'd get themself here sometime before Friday.'

If I'm a bit surprised by Dex arriving a week early, I don't let it show. Sure, it would have been nice for them to miss their flight or come late and make an example of themself, but I guess this version of events is nicer for Serena.

'Way to hold out on us. You've known for a fortnight and didn't say anything.'

'I didn't think it would matter.' That's bullshit and we all know it. Dex is as much a sibling to the twins as I am. While the boys were that bit older and cooler, Dex was right there with us, walking to school, playing the floor is lava with us and the cousins during Durga Puja or begging for penny sweets when we went to the local shop.

22

For years when we were kids they both acted as though the sun shone out of Dex's arse and Dex adored them back. It would have bothered me, I'm not great at sharing despite how much practice I have, but Dex always came back to me. That meant something. And if it made the girls like me better, well then, who was I to sniff at it? 'They've been gone two years, it's not like any of us are close any more.'

More lies. Pom and Pri talk about Dex's hijinks constantly. When they stopped going by their birth name, the girls were the first to tell me. They correct everyone's pronouns constantly and somehow found a way to get a postcard from almost every sodding country that prick has been to over the last couple of years. It would almost be cute if I didn't resent Dex Carpenter-Brown so much.

'Speak for yourself.' Priti sniffs, the faintest glint of hurt shimmering in her eyes as she turns her back to me.

I shift in my chair, trying to ignore the inevitable guilt I'm going to feel about upsetting my younger sister. It's always been this way. I'm brash and sharp. I'm too busy trying to protect them to show them love, and one or all of us end up hurting. Whoever it is, I end up feeling like even more of an arse than I usually do.

Once, when we were kids, some of the neighbourhood kids bet Pomona that girls couldn't climb the trees in the park as well as boys. She's stubborn and far too like me for her own good, so she raised the stakes. She bet that she could climb to the top of the tallest tree before any of them.

She won. Beat them, hands down, her scrawny little legs pushing her higher and higher, right to the fresh, weaker branches at its peak.

Because they're in almost all of my childhood memories,

Dex saw it first. Caught Pom yelling and waving her arms in a gloating celebration, which is how we all ended up watching as the fragile bark cracked beneath her. Even now, I'm convinced she fell in slow motion. I can still see it when I close my eyes, her small limbs waving on the way down, how her hair was snatched up in twigs and branches.

We ran to her, and before I knew what was happening, I was yelling.

Telling Pom how stupid she was as she wept. I kept saying how short-sighted she had been. Pointing out that it was because of her actions that she was hurt. I don't remember what else I said, but I didn't shut up the whole walk home, with her snivelling into Dex's shirt as they carried her back to the house. I kept going as Priti explained that the boys had dared her, and it wasn't Pom's fault.

I don't think I stopped until Mum loaded us into the car to go to the hospital, and she started yelling at me.

It was my job to look after them. They were younger; they needed me to protect them. All the usual shit that gets dumped at the doorstep of an eldest daughter.

Pom hated me for weeks after that, glared at me across the dinner table, and sniped at me while I did her maths homework for her. But Dex got thanked by everyone, just for helping me carry her home.

In fairness, I did also catch them threatening the little shits who dared her the next time we all went to the park but only I saw that.

I never thanked them. I needn't bother now.

It's just another perfect example of how I fail to fit in with our family while they thrive.

Watching my sister's buzz with excitement, I realise I'm

going to have to put on a brave face for the next couple of weeks. My slow-building resentment might help me sleep at night, plotting revenge, the madwoman's answer to counting sheep, but it had the potential to make this holiday tense.

'I'm sure Kyle and Serena are thrilled.' I offer in my least hostile tone. The tiniest olive branch.

Pomona looks between us both, her perfectly lined eyes scrutinising me in an all too familiar fashion.

The three of us are all named after divinities Mum learnt about in her travels, collected from all over the world, with elements she hoped we would each carry with us. At least that's what we were told as children.

Priti is the younger of the twins, three minutes younger and three miles softer. She's round in every conceivable way, the same curving body as me and Mum's sisters, Auntie Afsana and Anjali. The same proclivity to gain weight in the blink of an eye and put it all on the boobs, hips, and cheeks. She's round in personality, too, welcoming, warm, and smiley. Named after the Hindu goddess of love and affection, she's forever been the kind and gentle sister. A fact only further proved by her studying Marine Biology with only the grand dreams of helping sea creatures to motivate her.

Whereas Pomona is named after the Roman goddess of gardens and orchards, and couldn't be less fitting if she tried. The only characteristic she shares with her namesake is the lack of a counterpart. Pomona has no Greek equivalent; she exists only as herself in this one world. That sounds more like my sister.

Pom is a human hurricane. From age two, her favourite colours have been gold and hot pink and everything in her life makes that make sense. She doesn't do anything by halves.

Sometime during the pandemic, she became famous for the easy way she does the most elaborate make-up looks. She dropped out of uni to pursue semi-fame on the internet, but she doesn't seem to care about it. It's all just a backdrop to her life. She has a sharp-cut jaw, an even sharper wit, and the same kind of easy beauty with which Mum carries herself. If she weren't my sister, I'd hate her for it. Instead, I love her and try to keep the envy to a minimum.

Even though I'm the oldest and should have forged my own path, I fall somewhere in the middle of them. My namesake is less of a person than a concept. Daena, an ancient Persian divinity of conscience. She's supposed to signify intellectual and spiritual enlightenment or growth, not that any of that feels relevant to my life. I'm just a muddle. Half Muslim, half Hindi, practising in neither, fluent in English but not Bangla, a high-achieving child but an adult disappointment, a lesbian but not practising in that most of the time either. I've got the same heart-shaped face and arched nose as Pom, with the awkward body that Pri calls mid-sized.

I am neither one thing nor the other. Caught between strong personalities and falling entirely flat.

Dex and I were tomboys growing up, unruly in a way that other people understood and, with time, that morphed into practical, comfortable styles. I wear a lot of jumpsuits and dungarees, things that I can wipe my hands on and not ruin. The girls and I all have the same hair, long, thick and brown, but mine remains puffy and pony-tailed or lashed back in plaits, while the girls both know how to make it look beautiful.

That probably plays a part in the near-constant threat of makeovers I get from my sisters.

I see the question brewing now before either of them asks it.

Pom's eyes are taking me in, lingering on the rumpled t-shirt I'm wearing, lips sneering as she catches the stain I'd hoped wasn't too visible on its left side. Priti's gaze is less cruel, but I can still see the glimmer of child-like joy in her as she meets her twin's eyes.

'De,' they sing-song, stretching the shortest version of my name out into a screech.

'No.' I snap to attention, whipping my laptop open to remind them I'm very busy.

'Please?' Priti bats her unnaturally long lashes at me.

'Nope.'

'But-'

'Nah-uh. No way.'

'You don't know what we're going to ask.'

'Yes, I do.' The urge to walk away is unbelievably strong. 'You are going to ask to give me a makeover. Same thing you always ask.'

'Well, you need one.' Pom folds her arms.

'Oi, watch it.'

I've been down this path with my sisters enough times now to know how this will end. They'll keep pushing until they call one of our parents in, and then, depending on which parent they get, I'll be met with apathy (Mum) or tripled pressure (Dad) until I dig my heels in and refuse them all. Then I'll get annoyed with their probing comments and back-handed compliments, and I'll leave and head back to my flat, forgoing Dad's shorshe ilish in favour of whatever microwave meal I happen to have in the back of the freezer.

It would be more helpful if I didn't share that flat with Pomona, but at least she'll bring me home a bag of leftovers.

'Please, just a teensy little revamp.' Pri begs.

27

'I don't need a revamp.' Pom snorts, and I thank her with a smack. 'I'm perfectly happy with my life the way it is, thank you very much.'

'But you're stuck in a rut.'

'Dropping money I don't have on a new wardrobe isn't gonna help get me out of a rut.'

'So you admit you're in one then?' Pom Regina Georges' me.

Why the fuck did my parents have to make smart children after me? Couldn't they have been content with one genius eldest and stopped producing brain cells in their offspring after that? It would make my life much simpler.

'I'm just mimicking your words back to you and pointing out the flaw in its logic.' I am a big fat fibber. 'If I were in a rut, which I'm not.' Definitely am. 'No amount of new clothes or hairstyles would change that.' That part is true. 'And I couldn't afford to if I wanted to,' also true. 'Which I don't.' Half true?

Pom sniffs, her smile staying plastered to her face like a low-budget supervillain. It's putting me on edge.

'I mean,' Priti plays with the chipping polish on her nails. 'It might help with your self-esteem problems.'

I spin my head around to glare her down so hard I almost get whiplash. 'I do not have self-esteem problems.'

'You kind of do.'

'Says who?' I ask and then think better of it. There are several nosy aunties, family friends or relatives who might have discussed the topic of my self-esteem. Knowing about it won't make me feel better. 'Actually, don't tell me. You can tell them, whoever it is, that I like myself perfectly well. I find myself very tolerable and not at all repulsive to the eye.'

'Oh yeah, because that little speech is gonna be so convincing.' Pom laughs.

'You're not supposed to tolerate yourself!' Pri pats my hand lightly, pityingly. 'You're supposed to love yourself.'

'I do.' Another big lie.

'And you're not meant to just not be repulsive. Where is the bar, in hell? You're supposed to be your own biggest fan.'

'And I suppose you both look in the mirror and fancy the pants off of whatever stares back at you then?' I half-joke, surprised when they both nod.

When I catch my reflection at the end of a long day, so most days, I have to fight the urge to flinch.

'Exactly!' Priti shrieks. 'When I look in the mirror, I don't see all the things I hate, or if I do, I push them away, I focus on the things I love about myself, the pretty parts, and suddenly that's all I can see. A very capable, sexy woman reflected back at me.'

I blink, mind-blown by the idea of immediate self-acceptance, and turn to look at Pom for confirmation. She simply bobs her head in response.

'Oh, I know I'm perfect. Frankly, everyone I've ever dated is punching up.'

'Well, whatever,' I say, shaking off the weirdness they've woven into my thoughts. 'I like me. I don't need or want to change who I am or how I dress.'

'Or where you work or who you date?' Priti pushes.

'Or how little you have sex?' Pom ramps it up. When we both turn to look at her, appalled, she just rolls her eyes. 'We live together. It's not exactly like I can ignore that you haven't gotten laid in four months.'

'Four months?' Priti gasps.

'That's a normal length of time.' My protests are muted by the way they both stare at me. That look of pity again.

'Not since Liana?'

I bite my lip at the mention of Liana. How she just ghosted out of my life without a word until I saw her in the shops a month later with her new girlfriend and their puppy. I mean, who brings a puppy into TESCOs? That's just not sanitary.

'I slept with Callie last month while Pom was in London. So there.' I stick my tongue out like a kid.

That part is true. I just wish the sex had been more satisfying than the feeling of proving my sisters wrong.

'That's good.' Pri pats my arm encouragingly, but Pom stays suspiciously quiet. I get the unsettling feeling that she knows exactly what I'm thinking, and I wonder just how thin our walls are.

'I'm focusing on myself at the moment,' I say defensively. Hoping largely to get the topic off of my sex life.

'Which is why you should be improving yourself!'

'A job you like-'

'I have a very good job-'

'Which you hate.'

'I wouldn't say hate.'

'And you haven't changed your wardrobe since 2019.'

'It's eco-conscious.'

'It's ugly is what it is.'

'I'm fine like this!'

'If you say so,' Pom stands up, clearly tiring of my resistance. 'I just thought you might like to show Dexy just how new and improved you are.'

'I don't owe them—wait, what?'

'At dinner tonight? Surely, since you know everything, oh

30

wise older sister, you heard that Dad is cooking a big family meal down at Serena's beach hut to celebrate Dex coming back into town.'

Shit.

I sit mulling that new evening plan over, and all I can think about is the stain on my shirt and the fact that there's no time to go home and change it. I hate when my sisters are right!

Chapter Five

Dex

Not to be that wanker that leaves their home town and returns all 'nothing changed' but it's genuinely surreal to be my new self in all the same settings.

I'm thrown by the simple act of walking around the same shops that I spent my developmental years in. I'm startled by the reflection of myself in my parents' slightly dusty hallway mirror that was brought down for my prom and hasn't been moved back upstairs since. And nothing prepares me for sinking into the camping chairs at the beach hut, my old one with the hole in its cup pocket and the wonky back foot that I broke during the summer of year ten when Dean and I camped away from the families and got ourselves drunk on WKD till she sicked up a blue horror show.

Everything is so similar that the few things to change feel almost earth-shattering when I spot them.

Our local post office closed; the building's all derelict and empty now.

Liam's grown a beard, a horrible straggly thing that I immediately rip into him for. He's a little chubbier than I remember, but it suits him, a cosy alternative dad vibe that feels right. Archer looks older, his skin tanned from the sun, the smile lines on his cheeks and forehead more prominent as he joins me in mocking Liam.

Dad's gone grey. I'd seen it over Facetime, but in person, it's bizarrely beautiful, like a strange mix of silver, white, and steel that I can only hope I inherit later in life.

The grass around the hut is browning in the sun, and the flower beds that used to line the walkway down to the beach have been torn up and replaced with ugly sculptures of town landmarks.

To my surprise, Mum sort of looks the same. Her hair is pulled back in its same ponytail, exactly as it always has been when she leaves for work, and her glasses are propped on the bridge of her nose as she squints down at her phone to type with her index finger. She's still exquisitely done up, her nails filed and lacquered clear, her false lashes subtle and understated. The blonde of her hair hasn't changed, still ashy and warm in the sun, exactly how I always wished mine would be.

I didn't inherit the blonde gene, which is weird because despite the boys having a different mother, they all had naturally blonde hair at one stage or another. Everyone else looked the part of our parents' children, a miraculous mix of two people who didn't even know each other when they were conceived.

But most of me seems to come from Dad. We have the same auburn hair, almost red when the sun catches it right, although his has gone grey, and mine is looking lighter than ever from a spring of SoCal skating followed by a June of swimming. We have the same blue-green eyes, too far apart to be normal and the same stupid personality.

Growing up, Mum seemed almost upset by my genetic failure. She wanted to see more of herself in me than just her upturned nose and the echoes of her laugh.

I think she always hoped I would turn out to be a small replica, and I can't blame her. She took on three boys without question, three kids already making their choices and looking like mirrors of a woman her husband used to love. But I was all hers, or I should have been. The only girl. Ready to be moulded in her image.

She was so invested in my girlhood. The mother-daughter pamper days, the shopping trips where she begged me to try on something pretty rather than wearing Liam's hand-me-down t-shirts and Parker's spare cargo shorts. The older I got, the weirder I felt and the more pressure I put on myself to adhere. Sabina had three beautiful daughters, each one of whom behaved and wanted to be treated as a girl, and all my mum had was me. Her last beacon of hope for girl time.

In hindsight, it might have fucked me up a little.

My nieces and nephews are the change that almost beats me down, like a bitch slap right to the heart. There are five of them: Meggie, Roscoe, Martha, Leon, and Lois. Lois was only two months old when I left; now, she's chubby and toddling. Meggie, the oldest, has shifted from eight to ten and grown about a foot in the process. The second they walk up, I abandon ship to play with them.

Maybe I've missed two years of their lives; maybe I have only been there through phone calls at weird hours and birthday gifts sent via Amazon, maybe they don't know whether to call me aunt or uncle, but none of that matters because I can be here right now.

I take them to the sea. Hold Lois' sticky hand in mine as Roscoe helps dip her toes in the water. I wade up to my thigh, gritting my teeth as the denim of my shorts gets sodden and heavy, throwing Martha up in the air with each oncoming wave. We have timed races, where I check an invisible stopwatch, and pause for ice cream on the way back and not once does someone ask about work or pry into weird parts of my life that they missed.

It is perfect. Like all the best elements of hanging out with small relatives, compounded into a few short hours. We return to the hut dripping wet, covered in ice cream and smiling. I do the gentlemanly thing and buy Mum a 99, too, which I send Leon running ahead with so that it doesn't melt all over us as I carry the smallest.

By the time we reach them, Mum's ice cream is gone, her eyes threatening tears again, the BBQ is on, and my seat has been taken.

I put Lois down into my brother's arms, waving away his sugar-related complaints and feeling a two-fingered tap on my shoulder. Before I can turn around, I am pulled into a lung-pummelling hug by Priti, wrapped up in the familiar smell of their family detergent. I could identify the Ashraf family by scent alone, in a crowded room full of perfume stands and sweaty commuters.

When she pulls back, her lips upturn into a look of disgust.

'You're soaked,' she says, still laughing.

'And now you are too.' I squeeze her, closing in for a hug again and then make for Pom, standing behind her sister. She manages to dart out of the way.

'I'm good, thanks. I can greet you just fine without looking like the tide took me out.'

Her words are blunt as always, but I can hear the humour in them. It's the innate understanding you develop when you've known someone longer than they've known themselves. Her words can't hurt me if I watched her learn how to speak.

It's familiar and all too easy to relax into, this sense of knowing one another, but it's missing something important. Unconsciously, my eyes seek her out, looking for Dean in all the places she's missing. She's not standing with her sisters, she's not with her parents as they beckon me closer, she's not with my brothers.

She's in my chair. Her long legs folded up to expose shiny calves and perfectly white Converse. Her sundress is short and catching in the breeze as she sits, meaning she has to grab its hem in her fist as she talks to my nephew.

Seeing Dean in person after all this time is strange. My body vibrates as if I've touched a live wire, and weirdly, I'm jonesing to do it again. I'm torn between the impulse to run to her, pick her up in a bone-crushing, spinny hug, or run away from her and examine this feeling in private. I don't have a chance to do either, though, because before I know it, she's looking at me, her eyes just as wide and brown as I remember, and I'm grinning like a fool despite her unmoving mouth.

While I got lost in my head, my hand poised to wave, Dean's eyes move on behind her glasses, glazing over me as though I don't exist. So now my hand hangs, suspended in the air like a misplaced balloon above Disneyland.

I let it drop and feel the ball of hope in my stomach tumble with it. My cheeks are burning as if I've just chugged a vat of Tabasco sauce, and I scratch the back of my neck to hide my disappointment.

In front of me, the twins cough, pulling my attention back

to them.

I turn up the wattage on my smile and hope they didn't catch whatever the fuck that weirdness was.

'How have you been? Tell me everything!'

If the girls notice the falter in my grin, they have the good grace not to comment on it, which, if you know Pom, is a bloody miracle. Instead, they launch into a lengthy discussion of their lives. I hear all about Priti's coursework and the mother-daughter otter duo she's currently monitoring and nicknamed the Edies.

We chat about her attempts to learn Bangla, her studies, and her boyfriend, although I immediately forget his name and feel too bad to go back and ask about it again. She tells me everything she enjoys about living together as a couple and then everything she hates about living with a boy, which, it turns out, is a list as long as my leg.

'I mean, seriously, why can't they put the toilet seat down and close the cupboards? Like, it's not that hard to just close the door once you're done. One little tap and boom, easy as. Last month, he left the fridge open. The fridge, for Pete's sake! We had to get rid of everything, and the kitchen smelt funky for a week.'

'No one made you live in premarital bliss,' her twin rolls her eyes. 'You could have moved in with Dean and me and not become some doting housewife at twenty-three.'

The mention of Dean has me looking towards her again. She's grinning into the rim of her cup at something my mum is saying, and I'm filled with an inexplicable swell of jealousy. I don't understand why, and I would rather not consider what's made me jealous of my mother, but I'm self-aware enough to know it's an ugly emotion—the kind I haven't had in years.

'Like that would be any better. You two can't agree on what brand of toilet paper to buy, let alone important things.'

'Oh, we cleared that one up,' Pom says matter-of-factly. She turns to me, giving an aside of additional information. 'Dean wanted to go with the value pack, but I was pro-name brand.'

'Sure, makes sense.' I say because it does. Dean loves a bargain; she's always been semi-obsessed with spending the least amount of money and saving the most. As teens we used to call it her miserly habit. From anyone else, it might come off as shallow, but I was there when we were kids. I remember the days when there wasn't enough food to feed parents and kids. I recall the look of stress on Mum's face when I outgrew my school shoes and the fact that they were passed along to Dean in my stead.

We're from a poor part of the country, with too many people and not enough jobs. Even before the Tories ran us into the ground, we were barely getting by. Years of joint camping trips because that's all we could afford in summer holidays, and a complete aversion to jacket potatoes because they were the cheapest food that stretched the furthest.

I can still see the look on Dean's face when Sabina and Rami explained how people made big money. The way her eyes rounded out, awestruck, and her perfect cupid's bow shadowed her bottom lip as comprehension took over. That was when she understood what money did, how it worked and how someone could get it. It rewired a determined part of her brain irreparably.

'It might make sense to you weirdos, but if there's one place I'm not gonna scrimp it's on something that touches my butt.' Pomona levels a terrifyingly spiked eyebrow at me, and she's never looked more like her sister. The reminder of Dean hurts in a way I can't comprehend.

She's just sat over there, out of reach, refusing to make eye contact with me. If I wanted to, I could just go over there and make myself unavoidable.

But I don't want to *make* myself anything in her brain. I hoped that she would come to me. Maybe it was silly, but I thought I'd get at least a perfunctory hello. We haven't talked in a long time. I assumed she wasn't interested in hearing from me.

I didn't realise that her apathy had turned to dislike.

'You know,' Priti's voice drags me back to the present. 'You could always just go talk to her.'

'Who?' I answer, despite the heat rising to my cheeks.

'Bloody hell, we've progressed from playing naive to feigning absolute ignorance, have we?' Pom says, sounding, once again, disturbingly similar to her older sister.

'No.' Priti held up her hand, delicate painted nails flashing in the sunlight. 'We're all adults. There's no need for game playing.' I was pretty sure I could *hear* Pom's pout. 'I'm sure that Dex can put on their big boy pants and go talk to Dean in a perfectly reasonable, not at all childish manner.'

'Sure, they can.' Pom says with sarcasm that suggests otherwise.

Unsure that I agree with either sister. I preoccupy myself with the event. I circle the group, helping people get food, playing with kids, and answering all the basic questions people have when you've spent the last two years anywhere but here.

What was my favourite country?

'For sure, Greece.' Don't mention the transphobia that made me leave.

Which was the prettiest?

'Barcelona.' Neglect to mention that it rained two-thirds of the time I was there.

Which had the cutest girls?

'Trick question, there are cute girls everywhere if you just know how to find them.' Skip over the near-triple-digit number of one-night stands I tried my hand at. This is a family function; there are some things my parents don't need to know.

Where did I enjoy skating the most?

Easy. So incredibly easy to talk about. I tell them all about America, about following my friends and acquaintances all over the place. Bunking rides in shitty cars, stuffed with more people than legal, taking buses and cross-state trains to see the skate parks, competitions, and historic sites I always dreamed of.

In any other crowd, this wouldn't impress, but I know my audience. I built these dreams in the shadow of my brothers and learnt about Love Park and Hollywood High from them. While I was travelling, I was aware that I was living their dreams just as much as my own. I sent them so many photos of things no one else would care about, captured every fucking moment I could just in case I never got to go back. I even stole a handful of pebbles off of Venice Beach just because it felt right and brought them back in the front pouch of my backpack.

Everyone else nods along politely, letting me have this moment. These are my people, as far away as I've been, as long as I've gone without seeing them, they still know what these places mean to me.

When I left home, I expected my family to grieve the loss of their daughter, but it never occurred to me that I might feel a ripple of that grief in my own way. Alone, travelling the world without my family to talk to, I was haunted by our strange shorthand and inside jokes. I was desperate for someone to understand the things only they would.

It's nice to be seen by them again. I'm grateful.

And if Dean rolls her eyes or averts her gaze every time I show another picture, I don't notice. I definitely don't commit the sharp sting of hurt to memory.

Chapter Six

Dean

I knew they would be here. I came to the beach hut with that express knowledge, and yet I'm still seething at the sight of them.

Every few minutes, I can feel the weight of their gaze land back on me, and it pins me in place, squashing me between Dex and the earth's centre. When we first arrived, they were nowhere to be found, and I part hoped, part feared that they'd run off again to chase some new, more exciting adventure. It would have been an expedited way to prove my point but it also would have sucked for Serena.

As it turned out, they were just looking after their nieces and nephews. As if they knew exactly what would win everyone over and wanted to make the best possible impression upon re-introduction. So when they returned to our little circle, covered in ice cream and holding the smallest Carpenter-Brown child by the hand, even Dad cooed.

It took all my willpower not to groan, and, in fear of slipping up, I looked anywhere but at them. Pointedly not taking in the way their band tee was cropped just above the waist of their trousers or the soft strip of freckled skin it exposed as they lifted the littlest Carpenter-Brown onto their newly broad shoulders. I certainly didn't look at the muscle they had built up in their absence, the way their new tattoos rippled as their biceps moved.

I tried not to focus on the odd twinge of hope in Dex's eyes as they saw me. I'm not sure what I expected of them, anger maybe, or indifference like I was trying so hard to feel, but not excitement. What the fuck was that about?

They just abandoned me, first for that horrible woman and then for a million different skateparks, and now they have the audacity to be excited to see me. Seriously, make that make sense.

You can't, which is why I've spent the last few hours systematically being everywhere they aren't. I've made small talk with distant Carpenter-Brown cousins, played games with the kids, bullied my sisters, talked to Serena and Kyle, and stomached a weird conversation with Serena's aunt Marilyn about AI, all to escape them and the low rumble of their voice.

Until now.

I'm in the process of spooning more potato salad than one human should eat on my grandmother's plate when a shadow darkens the beach hut doorway.

'Can I help with anything?'

Fuck me, I think and barely refrain from saying. I manage to keep it in, though, because I'm in the presence of an elder and not a complete heathen.

'Dexter.' I say, coating the elongated name with venom.

'Dean.' They don't bite.

Within seconds, Dadu is waving her wide arms in the air and reaching to wrap them around Dex as if they're old friends.

43

Dadu pulls back, petting their cheek idly and squeezing as she did when we were kids.

'Oh, it's so good to see you. And the two of you,' she pulls me in, taking my cheek in her free hand so that Dex's face is squashed next to mine. The contact makes my skin burn. 'It's like old times having you together again.'

I suppress my sneer and try to pull it off as a smile.

I'm sure it's nice for her to reminisce.

My paternal grandparents moved down to live near us and my cousins when I was small. Because they were retired, and the parents were always busy, Dexy and I spent a lot of time at their house. Dada passed away a few years ago, an ache that hasn't quite faded from my heart, but ever since, Dadu has been nearly obsessed with seeing all her grandchildren happy and settled. She talks about Dex at least once a week, as though they're included in our family, and worries about them travelling constantly. This means that once a week, I am forced to remind everyone that Dex chose to run away.

People who abandoned us don't get the honour of being called family.

'It's so nice to see you smiling again after all that misfortune with the wedding. Ah! You look good, Lipa.' She whips the nickname out as though nothing has changed, and we're still eight-year-olds giggling into our absolutely-off-the-record-secret sundaes. 'Dean, don't they look good?'

'Yeah, grand. Real knight in shining armour.' I say, dropping my eyes to the mayonnaise-laden spoon still clutched in my hand and about five seconds away from dripping on the dress Priti let me borrow.

'Oh, don't mind her. Daena is just bitter because her girlfriend couldn't come today.'

'Dadu!' I gasp, mortified that the thought would cross her mind, let alone be spoken aloud in front of my mortal enemy.

In my horror, I dig my thumb into the paper plate, tearing it clean in two in my fist. The resulting explosion is a potato salad volcano of apocalyptic proportions. Mayonnaise is strewn across my arms, dress and face. Dadu has a rogue onion chunk in her neatly permed hair, and the floor is covered in potato debris. I stammer out my apologies, as if this isn't secretly Dadu's fault for throwing me under the bus of social interactions. Then continue yelling them as she totters away to clean up, not so subtly muttering 'pagli' with a shake of her head.

Hanging my head, I try to consolidate the remaining food onto one of the plate halves and wait to be mocked ruthlessly. I squeeze my eyes tightly closed, readying myself for whatever cutting remark Dex has lined up for me. To my surprise, nothing comes.

When I open my eyes, they are on their knees in front of me. They're bent picking up my mess, but the shock of it is still enough to make my cheeks flush, although maybe that's just the lingering embarrassment. They have a few rogue splotches of mayo on their clean black shirt and shorts, and I feel bad for making a mess of them as well as me.

And then I'm mad because how dare they come back here looking so damn good. How dare they look this fine, even covered in mayonnaise and with a wedge of spud on their chucks. The gall!

They stand, blissfully unaware of my indignation, and drop the mess into the bin bag before turning back to grin at me.

Being hit with that smile can only be compared to running into the lower half of a stable door at full force. It's as if my body is forcibly split in two. It winds me enough that I fight the compulsion to hold my core and check my pulse.

It's not fair that I missed this smile. It's an injustice and somehow insulting to feminism.

'Girlfriend, huh?'

The mention of Callie pulls me back to the present. My disappointing reality. I want to deny it. Tell them that I'm not dating Callie, but I guess maybe I am. We've been seeing each other for months now. We go to the cinema together, occasionally to a restaurant after work, and we have lacklustre sex once every few months just to grease the wheels and because it's what women my age are supposed to do. The truth is, though, I don't think of her as my girlfriend; I don't think about Callie at all. She's not at the beach hut with us today because I didn't invite her. It didn't occur to me to mention it. Should it have?

Am I a girlfriend… and a bad one?

'Uh, yeah.' Is the intelligent response I manage to grunt out.

Dex nods, unfazed by the sudden dip in my IQ.

'Lucky girl.' They say with a slightly dimmed smile, the wattage turned down just ever so slightly from the brilliance they usually manage. It's the kind of thing you wouldn't notice if you weren't paying attention, if you didn't know them painfully well, but unfortunately for me, I still know them better than I know my scar tissue.

They reach out then, their hand is veinier than I remember, strong looking, with a ring on the index and pinky fingers. They move towards me, seemingly in slow motion. I watch, suspended, unsure of what they're about to do as they scoop a fleck of potato salad off of my cheek and then bring their finger to their mouth to suck it.

My jaw drops slightly. I am, for the first time, speechless.

I'm itching to chide them, to tell them that was gross, or that they don't know where I've been or know me well enough to do that. But they do. They just did. And a small part of me is too stunned by the way their cool touch sizzled against the burning skin of my cheek to protest.

So I just stand there, staring silently as their cheeks pull in, exposing killer cheekbones, and their eyes close briefly like Dad's sun-warmed potato salad is the most heavenly thing they've ever tasted.

It's unfair. Ungodly. Downright pornographic.

And I don't know why.

I've never been particularly attracted to sucking things off of one's fingers. This is proving a notable exception.

I certainly didn't expect to feel some kind of way about Dex's fingers. We weren't ever that kind of best friends with secret sexual chemistry and long-hidden yearning. I wouldn't say we were siblings; it felt different than that, there were thoughts, blips of attraction, but nothing substantial.

We did everything together; they were privy to every thought that ever flitted through my head. Well, almost every thought, with the notable exception of when I developed sexual desire spontaneously at seventeen. I remember it vividly. A lightbulb sparking to life and illuminating everything that had been hidden in its depths.

Up until that day, I had been, as my mother put it, 'a slow burner' on the puberty front.

When my friends started getting crushes around age seven, I thought they were just assessing the cutest boy in each band and picking a strategic alignment that said more about their persona than any real romantic interest. And Dex was right there with me, telling people they would date Danny Phantom because they thought he was fun.

Turns out that was secretly queerness othering us from our peers. By twelve, Dex had figured out some part of the crush thing. They were far more interested in women than they were in men. And thus, crushes became less about celebrities living worlds away from us and more frequently featured girls older than us in school or that we saw on the bus.

It didn't bother me that I still didn't feel that yearning for love. All Dex's crushes seemed to do was cause them anguish and, occasionally, social embarrassment. I got enough of that on my own. But then, at sleepovers, Priti piped up about her pre-teen boyfriend. A scrawny white boy named John Michael, whose family I still see in our local Sainsbury's sometimes. She was in love, so she claimed. It was strange to be surpassed in something that felt like it was attached to age by my younger sister. As if I were falling short of some metric of maturity, while she exceeded expectations.

I had hope that I wasn't alone until I saw Pomona's pharisaic eyebrow. She's always had a killer arch to them, passing judgment over our decisions with shrewd discernment. She wasn't just judging me for not having hit the supposedly essential marker of teen girldom, but she was looking down at John and Priti by association.

'Do you want your first love to forever be a boy that once sat on a juice box for fun?' Her words were barbed, and, despite John doing that way back in year four and it being an accident, the happy couple broke up a week later.

From there, things only got worse.

I have lived my life surrounded by crushes. Priti kept dating, a stream of intense loves one after another. Pom was the

48

opposite, scaring away everyone she thought unworthy of her time, but striving to better herself for whatever famous goal crush she had. While Dex had crushes similar to hyper-fixations.

Every month, there seemed to be someone new, a fling, a seasonal obsession I heard about, witnessed snogging, and just generally third-wheeled with. It was always love. They never stopped talking about love. Whether it lasted a month or an afternoon, Dex was besotted. A ready and raring Romeo jumping from Rosaline to Juliet with the same implausible passion and intensity. They struck out a lot, especially in those early days, but the older we got, the more charming Dex became, and it was obvious that their shimmering energy was on an ever-upward trajectory. They could make old ladies blush when they winked. They certainly weren't pursuing them, but have you ever heard an elderly librarian giggle?! Unfortunately, I have.

Everyone was crushing and lusting and just generally feeling the things that you're told are supposed to come with raging hormones. Everyone, apart from me.

I was an island of pubescent apathy.

Crushes still felt as foreign to me as they had at seven. I could pick the best boy out of a line-up, but I had no idea what I was supposed to do with him after that. It wasn't that I didn't want to have sex; I sort of did in an amorphous, far-away thought. I just hadn't felt the feelings that would lead me to desire. I didn't know these people. I couldn't imagine sharing that intimate part of myself, that strange naked experience, with someone I didn't know, let alone like. Dex told me about one-night stands they had stuffed into bathroom stalls at house parties or sneaking out on Sunday evenings to hook up, and I just didn't get it. How was I supposed to know that I wanted to fuck someone if I didn't know the basics about them? What was the spark of lust supposed to feel like?

And then, it hit me like a fucking freight train and I was mortified.

So mortified that I never shared it with anyone. Especially not Dex.

Eventually, things fell into place. I came out as a lesbian in my last year of school. Dated a bit throughout uni and got that awkward first time out of the way, realised I was demi-sexual on top of it all, but I never felt lust the same as that first time. An invisible string pulling on the lower part of my abdomen, dragging me towards someone else.

At least, I hadn't until now.

I'm still staring at Dex's fingers as they emerge from between their plump pink lips. The tip of their index finger is slightly slick, the afternoon sun catching it and almost blinding me.

As if they sense my reaction, Dex sidesteps to block me from the sun's harsh light. I'm not wearing sunglasses; they're outside somewhere, abandoned in the cupholder of an old camping chair, and without any buffer between my eyes and the light, Dex's silhouette is creating a kind of optical illusion. They're shadowed now, mostly just the outline of my ex-best friend, but haloed in a glowing warmth like some kind of angelic figure. The statue of Apollo or Eros or one of those bloody Greek gods they were always yapping on about. I'm too thrown by it to remember which one. All I know is that the luminous light of summer is highlighting the outline of their nose, the straight line that curves up to a slope at the end. It's illuminating the two raised lines of their cupid's bow, and I'm right back to thinking about Eros again, innocent Greeks being struck with an arrow and having no choice but to fall in love, and that damn string is yanking on my tummy, and I'm whacked in the face with the memory of being seventeen and wanting to pant for the first fucking time.

What the fuck is wrong with me?

For the last two years of my life, I have prided myself on my disdain for Dex Carpenter-Brown. While the rest of my family fawned over their measly gifts and pandered to their pathetic postcards from their glory days, I have known better. They're a coward. Too afraid to be themself even with a family that loves them. Too afraid to speak up for what they want when nothing but their stubbornness stands in the way. Too scared of change to stay in place and change with us, with their family, with me. They ran away from vulnerability and became a new, improved person out there in the great wide world. They abandoned me here, and I have hated them for it. Every fucking day.

But what does it mean if I don't hate them?

What is this incessant tugging at my gut?

Have I read this all wrong?

Am I the coward here?

Should I be scared?

I'm unsure what to do with any of this, so I do the easiest, stupidest thing I can think of and steal a page from Dex's playbook. Faced with danger, staring down the barrel of change, I run.

I don't explain myself or stop to make excuses. I just bolt. Away from the beach hut, past our families, past trees and picnics, along the edge of the toilet block and I don't stop running until I hit the shallows of the sea.

Like a fucking coward.

Chapter Seven

Dex

'So, tell me,' Parker says, smiling through a mouthful of Cheerios. 'Who was she?'

I pause with my spoon halfway to my face. 'Huh?'

'The girl that finally sent you packing.'

'What?' I don't follow at all.

'Oh come on. Every place you stayed, there was at least one fine young lady. And those're just the ones you deigned to tell your poor, dateless older brother about. Every bloody city or suburb had a girl to be flung. Which bird finally did you in and had you longing for jolly old England?'

I drop my spoon entirely and blink.

Maybe I'm dim, but it never occurred to me that my family would pick up on my non-committal relationships. It's something I was thinking about discussing in therapy rather than over cereal dinner with my brother. But I haven't seen him in years, I suppose the least I owe him is a hint of emotional vulnerability.

'The truth is I kind of got tired of...flinging.'

'No shit.' Parker grins at me as if this is the answer he

expected, and I don't get it. How is it possible that, after all this time, after changing my name and travelling a quarter of the world, he still knows me this well?

Sometimes, it feels as though my family comprehend the inner workings of my brain better than I can. Like, I live to embody their version of me. It's a lot to live up to those expectations. Overshadowing almost.

It makes me wonder if it took me so long to recognise my identity because they couldn't see it.

I'm lucky to have an incredibly understanding family; while they might not always *get it*, they're on board and trying.

They took my coming out in their stride. The only person who cautioned me against it was Mum, but she came around eventually. Frankly, running away and taking space to prove myself helped with that.

Growing up, I took for granted that there were loads of queer people related to me. Two gay cousins, a very sexually fluid uncle, a statistically improbable number of trans relatives.

Mum's aunt Marilyn came out in the 80s and is the first trans-woman I ever met. I was even too young to remember most of Parker's comings out. He socially transitioned when I was small. I've only ever known him as my brother. I also can't remember when he first announced that he was bi, but I do recall the conversation about him being poly. By all rights, I had a pretty fucking easy journey, the path was laid out for me. Plenty of people laying the groundwork ahead of me.

But I didn't see it. I couldn't catch my reflection in those more binary stories. Maybe I'm just stupid. That's a very real possibility. I prefer to think these feelings are different for everyone. It's impossible to rush the process of becoming yourself.

I understood my sexuality from a relatively young age. I have always loved women. I saw Velma in that vinyl jumpsuit and knew that the buzzing between my ears, the warmth in my cheeks, was something special.

I've been chasing that infatuation ever since. And I would still willingly wrestle any man for the chance to treat Linda Cardellini right.

Sexuality was easy. Romantic attraction was less clear, but still, mostly femme-leaning. Which lead me to being butch. Not because I had to be. In fact, for a long time in my later teens, I was trapped in the femme-for-femme world, answering the demands of what other people wanted me to be. Khloe wanted to 'defy stereotypes', as if being butch was somehow a harmful image to project onto the community. As though defying gender conformity isn't one of the bravest acts a person can do with their body.

Deep down, I knew that I didn't fancy butches because they are hot (they emphatically are), but that feeling was misplaced. I wanted what they had. I have always wanted the almost camp version of masculinity I recognised in butches.

When I realised I could just be butch, no other identifier, all the voices in my brain fell silent. All those other versions of me that people saw were put on mute. I could finally see myself.

So I took the Dex I had been, wedding dress laden and using lipstick as a shield and carved out the Dex I would become.

And then I chased that buzzing again, and it was all the louder for being seen as me.

But somewhere across America, the bubble of joy I felt at making a woman smile started to get fatigued. Not because the act was tiring, I can give myself all day long and come away replenished if I'm receiving appreciation and affirmations in return, but because I was never chosen.

Exactly as Parker suggests, I was always a fling on my never-ending summer holiday. I chased the sun, I chased women, but at some point, I realised no one was following me. Maybe the chase was more of a run.

The women I dated wanted temporary, and I was happy to be that. I am painfully good at temporary. But as much as there is a thrill in the chase, eventually, your legs get weary.

Hearing the words 'I could fall in love with you' across continents and several short relationships makes you wonder what stops could from being would.

'If you're so smart, how come you didn't tell me to cool it?' I ask my brother, reaching out to punch him lightly on the arm.

He slurps milk up from his spoon, dodging me.

'It's none of my fucking business if you shag your way through half of Europe…and America…and Australia.'

I shrug. 'Well, I had to branch out somewhere else. Between you, Liam and Arch, half the women between forty and twenty-five in Portsmouth have already slept with a Carpenter-Brown.'

An unfortunate side effect of having a big family in a relatively small city is the awareness that everyone knows someone you're related to. Park is only eight years older than me, which means that while we weren't in school together, my high school was littered with stories of his mayhem and older kids who still had lingering crushes on him.

By virtue of having him having a decade on me, I didn't hear about Liam's dating life until I was in my teens, already sneaking out to bars.

On one particularly horrifying occasion, an underage me hit on a uni student, only to be told I looked familiar. I was smart enough to already be wary, but when my brother walked out and put his arm around her waist, I knew I was in deep shit. Both for sneaking out and hitting on his girlfriend of the month.

Let's not forget Archer's impressive legacy. A father at twenty-one, with a woman he didn't know the last name of. Cami, my niece, came along when I was nine. Although Archer only sees her every few weekends, the single dad title worked wonders for his dating life. He didn't settle down until he was thirty, so despite having had a wife for a full nine years, I still regularly run into women who dated my eldest brother and have some choice words for me.

The Carpenter-Brown shadow is a lot to fill and far too big for the small city we live in. But the problem with running away from your own shadow is that it'll always stick to you. Even when you can't see it, it's right behind you, holding your shape. Occasionally, it's ahead, stretching out before you, a prophecy of things to come. It'll catch up with you no matter how far or fast you go.

Parker sniggers and continues munching.

'I bet you're thrilled to be spending a solid fortnight with us then. One big family holiday must be exactly what you were looking for.'

I suppress my groan. I love my family, truly, and I've missed them, but Jesus. Two full weeks, no breaks, no escape. You might be asking yourself, what kind of sadist planned this? The answer is simple: Kyle Carpenter.

The doting husband that is my dad.

This is his grand plan. Two weeks of birthday fun for Mum. Kicking things off with a home-cooked dinner, then a ferry to France, a week in a château, touring Mont Saint-Michel and six days in Paris before catching the ferry home again. It's a group holiday unlike any other. Just the two families, intermingled for two whole weeks.

As far as I can tell, people have been saving for this trip for at least half a decade.

We've only had one full holiday abroad. The Ashrafs are similar. I don't think they've ever done a family trip out of the country.

None of this felt odd to me until my teens. We weren't skiing people. We didn't take trips abroad every summer. We went camping. That was all I knew. Camping was fun.

It never occurred to me that we couldn't.

When I turned thirteen, I started to see the way other families lived. The holidays they went on, the look on their face that told me they would be disappointed with what I had.

The funny thing about being poor is that you are aware of money at every age. You don't have the luxury of not knowing you don't have it. It just takes a while for the societal expectation of that to set in.

You can be eight and know that you don't have cash for that new doll you want because your parents are still paying for your brother's braces, and the boiler is on its last legs and needs fixing before winter, and none of that will bother you all that much. Then suddenly you're fourteen, and a girl at school jokes that you're the British equivalent of white trash because your mum is the only person in your family who's finished uni, your brother had a baby young, and your idea of a fancy shop is Co-op rather than M&S.

57

That's how you learn what being poor truly means. People will look down on you for it, even though you have no control over it. Even though half the sodding country is struggling, the economy is wrecked, and the class divide is stronger than ever.

They'll act as if it's funny. They'll make jokes at your expense, mocking the fact you mistook 'innit' for a dictionary word rather than a contraction, and laugh at your hand-me-down clothes. Until you're in uni, when they all adopt your accent to talk about being skint all the time, and second-hand clothes suddenly become thrifted.

By then, you'll have worked it out. It's not funny, and it's not some cute aesthetic. Being poor is nothing to be ashamed of; it's a fluid state, but it's something that shaped you. At the end of the day, people might play at broke for liberal social points, but watch them— it won't be so cute when they're in their late twenties. They'll start getting solid jobs, pulling in family favours, and making real people money while you struggle to pay the same bills that your parents couldn't afford two decades ago.

So, this will be my first full family holiday abroad. Trapped on boats and trains, and cars with my siblings, my parents and Dean. People I haven't seen in two years.

A strange heartburn sensation takes up residence in my throat when I think about it. Is it normal for guilt to do that?

As if he can sense the direction of my thoughts, Parker smiles.

'What did you do to Daena, by the way?'

'Pardon?'

'Yesterday at the hut. Dean darted out of your conversation pretty damn fast.'

Oh.

I would like to say I did nothing, but I'm not sure that's true. I didn't hurt her. Not deliberately, at least. But I did lick potato salad off her cheek, and that's something, I guess.

I wasn't thinking it through when I did it. It was just there, and I—well, actually, I short-circuited. She looked so put out, and the potato salad was going to go to waste, and her cheeks were so round. I just acted on impulse. Something I have been doing a lot over the past few years.

'I think she's mad at me.'

'For what?' Parker turns, dropping his bowl in the already full sink.

'Oh, you know.' *Running away on my wedding day. Practically begging her to be my accomplice and leaving her to deal with the shit when it inevitably hit the fan. Asking her to be my bridesmaid despite not having spoken one-on-one in years. The way I abandoned her long before that. Not moving across the country to follow our plans at eighteen.*

'You think she's still pissed about what everyone said at the wedding?'

'I'm not—wait, what?' Parker's words stop me dead in my tracks. 'What did everyone say at the wedding?'

'Well, not everyone but Khloe.'

I place my spoon back in my bowl with a clank.

'What did Khloe say?' I ask again, keeping my tone carefully neutral.

My brother's eyes go wide, suddenly aware he's waddled his way into a tense situation. He coughs and retreats into his hoodie.

'You didn't know?'

'Didn't know what?'

59

'Oh, uh, well. When you... bolted.' I have quite literally never seen Parker trip over his words this much. It would almost be amusing if my nerves weren't straightened and ready to spark. 'Dean had to-to tell everyone.

'It was fucking awkward. We were all in the bar and she came in in her fancy dress. She said she'd gone to pee, and while she was in the en suite, you popped the window and, well, you know.' I've heard parts of this lie before. The little white one Dean gave when I leapt through the window, so that she didn't have to explain how she'd opened it for me. 'It wasn't pretty. Mum and Dad freaked out about the money, and then about your safety. Liam tried to go look for you. Then we had to find Khloe and tell her. That was worse. Well, Mum was worried, and Sabina was frantic, but Khloe was like... mad. Like, I've never seen someone that mad. She didn't exactly look surprised or sad, I guess. It was weird. She said some mean things about you, about our family and—and then she zeroed in on Dean.'

'Zeroed in how?'

Parker exhales as though dragging forth the memory is a challenge. 'I don't know, dude. We were all busy trying to make sure you were safe, but it sort of sounded as if she accused Dean of being jealous. Said shouldn't have even been there. Then Khloe's sister got in on it, and she was a piece of work. It was messy. Pom stepped in eventually and told them to back off. Said that if you left, that was your decision, that maybe Khloe should take a look in the mirror before blaming other people for her relationship ending. There were a lot of tears.'

I push back in my chair, digging my spine into its back with enough force to make the wood creak.

60

There's too much energy in my body to think clearly.

I want to track Khloe down and retrospectively yell at her. I want to turn back time and slap past me. I want to never have been the catalyst for all this shit. I'm hoping that bearing down on this chair until my back hurts will prevent me from doing those things.

When I left, things were a mess. I refused to see family. I didn't want to talk to my few remaining friends. Even though it was me who jumped out the window, I was just as distraught and confused as everyone else involved in our relationship.

There is no excuse for my behaviour. Truthfully, some part of me was hoping that, by behaving badly, I had ensured myself a breakup. The idea that one bad action would make me undesirable to Khloe.

She returned to our flat while I was packing up my things. She yelled. I apologised. A couple of plates were thrown at me. I've muddled through this with my therapist over the years since. But almost all of it was a rehash of previous fights.

I was a bad partner, selfish, unable to give her the life she wanted, and my family never accepted her as one of us. I don't know what parts of it are true.

When I said how I'd been feeling, how I had tried to voice my concerns as we planned the wedding, and explained that gender was a part of it too, she claimed that I was just confused. Said I would regret getting married in a suit or cutting my hair.

The sad truth is that was standard fare for that relationship. I don't believe Khloe loved me all that much by the end of it. We were both just going through the motions we thought came next.

She only said one thing about Dean in the argument: that I

would never let anyone into my life completely while she was around. We had trodden that path before. Khloe hated our friendship; jealousy isn't an adequate word for the way she felt. It went beyond that. And maybe she had some right to feel that way, but the repercussions should have never gone to anyone but me.

In the time it takes for me to process these thoughts, I'm practically vibrating with rage. I feel pale and shaky, and I'm freaking my brother out.

'Are you alright?' Parker asks tentatively.

'I didn't know.' The words come out strained as if each one carries the weight of my mistakes. They land in the room like stones, heavy and unmovable. My burden to bear.

Fuck.

Things make more sense now. The way Dean avoided my eye, the pointed glare she sent my way when I did catch her looking. I'm piecing together what happened from her side, and I'm liking myself a heck of a lot less.

I bet she was hoping I would apologise. Or that I wouldn't ever come home, save us both the trouble of dealing with this.

I can't change Khloe's past behaviour, but I can make up for my own. I have to find a way to explain, to apologise in a meaningful way. Tonight. Or tomorrow. Definitely sooner rather than later.

Dean has waited long enough.

Apology rapidly incoming.

It's a good thing we have two full weeks of uninterrupted time together. That definitely won't make things weird if she doesn't want to see or forgive me.

Chapter Eight

Dean

There are a million people in my parents' house—at least, that's how it feels until the doorbell rings, and the millionth and one person enters with a wave and a hug.

This was supposed to be a small, intimate dinner, just the two families pressed together, but we forgot that those two families make up half the population of Portsea Island. I fucking hate it.

I'm crammed into the narrow hallway, smiling at the OG Mrs Carpenter, Serena's mum and trying desperately to sip my drink in small, lady-like gulps that'll get me drunk fast without ruining the vibe. OGrandma has known me my whole life; I have a photo of her changing Dex's nappy somewhere whilst a fat baby me giggles in the corner like it's the funniest thing I've ever seen. I was zero; it probably was. Yet, somehow, she can't ever separate the lives of my sisters and me. After the third polite correction on my studies, I excuse myself to refill my abysmally empty glass.

I may be a smidge anxious about tonight's dinner. I'm still living down the embarrassment that was legging it out of a family gathering earlier this week. I haven't come up with a good excuse yet, so I keep avoiding adults who might pry.

Based on the way Dad asked if I was feeling better, I'm willing to bet Pom told them I had some kind of food poisoning or tummy bug. It's a toss-up as to which version is more embarrassing, fleeing from whatever Dex made me feel or running to the nearest bathroom in an emergency.

Cringing, I neck back another gin and tonic and eye up the main source of my stress this evening.

There, stood between the monstera plant I gave Mum last Mother's Day and the cheese plate, is Callie. She's smiling at Kyle, laughing as if they have a world of things in common over their cracked beer cans. Who knows, maybe they do have a lot in common. One thing I've realised since she arrived at my door this evening to 'talk' is that I know absolutely nothing about this woman I may or may not be dating.

She only got invited because Pom is a nosy cow who likes to see me squirm. We were dressed and ready to leave when the doorbell went. I was on all fours, trying to locate my lucky lipstick that I'd unluckily dropped behind the bathroom vanity, so I had Pom answer, and she decided, since we were heading out anyway, that Callie should come with us. What could I say but *great*, *fine*, just fan-freaking-tastic! So now here she is, shaking hands with the Carpenter-Browns, smiling, looping her hand around my waist when I stand with her.

It's awful.

There's about a 0.01 per cent chance that we aren't dating. I'm sure of that now. The other 99.99 chances all point to an emphatic yes. It would be alright if this weren't a big deal. But it is. I've never brought someone home. I've never so much as voiced a crush aloud to my parents, and now, well, Callie.

She's all perfect smiles, curly brown hair and neat teeth, and I'm not attracted to her. She's a hot, shaggy-haired masc and objectively pretty good in bed, enthusiastic if not always a bullseye. But she leaves me empty inside.

Watching her make even Pom blush has me considering whether I might simply be dead inside, a hollow husk of a woman without sexual desire at all.

I am broken, faulty machinery that needs to be pulled apart, individually tested and reassembled. If only it were that simple.

That I could manage, but sadly, my body isn't a machine; my vagina isn't a sputtering Chevy I can rigorously test and then order a fully functioning replacement. Well, I'm sure I could if I had Kardashian-level money, but that thought is too strange to linger on.

To my immense relief, I feel a brush at my elbow, and I'm faced with the other living cause of my heart palpitations.

'Sense a second prohibition coming, did you?'

I see Dex's hands first. Those same rings, on those same fingers, the way their veins pop as they reach for the bottle of Jack, Liam brought before moving to the Coke.

It's slowly done, an idle hedonic pour, lavishing in more than a single's worth.

I turn to them, blinking as I process their words.

'With the current rise in fascism, I wouldn't be surprised. Although we'll probably be rounded up and sent somewhere remote first.'

'We?'

'Queer people, people of colour, the mentally ill.' Of which, I am impressively all three. 'Anyone with a disability.' We're going for bingo here.

65

'Glad to see you haven't lost your dark streak.' They laugh, and it's a paradoxically bright thing. It irks me. 'So if you're not knocking back the drinks for fear of shortages, is lesbian loverboy the cause?'

'Loverboy?' I frown, brought back in time to a memory deep in the recesses of my brain. I wonder briefly if they remember it, too. If that word conjures up the same thought to them as it does me, but the meaningless mirth holds no sign of it, so I drop it, burying the thought behind forgotten classmates' names and GCSE knowledge I wilfully parted with.

It's time that I admit to myself that nothing with Dex meant anything to them. All the moments between us that I held dear over the years are just fodder for their romantic origin story. I am just a part of their lore, a footnote in the story they tell to woo girls, along with their childhood cat, Beans, or their brother's too-big hand-me-downs.

'You mean Callie?'

'Do I?' Their eyebrows dart up, auburn and straighter than I remember them being. I stare at them, momentarily transfixed.

Then, I drag my eyes from their forehead back to my girlfriend(?). She's hugging Dadu now, or rather, Dadu's hugging her, hunching Callie over to her five-foot nothingness and enveloping her in a squashy cuddle, overly familiar and far too heavily perfumed. The poor woman can't get a word in edgewise. She's met Dadu before, once when she bumped into us in town one day. She helped carry her shopping out to the car, very chivalrous, and I'm reminded again that I'm completely fucking unworthy of a girl this...perfect.

She's smart and kind and pretty, and I forget she exists most days. Time to humour the idea that I might be a cold-hearted bitch after all.

Beside me, Dex snorts. They know exactly what a Dadu hug feels like; they've been engulfed by her wide arms more times than they deserve.

'Careful,' they lean into my shoulder, their breath grazing the hair around my earlobes, 'or she'll drown in the smell of patchouli.'

I fight against my laugh. They're right, but I don't want to admit it, so I charge forward. I'm tall and wide at the hips, so it's more of a barrel, and I almost send poor Callie flying as I lock my hand around her wrist and pull her away from my grandmother's clutches.

'What are you doing?' we ask each other at the same time and then stop.

'What am *I* doing? I'm rescuing you.'

'What am I doing? I was fine. You just hauled me away from a perfectly nice conversation.'

'Perfectly nice?' Has the girl gone mad, or did she speak to a different elderly Bangladeshi lady in my parents' house? Dadu is funny, eccentric, and caring, but also a little mean. She never hides her true thoughts, even when you desperately wish she would, and we've only just trained her out of saying some of the more inappropriate ones.

'Yes. That was very rude, Daena.'

My insides wince at the use of my full name.

Here's the other thing I should probably fess up about. When I first met Callie, she bugged me. She kept beating me to the right answer in class. I'd bicker, and she'd ignore it. So when I realised she only called me by my birth name, I thought Callie was toying with me and the nauseous sensation I felt at it, well, I mistook it for butterflies. I thought maybe I was finally experiencing excitement. Turns out I just hate it. I haven't worked out how to tell her yet.

'Don't worry about being rude,' I say in a smiled hiss. I am hyper-aware of my nosy family's presence, and I don't feel like becoming the subject of another spectacle.

Around us, Dadu has moved on, unbothered by my apparent social transgression. She's currently hassling Kyle about something on the meat platter. Dad and Serena are talking to Priti and Liam. Archer and Parker are in the hallway chatting over beers. Only Dex remains close enough to overhear our conversation.

'I was trying to rescue you.'

'Daena, I like you. I would like to get to know your family.' At her own admission, Callie's eyes go all gooey around the edges. The idea of her liking me evidently enough to make her feel the warm and fuzzy feelings I've yet to experience.

By all accounts, Callie is perfect. So why can't I bring myself to fancy her? She's exactly the sort of woman people want me to end up with: smart and sensible, respectful, she's never been late to meet me, we work well together, and most importantly, she's going to make a lot of money.

Wait. I've just heard that back. Something is wrong with that logic.

I guess those are the traits one looks for in an employee, not a long-term partner. *Shit*.

My face gives way to a frown. The kind of expression my family has always joked about speaks volumes without me needing to open my mouth.

Callie shifts her weight then, which is when I realise she is wearing boat shoes in my parents' crappy kitchen. Boat shoes! Indoors! There are two major problems with this.

First of all, boat shoes are one of the single worst choices of footwear available to anyone. A crime to both eyes and feet. And secondly, she's indoors, far away from the ocean or potential boats.

We're not exactly a fancy family, but Callie came in on the heels of Pom and I. How did she miss the part where we slipped off our shoes at the front door before walking through the rest of the house?

It's enough. An excuse I can use to segue my confusion into another feeling. The crumb I can use to demolish the whole bloody cake.

The boat shoes settle it. I'm going to end things with Callie tonight. Now maybe. Yes, I give my arms a shake, readying myself to make the first move.

Until Dex sweeps in.

They're smiling, offering a cider to Callie in an extended hand. I glare at them, appalled at their timing. I was just working up the verbal responses to end this thing, and they chose now to interrupt. As if I could hate them anymore.

'Trust me,' they say with a conspiratorial smile, the one that dazzles everyone. 'You were about to get a full FBI-scale interrogation from Dadu if you stayed there. She'd be trying to get you to adopt a pug before the conversation even started.'

Callie, to her credit, smiles back at this person she knows nothing about. I wonder if she's sizing us up together, collecting the creases of their smile lines, the freckles scattered across their sun-kissed cheeks, assessing whether their eyes look as if they could be a cousin of mine. Our house is filled with Ashrafs and Carpenter-Browns alike; for all she knows, we might be one long, convoluted bloodline.

'I'm Dex, by the way.'

'Dex?'

'The prodigal Carpenter-Brown child.' They offer as if that will trigger a response from this woman who doesn't understand who the Carpenter-Browns are to my family. I wince as my oversight in explanation becomes clear to them both. 'It's my mum's birthday dinner.' They finally offer, trying very hard not to show the disappointment that I can see gathering in the downturned corner of their mouth.

Damn, why is being responsible for that such a gut punch? I didn't tell Callie about them for a reason. They weren't important to me. They disappeared and had no place in my life for years. That was their doing. Being excluded from the narrative of my life is a natural conclusion, and hurting them was kind of part of the plan.

So why do I wish I could take it back?

I look down and realise the glass in their other hand is a gin and tonic. They're offering it to me. *What the fuck?* It's like they insist on being inconveniently kind just to make this harder.

As if to prove my point and because the universe hates to see me succeed, Dex's eyes dart to the floor—no, the boat shoes. Of course, they would also notice exactly the one thing I had about Callie.

They look back up at me, the slow flush of red inching up my neck in anger and then back to Callie.

'Oh hey, mate, this is a no-shoes kind of house.' Dex says with authority that suggests my parents' house is as comfortable to them as their own.

'Oh, really?' Callie's voice hitches in surprise. Her eyes dart to me.

It's weird, and something in the air between the three of us shifts. Callie looks from her feet back to Dex and then back to me. I would let it pass if the silence didn't feel so heavy. And then her eyes go back from me to Dex, lingering as though a spider web string connects the two of us, and suddenly it all makes sense.

Callie is sizing Dex up, working out what we are, were, and are again.

Self-conscious, I bring my hand up to my hair and break the eye contact triangle we've been living in. I'm beginning to have immense sympathy for Bella Swan's twitchy attitude toward romantic entanglements.

Thankfully, Dex's annoyingly friendly demeanour never slips. 'Yeah, best slip those off and put them by the back door while no one's looking, bud.'

Just like that, Callie drops the rigid stare, evidently at ease with Dex's presence once again. 'Oh, thanks. Lifesaver!'

As Callie slips the shoes off and makes an undignified scuttle barefoot to the back door, I look at Dex, outraged. They're grinning again.

'Bud?! What are you, a middle-aged divorcee?'

'What? I'm playing nice.' They give a careless shrug that projects a kind of innocence it has no right to.

'You're always playing nice.' I mutter mostly to myself.

I turn so that we're standing next to each other, just a hairbreadth apart, both watching Callie's hurried return.

'Ten quid says Dadu saw the shoes and thought they were house slippers.'

Against my better judgment, I cackle.

'You're on.'

71

Chapter Nine

Dex

'Did you apologise to her yet?' Parker yells from his bedroom.

'What?'

We're both frantically stuffing clothes in our bags last minute because, naturally, Park and I agreed we'd pack when we got home last night and then didn't.

Turns out, when you've spent two years away from your family and friends, you have a lot to catch up on, and that requires a shit ton of alcohol.

Every cousin, uncle or neighbour wanted to ask about my travels, a question which somehow always had a clunky segue leading into the wedding and their thoughts on my romantic history.

I was asked three separate times how many deposits I got back, and three separate people were horrified to find out the answer was none. It was exhausting.

I tried to beg off at the semi-respectable hour of eleven, but Dadu showed me her new foster puppy, Cilla, and well, that couldn't be rushed.

Mum doesn't talk to her parents much, and Dad's both

passed away when I was young, so Dean's grandparents, Dadu and Dada, have been practically my own for as long as I can remember.

Since Dada died, Dadu began fostering puppies for something to do. So far, she's kept three of them, Barkbra Streisand, Madogna, and Tom Bones, but I think Cilla Black-Lab might take up permanent residence with her as well. She says she enjoys finding a stray a good home.

So here we are, my clean underwear spread out on the bed, my socks scattered across the floor, and my backpack open as I try to decide if I have anything formal enough for Parisian society. Maybe I should have thought about this in advance.

Formal is not my forte. I don't clean up well. I've learnt that I'm sexier in the dirt anyway.

'Did. You.' The words come out loud and staccato as if that will help me hear over the sound of Park hairdrying his boxers. 'Say. Sorry. To. Dean. Yet?'

'Not. Yet.' I return at his bonkers volume.

'Dip. Shit.'

In theory, crashing in Parker's spare room is better for me than trying to squeeze myself into the childhood bedroom Mum converted into an office the second I left home. His last flatmate moved in with his boyfriend in June, and he hasn't found anyone to fill the room yet.

I think the ever-revolving door of flatmates is beginning to fatigue him in his old age. There's no age too late in life to have a flatmate, but by your thirties, having to adapt to someone new in your space every twelve months seems exhausting.

In reality, Parker is giving me a much harder time than I expected. He's very emotionally attuned, far more than I gave him credit for, and he's revelling in having someone less put together than himself around.

I'd complain, but, hey, he's not charging me rent, and I get it.

His kid "sister" ran away from a wedding, changed their gender and never fucking looked back, leaving him in the dust and out of the loop. Initially, I didn't communicate with anyone.

When I first bolted, I went to Greece alone. On the defunct honeymoon. It was objectively idiotic, and I'm unclear what I would have done if I hadn't met Hawa.

What started as one tourist helping another order a drink in a bar turned into the kind of friendship that will last me a lifetime. Hawa took me under her wing, made sure I wasn't getting lost, helped me to gather my measly savings and let me return with her to the US to crash in her flat.

It was just luck that she happened to be an ex-professional skateboarder. Happenstance, that she knew who I was via a friend of a mutual on social media. Chance that she was planning to teach a spring course to kids and was down a tutor. Our connection, though, that shit was kismet.

Hawa and I couldn't be more different on paper. She's an Ethiopian American trans woman who gave up her Olympic prospects to transition and has avoided the internet like the plague ever since. I was a chronically online British butch without an ounce of worldly-awareness, skating by on a large social media following. But you don't have to have the same story to make strong bonds.

The Venn diagram of our interests is practically a circle: skateboarding, pop-punk, Avatar, fat crushes on Hayley Williams, affinity for the colour blue, and queerness. Spending time with Hawa is like being alone, and that's the best compliment I can think of giving.

Just thinking this, I miss her.

For the last two years, Hawa has been my home base, the person I've trusted to tell me when my head isn't on straight, and I attempt to be that for her. So, when I said I felt my travelling days were coming to a close, she put my backpack on my bed and sent my arse packing. Her daily texts keep me feeling sane. Her commentary on how hot my brother is, I could live without, but, hey, that's friendship, unfortunately. You take the great with the icky and learn to shut the fuck up.

It was Hawa who made me reach out to my siblings after hiding out in the US for a month. I'd spoken to my parents, told them where I was, what to do with the boxes of my shit that Khloe kindly dumped on their front doorstep (mostly bin it all, since it had been raining), but my brothers were too scary.

It's hard to explain the fondness a substantially younger sibling has for those older; it's two parts adoration and one part regular sibling irritation. I love them; they drive me nuts, but even at their worst, I pretty much think they are the coolest people on the planet.

My whole childhood, my skateboarding career (if you can call influencing that), had been defined by my want to be seen in the likeness of Archer, Liam, and Parker. It feels painfully desperate at times.

So the idea of calling them out of the blue, explaining my newly fortified gender and my half-baked plan with no warning, no sign that I would succeed, was mortifying. I avoided it for as long as I could before Hawa finally called me out for being a chicken.

She might have said something similar about the Ashrafs,

too, but that was less scary. Or at least most of them were. Pom was prickly at first, but Priti replied to my postcards right away. Dadu was always easy. But Dean, well, you can see what I see, and now I understand why.

When I emerge from the spare room, my clothes are packed away, and my e-reader is loaded up with novels I almost certainly won't have time to get to. It's just second nature at this point, a way to guarantee I'm ready to go anywhere at a moment's notice.

Parker, on the other hand, packs like a man who's never left the postal code.

He has a full suitcase laid out in front of him, grubby, busted wheels on clean sheets.

'What the fuck are you doing?'

He looks up, uncurling his spine sharply like a pocketknife extended with a snick. 'What does it look like I'm doing?'

I eye his mound of socks suspiciously, the hoard of trousers piled up next to him and the stack of swim trunks.

'We're not moving to France, bloody hell, dude. You don't need all that.' I step forward, ignoring his protests, as I toss in a week's worth of socks and discard the rest. 'You can do laundry in the château.'

'Did you just say laundry?'

I pause, rewinding my own words in my ears. *Shit.* Yeah, I guess I did.

'Huh, that's new.' It's a small shift in my sense of self, but it's as though I've just missed the bottom step and plummeted free-fall to the floor.

'Well, here in Britain, it's called *washing,*' my brother replies pointedly. 'And I don't wanna do it on holiday.'

'Then I'll do it.' I say, chucking a washing pod at him.

Parker truly is a dichotomous person. Sloppy and careless actions, mixed in equal measure with methodical and meticulous habits. I kinda forgot how much I love him for it.

Maybe that sounds bad, but after so much time away, it was easy to start doubting my memories. They began feeling false, like childhood scenes you know you can't possibly recall because you were too young, but you've intricately reconstructed, regardless, based on everyone else's detailed accounts.

When I thought about Liam's laugh, the way Parker always wrapped his laces around the ankles of his Converse before tying them, or how Archer has always worn Granddad's ring and one of his own on his index and pinky fingers, I questioned if those things were still accurate, if they'd ever been true, if I knew my family at all.

Eventually, I started hoarding those details, building my new identity out of bricks of them, bit by bit, until I'd constructed solid foundations to develop.

Seeing Park be his usual weird self inches away from me, inconveniencing me, is borderline miraculous. I try hard not to let it choke me up. That's a one-way ticket to getting bullied.

'You're volunteering to do chores….for me?'

'Yes?' I face him, unsure why this is surprising.

'But you hate doing chores.'

'I've never hated doing—oh, hang on, you can't base that off of when you lived at home. I've been doing my washing since I was twelve. It was never that I objected to.' I neglect to mention that the chore I loathed the most, washing up, is still something I'd do anything to dodge. 'I've been a semi-functioning adult for over a decade now. I don't appreciate this doubt.'

77

Parker leans up; he's an inch or two shorter than me now, and he stretches to rest the back of his hand on my forehead in a mimicry of checking my temperature. 'Are you sure you didn't come back with some kind of travel sickness that changes your personality and makes you grow up?

'Ha ha. I look forward to a fortnight of pissing-taking, but if you keep it up, I won't wash your laundry.'

We spend the next thirty minutes bickering like children as we walk to meet everyone at the ferry port. Parker is desperately trying to win me over, not knowing that I only have enough underwear for one-half of this trip anyway, so I have to do laundry at least once. Still, I make him work for it.

I love my brother, but it's not all virtuous. What am I, Saint Dexy?

There is something very important you should know before I continue. My dad fucking loves a ferry ride.

It doesn't matter that it probably would have cost less to fly, that we would have gotten into Paris rather than docking and having to travel an additional hour in the car from Cherbourg to our Château, or that the flight would take an hour tops while the ferry takes five. My dad loves the ferry. He thinks it's one of the best inventions and conveniences of modern times, despite it being both quite old and only moderately convenient at best.

So I invite you to imagine five hours in a massive sodding tin can floating on the waves with nineteen members of your immediate family and their closest friends, six children, thirteen adults, a mix of whom are apparently seasick and absolutely no escape until you pitch up port side.

A special kind of hell, even for someone who enjoys their family.

I spend the first hour in the cinema room with my nieces and nephews. There's some threquel on, the conclusion to a series I appear to have entirely missed the first two instalments of. Roscoe attempts to explain them to me in the semi-hushed stage whisper of an eight-year-old, but the other guests keep shooting us deserved dirty looks and shushing us while Lois repeatedly spills the juice in her sippy cup over me.

By the mid-way point of the animated gerbil adventure, I'm damp and discontent and losing the battle with my attention span. So I wave at Meggie to watch over them all and excuse myself to the bathroom.

As I navigate the hallways, I can see the silhouettes of my parents and Sabina and Rami in a booth, talking to Nora and Liam, and hear the distant bickering of Priti and Pom in the gift shops on the main deck. It's kind of nice to know that, despite Brittany Ferries transporting roughly two thousand people from Portsmouth to Cherbourg, there are enough Caprenter-Browns and Ashrafs to successfully mark every available space for ourselves. Like ivy, we spread and claim. I assume that Poppy, Archer, and Parker have successfully found their way to the bar and fully intend to join them after I stop looking like I've peed myself.

In her infinite cuteness, Lois managed to cover my Dickies in, what I assume is, very watery orange squash. It's not water, but clear enough that I hope it won't stain them too badly. These trousers have been through a lot: skate injuries, blood soakings, wading into knee-deep water, sleeping on beaches, mud splatters, New York subways, nightclubs and numerous strangers' floors. I highly doubt that spilt drinks are going to be their final hurrah, but that doesn't change my urge to not embarrass myself. It's one thing to know I didn't pee my pants in public, but another thing entirely to expect my delightfully annoying family to buy that.

Which is precisely how I find myself crouching to angle my groin under the hand dryer as Dean walks into the bathroom.

I turn, expecting to have to offer an explanation to some poor stranger and hoping they'll find it charming and quirky rather than obscene, but my smile dies on its way up.

This is not how I was hoping to see her again.

We left things last night on decent terms, which seems miraculous given our prior interaction ended with her fleeing, but it wasn't exactly comfortable.

All night, Parker's words ran through my head, and my imagination did its darndest to conjure the vile things my ex would have said to Dean. I know my apology needs to be good, and for that, I need Dean to at least trust me.

Last night, she appeared to be alternating between a calm acceptance of my presence and a less subtle resentment. She laughed at my jokes and then sent me death glares like she begrudged the fact that I still knew what would tickle her. I'm not sure I blame her. I might hate me, too.

I was hoping to catch her this evening, maybe over a glass of Sabina's famous sangria when she's at her calmest, the whole trip fanned out ahead of her. Instead, I'm bent at the knee, angled awkwardly, with a warm citrus smell emanating from my now only moderately damp crotch.

We both stop what we're doing, frozen in place as our eyes meet. I'd like to smile and offer an explanation, but she just blinks at me coolly, recovering her distant air and walking to the nearest cubicle. So I frantically fan my trousers with the hot air as if I can dry them before she finishes peeing and straighten as the chain flushes.

I am not, by nature, an easily embarrassed person. Awkward, often, but ashamed? Never.

Apart from right now. I hate it.

I turn to face Dean, greeted with four mirror selves and only one reflection of her. The real Dean, my world one, doesn't deign to take her eyes off herself. Instead, I'm left staring at an inverted her, the mole on her cheek flipped to the right instead of the left, and her one raised eyebrow swapped sides.

She is no less beautiful than I remember backwards.

A weight settles in the pit of my belly, and I try not to puzzle it apart. I don't have it in me to know what that means when Dean still can't be bothered to meet my eyes.

'Lois?' She says, meeting her inverted amber gaze and running her fingers through the ends of her plaits.

This is one of my favourite Deans; collected comfort. Her long hair pulled back from her face, a full cat eye and pink lipstick, dewy skin and worn in denim dungarees that hug her hips and thighs but leave enough room to stretch and play. This is the Dean I see often in my memories, albeit older now. Coming out from underneath the chassis of a car, overdressed and uncaring about the oil stains, or red-cheeked and glowing as she runs around after numerous kids.

'The girl loves a silly little drink but hasn't got the finger dexterity to hold on to it yet.' She explains at my nod.

I try not to let the discomfort of her knowing my niece's messy habits better than I do sting. This shouldn't be news to me. I should know this. I should be coolly informing her of Lois's spilling capabilities whilst she dries her newly citrus-scented trousers under the hand dryer of an international ferry.

It's not fair, and yet it's probably utterly deserved.

The culmination of culpability and discomfort gets to me, and I feel the words scuttling out before I have a chance to assess them.

'I'm sorry. Not for my pants—trousers—not for that. Although this is embarrassing. I'm sorry for back then when I…when you…I shouldn't have. What I mean to say is that I didn't know, but I should have checked. Shouldn't have let you take the flak for helping me. I know that might not change anything, would've, could've, should've and all that, but I am sorry. Parker just told me, or well, two days ago, and I feel like such an idiot, and I was hoping that if you knew that I didn't know but that I'm sorry, so fucking sorry, that you might, I don't know, not forgive me because, you don't need to do that, not hate me anymore maybe?'

It's a cascade of crap, a waterfall of semi-conscious sentiments and whole-hearted apologies that ultimately feel both excessive and pathetic. It is, quite possibly, the worst speech I have ever made in my entire life. All of the words run into one another, I repeat myself, I swear and stumble and make a pig's ear of the apology I so badly want to be deserving of her.

From the blank expression on her face, the slow blink and inhale of disappointment, Dean agrees.

I step back, trying desperately not to see the slightly glassy-eyed stare of my reflection, the flushed cheeks drowning out my freckles, the hang-dog expression it bears. I consider running from it all.

I don't. I made a mess of things. The least I can do is stay to reap the repercussions.

So we stand, our four selves, looking, indirectly, at each other through the veil of the mirror and wait for someone to say something else, anything else, to set the tone of what is to come.

Neither of us does.

Time drags. The world turns to treacle, and I wade through it, impossibly slowly, clutching shame to my chest like a child does a favoured teddy bear.

Eventually, Dean breaks. Her expression doesn't change, her stoicism unshifting, but she tips her head towards the door.

'Wanna go stand on the balcony and heckle the dolphins?'

I am so thrown by this breaking of the ice that I don't have time to think of a witty retort or a meaningful follow-up, so instead, I say;

'I don't think the channel has dolphins, do we?'

Chapter Ten

Dean

The last thing I envisioned from this ferry ride was a hurried apology from Dexy. The second to last thing was to be holding back a teenager's hair as she up-chucks over the edge of the ship just minutes after that.

Of all the Carpenter-Browns, I probably know Cami the least. She's seventeen, no eighteen, maybe(?), and only ever around once in a while at family events. Kyle and Serena see her more, but at least, for the first few years of her life, her mother wasn't sure Archer should be involved. The last time we spoke, she was into Fortnite and K-pop bands I knew nothing about. Now, I'm attempting to keep the long strands of her hair clear of her puke as she hangs precariously over the edge of the metal railing.

Dex has their arm around her slight shoulders and is delicately rubbing circles on their niece's back in a way that they clearly hope is reassuring and not at all reminiscent of the seasickness that's taken over her body. I can tell that they only hope this and aren't sure, by the tight pull of their jaw and the way they're frantically questioning me with their eyebrows.

'How long have you been out here, Cam?'

The poor kid answers slowly between retches.

'Since—we boarded.'

She was bent double when Dex and I appeared on the deck. Not exactly giving either of us the time to delve further into the garbled mess that was her confession.

'Should we get someone?' Dex asks, mostly to me. 'Do you want me to get your Dad?'

Cami's hands brace on the red bars, the tips of her fingers turning yellow as another fit of it takes her, and yet another wave rocks the edges of the ship.

'No.' She coughs, the heaving of her throat slowing.

'Are you sure? He might have some travel sickness pill, or maybe we could just knock you out with a melly, and you'll wake up in France.'

'A melly?'

I blink at Dex, equally as perplexed as Cami.

'Melatonin?' They offer with a shrug. 'It relaxes you and makes you all sleepy. I use it all the time to get a kip on planes.'

Surely, I am mistaken. They did not just suggest drugging their underage niece to combat a little seasickness.

My fury must travel through my glare because they cease their back pats and raise both hands in surrender.

'Sorry, stupid suggestion. Ignore me.'

'No, why not give her some gummies and a glass of whiskey whilst you're at it? If we're gonna corrupt the young, why not go the whole nine yards and dose her too.'

'Hey, I said sorry.'

'Yeah, only took two years.' The words are out of my mouth before I can think better of them. Muttered mostly to my inner self, but just loud enough to be considered appropriately passive-aggressive.

Dex's hands are still raised as white flags, and it's an annoying reminder that I'm the difficult one here. Any high ground I had in my two-year-old grudge just melted away beneath the heat of my catty comment. I would love to say that this is surprising or out of character for me, but unfortunately, losing sympathy due to opening my mouth is familiar territory at this point.

Generously, Dex swallows their knee-jerk reaction and eases their niece's head over the bars.

'Alright, kiddo, the tank's gotta be empty now. Let's get you back inside. Maybe recline you on one of those big armchairs in the lounge area, and have your Dad fan you like a butler.'

The pair stagger towards the glass door as I catch Cami's whimpered 'That would be nice' and the tail end of Dex's laughter. Then it's my turn to hang my head over the edge of the ship.

Maybe if I dangle far enough, some kind of sea life will jump up and knock me in, and I'll get dragged away with the tide. At this point, it wouldn't be undeserved.

I shouldn't be so mean to them. I'm not saying they're innocent. My comment was cutting, but undoubtedly accurate. The accuracy is what helps to make it so harsh. But now, I'm also a dick. And they were all gracious about letting it slide. *Fucking unbelievable.*

I stand there, staring down at the slow peaks and valleys shifting beneath me, watching as they buoyantly ebb away from the line of the boat's edge (stern?) (bow?) (Christ, I know nothing about ships).

The afternoon sun is high overhead, shrouded in clouds and the sweeping silhouettes of seagulls. We're moving surprisingly fast, the water parting around us as if by magic, and I suddenly see myself from very far away. A bug floating along on one of those toy sailboats kids take into the bath. I wonder if that were true, where my journey would be headed; towards a great tidal wave or a surprise ship flip into the sea? Maybe an oncoming freak weather incident of bubbles and foam that I would have to blame on climate change.

The door to the deck creaks open again, and I feel the presence of Dexy coming to stand next to me. There is something so particular about their body, not just the scent but the energy they emit, that I could identify them blindfolded and backwards.

We stand parallel to each other for a while, both facing out towards the oncoming shoreline of France way, way in the distance.

Eventually, they break.

'Well, you sure know how to make a private dig at an inappropriate time.' They say not unkindly.

'It's a gift.' I reply stonily.

'It's something alright.' They sigh, curving their spine and resting the broad expanse of their forearms on the bar. The metal is horribly cold against my hands; I can't imagine it's pleasant pressed up against the bare skin beneath their rolled-up sleeves. 'Come on then. Let's have it out.'

'Excuse me?'

'We've probably got about fifteen minutes before another relative of mine comes out here to vomit, so chop-chop.'

'What on earth are you talking about?'

'Our dirty laundry, let's air it out. Get the wind in those knickers.'

They're waving their hands in front of us both, and I'm too

distracted by the glint of their rings in the sun to process their words in real time.

'Wind in my knickers? Air it out? What on earth are you saying and—hang on, since when did you say the word laundry?'

'Fuck me, has Parker been talking to you?'

'No?' I say, somehow more confused by this addition than the nonsense they were spouting before. 'You're British. We don't say laundry, we say washing.'

'Alright, well, it's an expression, and apparently, I do occasionally say laundry now. Is that alright with you?'

I shrug, still pretty lost on what this means to me.

'Alright, then. Onto the hard stuff. What I meant was, now that we don't have a green teen between us, I'm ready to hear what you've got to say.'

'About?'

'Me,' they answer as if that should be obvious.

'I don't have anything to say about you.' My walls instinctively come up. They aren't pretty, but they have kept me safe all my life. Maybe I could paint them pink.

'And that's what I'm talking about. You've been sniping at me since you saw me days ago, whispering snide little comments under your breath, and if glares could kill, you and I'd be single-handedly keeping the Portsmouth mortuary business afloat.'

'I wouldn't give yourself too much credit there. Pompey isn't exactly short on the grievously ill and close to death.'

'Keeping me humble and morbid, what would I do without you?' They pause, as if considering the rhetorical question a real one. 'Look, if you're not going to be honest, I will. I *did* live without you for two years and six sorta ones before that, and it sucked.'

Without meaning to, I straighten my spine, as though their words have inflated the vertebrae there.

'I've been so happy these last two years. The most me I've ever been, and the only dark spot, the only part I fucking hated, was you not being there with me. And I know it's my fault. I know that I let Khloe come between us, not at the wedding, although, yeah, but before that. She felt threatened, and instead of being an adult learning to talk through my problems, I bent to her will and slowly shut you out.'

I'm nodding because that's a relatively accurate description of the pain I felt in my early twenties. The slow, seemingly systematic way Khloe found to have a problem with every aspect of my involvement in Dex's life and the disarmingly abrupt actions they took to prioritise her comfort over either of our wants.

'I get it, or at least, I understand logically why you might hate me, and you have every right not to trust me again, but I want to prove that I care about you. That I can be there for you again if you want me. That you can trust me with your heart.'

The words press on an internal ache I didn't know I had, buried down deep somewhere beneath my sternum. It's as though I've waited decades for this moment, the sheer confirmation that I wasn't paranoid. I saw what was happening and called it out, and I got brutally crushed for having the bravery and common sense combo to call a spade a spade.

I take a second, assessing that ache, letting my brain check in with my body, my heart.

When I look over at Dexy, the ache dulls. I test that once

more, looking at the soft curls of the clouds around the sun and back to the dazzling brightness of their eyes. The ache is getting lighter every time I glance at them.

I'm not willing to say I feel better. I don't know if that could be true; there is a lot more for me to unpack, sort through and file away in the recesses of my memory, but I'm surprisingly weightless.

'Huh.'

The light auburn hairs of Dex's eyebrows are crinkled inward, each one edging closer together than I thought humanly possible. It's enough to crack a smile from me.

'So, you're sorry?' I try to keep my tone even. I deserve to have one final second of fun playing with my food before I let them off the hook.

They angle their body, and I know they are making a conscientious effort to be present, to meet my eye, to bring their whole self to this conversation.

It's another one of those facts I might have missed if not for the decades of knowing them. Dexy has always had a hard time reacting to things. They spent most of their time in their childhood being told off for not showing they were listening, even when their work was done and they could prove that they were. Then they used our teen years to piece together an exquisitely crafted carefree demeanour, nodding, smiling, laughing at all the right points just so that they could be perceived as responding in an appropriately human register. It's always harder for them to display that concentration in serious conversations.

I'm not suggesting that they're fake, their emotions a shrewd manipulation, it's the opposite. They care more than most people; their brain just doesn't always match up with their face.

It runs miles ahead at three times the speed and often forgets to read the signs aloud. It's just a part of Dex, something I've known about them as assuredly as the cluster of freckles and one mole that are closer together than all the others on the top right side of their cheekbone.

So, when they fix their eyes on mine and move that ocean gaze down to watch my lips periodically, I understand that they are trying to keep themself entirely focused on my reactions and how I might respond, giving it all they've got.

Still, the intensity of their stare is a lot to process. Their eyes, my lips, connected by a sparking invisible line of energy.

'I'm sorry,' they say with an almost scary earnestness. 'I'm sorry for a lot of things, but particularly, I owe you an apology for how I ditched you. You got shit for basically saving my life, and I never once considered how that felt for you or what people might have said. I'm sorry you got blamed for my rash behaviour and that I wasn't around or aware enough to defend you. And I'm sorry that I slipped away before that. It was stupid and short-sighted and, mostly, pretty fucking cowardly. I don't think there's a part of me that will ever not be sorry for that because I denied both of us a great friendship.'

I raise my eyebrows in silence. When I thought about dragging out my forgiveness a smidge longer to make Dex squirm, I hadn't accounted for the fact that they might go into more detail. I get the sense that if I let them, they would keep saying sorry and elaborating on their misdeeds until they run out of breath.

Opening my mouth to speak, I watch as Dex drags their eyes from mine to catch the words straight from my lips.

'You give a good apology, Dexter. Has anyone ever told you that?'

'Yeah, well,' they shift their weight to rest on their left foot, smiling at the old nickname. Their name isn't Dexter, it's an old joke between us. A sign of my trust. 'At this point, I've had plenty of practice.'

I wonder what that means. In the years I've been absent, a diminishing figure in the peripheries of their story, what have they possibly done to warrant a wealth of experience apologising?

'Not that I'm a bad person or anything, at least I'd like to think not, but I just seem to have a way of hurting women and putting my foot in my mouth.'

'Hurting women?' I scoff.

'They get attached, or I say something overly sentimental, and it all goes to shit. I'm not a long-term type of person. I'm much more tolerable in short bursts, easy to fall in love with, and easier to fall out of love with.'

I resist the urge to protest, to point out that if there is a trail of broken hearts across the globe, breadcrumbs to Dex's travels, they aren't as easy to let go as they assume, but they're staring at me again.

'This apology is different, though. More important feels wrong, but more personal. I know that I hurt you, and I bailed instead of taking responsibility for my actions. I want to make it up to you, whatever that means: space, time, answering your questions, a willing servant for the next fortnight.'

I nod because, to my surprise, I believe them, and then I scrunch up my face to contemplate.

'That last one is tempting. I'd have you carry me between the pool and the car, hold my many bags on a Parisian shopping spree, bring me iced tea as I lounge in the sun à la Sharpay Evans.'

'And I would do it.' They say, ducking their chin and making a mock bow. It startles an earth-shattering cackle out of me, which in turn earns a grin from them.

We turn in unison, then, looking back out to our approaching holiday on the horizon.

'Exactly how many girls did you upset on your grand tour?' I venture after a while.

They tactically do not look back at me. 'Uh, I'd have to guess about forty-three. The numbers get a bit shaky in the early stages of Europe.'

If I had a drink right now, I'm sure I would be a contender for the world's most iconic spit take. Come to think of it, a drink sounds really sodding good right now.

I'm still spluttering as I repeat the number back to them. 'That's like, two girls a month.'

Dex's eyebrows knit again, and they seem to analyse the statistic for a second. 'I've never thought about it like that. I guess you're right.'

'Of course you didn't. How would you have the time to crunch the numbers between romancing half of an off-Broadway theatre?'

They're smiling now, a low chuckle carrying their words. 'It wasn't that bad. It's not a monthly quota; several of them were closer together, some of them months apart.'

'How close together are we talking?' I jostle them playfully. They bite their lip. 'Seconds?'

And as easy as that, we're both laughing again. The weight of those years slowly sloughing away with the waves in our wake.

It isn't all miraculously better. The hurt won't go away overnight, but I think Dex knows that. For now, we can just make peace and maybe be friends again.

Chapter Eleven

Dex

When I was a kid, Mum's auntie Marilyn was dating this fancy bloke from Hampstead. I don't remember his name or any defining details about him, but I do recall his house in the south of France.

That is ingrained in my brain for several notable reasons.

Firstly, having a holiday home in another country was the wildest thing I could imagine as a kid. Secondly, when he lent it to us for a week in my sixth summer, it was the first time I ever left the UK. Thirdly, and most stubbornly burned on my psyche, I remember how fucking awful it was.

Much like this trip, we drove, taking our car on the ferry for a brief joyride. Except then, it was four children and two adults crammed into our tiny, loud hatchback. We loaded ourselves onto the ferry and then off again, only to make the trek hours away from the port to wherever the house was.

Parker and I both got car sick around the two-hour mark. I survived without incident, but Parker (and Liam's coat) weren't lucky enough to get out unscathed. Following that, the boys broke into an all-out brawl, and we arrived at the house

95

individually, furious or upset. Dad was upset we were ruining the holiday already, Mum was mad for the same reason, Liam was furious that he'd lost his favourite coat to his brother's poor constitution, Parker was upset that he was being blamed for something he couldn't control, Archer was angry that he was being dragged into the fight and made to take his headphones out, and I was upset that no one would include me in the argument. (Ah, the fate of the distant youngest child, desperate to be included even in the worst moments.)

By the time we unloaded our shit, two of the boys were grounded, and Archer had pissed Dad off so thoroughly that he was made to eat the same meals as Mum all weekend and go to bed/wake up on her schedule. (If you've ever seen a teenage boy forced to order a Caesar salad, no dressing, with his mum while the other kids eat chicken nuggets or steak, you can conjure that extremely strange and cruel punishment in your mind.)

The holiday only went downhill from there.

Liam and Parker had to share a room and a monstrous futon contraption. Archer was made to sleep on the living room sofa, while I had a roll mat on the floor of the master bedroom.

There was only one main bathroom that was technically an en suite, and an additional half bath hidden in the back of the downstairs coat cupboard. And by in the cupboard, I mean you had to part the coats as if entering Narnia to use it. It also had no light in it, so it could only be used during the daytime with the door open. Not an ideal situation for three teenage boys, a kid, and their parents.

The details of the rest of that trip are hazy.

We went to the beach a lot. Archer remained grounded and grumpy the whole time we were there. Liam got into a fight with some local kids because he thought they were being rude to him in French, and he ended up with a broken toe. Dad fell asleep on the sand and got the sunburn from hell, while Parker managed to get stung by a jellyfish, I almost drowned, and Mum got food poisoning of some kind.

Needless to say, it was not the joyous family holiday my parents envisioned.

Naturally, with my expectations for this trip so low, the fuck-off big castle we're staying in takes me completely by surprise.

Not only does it come with a heated pool and acres of lush green land sprawling out behind it, but it also has a turret, an honest-to-god turret and an elaborate glass dining room table big enough to seat a party twice the size of ours.

'I'm waiting for Mr Darcy to emerge from it,' I say with an appreciative whistle as we wander around.

Evidently, I'm not the only person gobsmacked by the extravagant luxury of the place because all of us appear to be awestruck by it. We each stand, taking in its marvellously imposing shadow and the wide, lush land.

Eventually, boredom wins out, and the kids return to their natural state of feral, which in turn means that my brothers are forced to charge after them, yelling about the things they absolutely must not touch. (Glass, statues, paintings, prickly plants, the peacock strutting around at the edge of the garden).

'Glad to see all those swanky hotels in foreign countries haven't made you numb to it yet, kid.' Rami claps me on my shoulder and hands me someone else's suitcases to haul inside.

I refrain from pointing out that, while I did technically stay in a few luxury estates and mansions, I was very rarely the intended invitee, so my last two years have been spent mostly couch-surfing the homes of the very wealthy, which doesn't exude comfort and settling into a lifestyle.

I expect it to be ornate inside, with arched ceilings and wainscoting that bleed into each other, old paintings, chintz sofas and frills on everything. To put it bluntly, I'm expecting the castle to deliver castle. I am sorely and wonderfully mistaken.

While I'm certainly struck by the profligacy of it all, it's decked out in the style of a sprawling mid-century build that would look more at home in Palm Springs than in France.

The stairs are a rich hardwood, meticulously buffed and cared for, nothing like the creaking, draughty floorboards of my parents' house post-2000s carpet, and peppered decoratively with slim, plush rugs. It's bright and vibrant with sharp-angled furniture, edging on camp, and I spy a Tom of Finland picture hanging in the sitting room.

On the first floor, I spot Post-It notes slapped on each door, my dad's scrawl informing us of the room's intended resident.

Now granted, I was the last-minute addition to this whole display, so I can't complain, but it occurs to me as I watch my family file into their respective abodes that there are only eight bedrooms and nineteen of us. I assume that the four younger kids will be based in the one housing bunk beds, which cuts them from the picture, but that's where things begin to go wonky.

Given our arrangement back home, I see Parker's name and assume I'll be sharing the twin room with him, but alas, my darling niece has beaten me to it. Clearly, Uncle Parker holds more appeal than a one-on-one week with me, which I try not to take personally.

Then, there is a sad, cupboard-like room worthy of a

children's story with its single bed and dark-panelled walls, which I discover Cami has claimed for herself. I consider fighting her for it, but she's still all shaky and pale from her brush with motion sickness, and my sympathy makes me weak. I don't have the heart to do it, so I end up leaving her prostrate on her bed, shoes and all, and head up the smaller stairs to the turret room where it becomes abundantly clear that my dad is meddling.

There is one round queen-sized bed in the mostly circular room, and Dean is sitting on it, staring down at Dad's Post-It as if her eyes can incinerate it.

'Did you see this crap?'

'I guess we're roomies then?'

'Ugh,' she throws her body backwards and closes her eyes, sinking into the hot pink duvet. This room looks as though it came straight out of Dolly Parton's fever dream. It's a bizarre mix of Western-themed decor and bedazzled show-girl items. A cacophony of colour, leaning heavily toward blue and pink with the saturation turned up to a million.

It's impossible to decide if I love or hate it. There is simply too much to take in. It doesn't elicit one feeling but a flood of them.

'I take one holiday! Two weeks with time away from school and work, and they make me share a bed in the Rhinestone Cowboy motel. Not just a room but a bed.'

I chew my bottom lip, feeling intensely as though this conversation is intended to be about me rather than to me. These are Dean's private thoughts; she's voicing them aloud, but it's not for my sake. If anything, it's kind of my fault.

'Sorry. It's probably the parents' idea of a joke, to set things up like old times when we'd share a tent or–'

99

'Well, it isn't old times, is it? We barely know each other anymore, and we're adults. Sharing a bed is weird; it crosses so many boundaries. What if you snore and, oh my god, Callie? Am I going to have to explain this to Callie? That's going to make everything so much more complicated.'

'Woah, woah, woah. Hey!' I slap my palms down on her knees and shake until she props herself up on her elbows to look at me. 'No stress. There's got to be a bunch of sofas in this place I can sleep on, some armchairs, that cloud-shaped chaise in the corner, maybe, I bet the bathtubs are more comfortable than some of the places I've slept. We don't have to do this. I can sleep on the floor or anywhere.'

'But if you sleep somewhere else, we'll have to tell why and I'll be making a faff and ruining Serena's holiday.' I can see the stress closing in on Dean, the familiar echo of her teenage meltdowns about exams and university admissions. Left to her own devices, she'll fret herself into a knot of anxiety and break down in tears by tomorrow at dinnertime—privately, of course. She would never let anyone else see her fall apart.

'It's alright. Don't worry about it.' I bring my hands up to cup her face and stop the panic, before I can even consider the intimate repercussions of the act. The skin of her bare cheeks is soft, plump with sun cream and moisturiser; it dips beneath the pressure of my thumbs, and I narrowly resist moving them in a rubbing motion.

This is too much. Too close. Her eyes are wide and fearful, and I can't afford to get lost in their rich depths right now. I glance down at Dean's lips and regret it. God, they're gorgeous. She's gorgeous.

I force myself to break away and cough for good measure. Nothing ruins a mood like a good throat clearing.

100

'Okay, so the brown cloud-shaped chaise it is.' I point to the corner of the room by the window. 'No need to worry, everyone else or force yourself to spend time with me. It's all good.'

She stays as is, perched at a forty-five-degree angle, but gains a sceptical look.

'I couldn't make you do that.'

'I offered. You're not making me do anything.'

'No, this is your holiday too and-'

'Remember,' I say, crouching in front of her and poking my chest. 'Wracked with guilt. Much making up to do. A bit of sofa sleeping is the least I could manage, all things considered.'

'If you're sure you're okay with it?'

She sounds as dubious as she looks, so I put on my best convincing smile and launch my body onto the plush curved seating. When I land, I wiggle a bit before breaking into excessively loud, fake snores. I let them go on for just long enough to be too long and crack one eye open to say, 'See, happy as Larry,' and snore again.

It works, though, because I hear her laughing, and I feel a throw cushion make contact with my face as it lives up to its name.

'It's a mountain by the way.'

'What?'

'The chaise. I think it's meant to be a mountain outline, not a brown cloud.'

'Oh. Well, I'll be fine on the mountain. No need to go telling Loverbutch unless you feel compelled to.' I clutch the pillow to my chest, letting its teal fluff sink against the push of my breathing.

We both lay on our respective beds with only the soft huffs

of our breathing between us, gazing up at the ornate diamond chandelier that might be shaped like a cowboy hat.

'You don't have to keep calling her that, you know.'

'Huh?'

'Loverbutch or lesbian lover-whatever. It's not...we're not... she isn't...'

'You aren't in love with her?'

'Definitely not.' She says with a weighty exhale. 'I'm not sure we're even officially dating.'

'Oh?'

'And I don't want to be. I was about to break up with her yesterday, right when you butted your big head in and started making nice.'

'Ouch. You're not even dating and already at the breakup? Poor Callie.'

'Hey! You don't get to judge me, okay? I have one almost-girlfriend in the last five years; meanwhile, you're leaving a stream of broken hearts across half the world.

I nod, conceding to her point. 'Duly noted.'

'I'd like that ouch rescinded.'

'Consider it struck from the record.'

'Thank you.' She says curtly, her body flopping back into the bedding with a creak of the springs.

I take a second to process the information Dean has offered up. No serious partners in the last five years. What must that have been like? How is it possible? Dean is stunning, all sharp wit and features juxtaposed with the classic curves of her body. She's got this effortless wave and bounce to her long hair, and she's pretty much the smartest person I've ever met.

I've seen Dean in every stage of life: when she was a beanpole in childhood, all knobbly knees and jutting elbows, her awkward pre-teen years with the braces and perpetual Katniss braid, then the later teens where she freaked out about gaining weight, not realising that it all made her look so...there's not a word for it.

It just suited her.

She looked right suddenly. Her hips and thighs were full, her chest distracting enough that I witnessed more than one of my friends take a tumble on a board when she wore low-cut tops.

Our mums always called it 'filling out'; other girls made comments as though it were undesirable, but, even now, the older Dean gets, the more beautiful she becomes. And she firmly falls into the category of desirable. She's basically the definition of the word.

I don't see how anyone can see her as anything less than the most beautiful person in the room. I'm just her friend, and still, every time I've laid eyes on her in the last week, I've succumbed to the gravitational pull of her presence.

There is no reasonable explanation for her staying single this long. I'm so baffled that I couldn't tell you how long we pass in silence.

'She's just so...nice. I'm not saying that I want someone mean. I'm not an enemies-to-lovers kinda gal, but, if I'm being honest, I only let it get this far with Callie because I keep forgetting she's there.' I have to physically reign in the pity my face expresses, and I'm suddenly incredibly grateful for our parallel ceiling staring. It might stop my second ouch from being noticed in my facial features.

'So how did you meet her?'

'We're in some PhD classes together. We were paired together a lot in the beginning for group work, and then one day, she asked me to get a drink.'

'Smart kid.'

'She's older than you...I think?'

'You think?'

I can hear the eye roll coming from the bed. 'I haven't retained much of what she said that wasn't school-related. Outside of class, I was much more focused on the sex part of it.'

My spine stiffens unconsciously against the cushioned support of the chaise. This is not a familiar topic for us; the ground of sexual exploits is very much untrodden, or well, Dean's is.

There was a time, well over a decade ago, when I told Dean everything that ever happened to me. Told her all about my first kiss with Mara Evans, my first-hand hold with Lizzie something-or-other in year ten, and the way my chest felt full to bursting with the excitement of it all. I went in-depth on the topic of second base as soon as I had enough experience to feel strongly about it. Dean was trying to imagine how it would feel, and I'd taken it upon my teenage self to become an expert in both practice and theory (make of that sentence what you will). Then came sex, and a veritable barrage of questions from Dean about what that meant to me, how I knew when it stopped being foreplay and became the infamous *it*. For a while there, it was the topic *du jour* in our adolescent minds.

Dean was always cautious about it. Curious, sure, but cautious. She wanted to know what to expect, but she exhibited no real interest in testing out that knowledge. In the years since I have wondered if that was the rooting sign of blossoming asexuality or just a late bloomer. The two things can go hand in hand or be remarkably similar. It would probably be impolite to ask outright, but her words have me intrigued.

Until this moment, the closest we have ever gotten to discussing Dean's libido is a drunken conversation the summer she returned from University when she told me she could only masturbate to videos of real couples. Fake scenarios turned her off too much to look past it.

I mused over the novelty of a brain I knew inside and out functioning so differently from mine, and then I echoed that thought aloud and later loosened the first rock in the avalanche that was mine and Khloe's relationship. I've been told that it's not normal to discuss masturbation details with our single friends.

'Okay?' is all I can muster up in reply.

'Sorry, that was weird. I shouldn't have said that.' She adds hurriedly.

Now it's my turn to prop myself up on my elbows. I have a choice here; we can either continue to be weird and avoid intimate life topics with each other, or I can take the first steps in rebuilding an actual relationship with Dean as friends who know the ins and outs of one another's lives.

'No, no. Go on if you are comfortable. We're both adults. I sleep with people, you sleep with people, or well, Callies?' I offer.

She snorts softly, and I am immediately gratified by the dissipation of tension within the room.

'Not just Callies. There was an Ingrid once, Liana and a couple of half attempts with a boy named Michael in uni just to check I wasn't into men.'

'You're technically still in uni, De. Isn't this your fourth degree?'

105

'Third, and I mean way back, in second year, so-' She drops her head to the side to face me and sticks out her tongue like a kid.

It makes me laugh.

'So what was the verdict?' I attempt not to channel the air of a prying auntie. I don't succeed. 'On men.'

Dean tosses her head from side to side. 'Not for me. With very rare exceptions.'

'So, do you have a type?'

'Oh, come on!' She looks affronted by my question. 'I told you about my Shane crush when you made me binge The *L Word* with you.'

'That's just called having eyes-'

'Kristen Stewart!'

'Who doesn't?'

'Kate McKinnon!'

'Again, duh!'

'Samira Wiley.'

'Common sense.'

'You are so frustrating.'

'Thank you, I'm glad my work is finally getting the appreciation it deserves. So you lean masculine then?'

'Mostly, I guess. Oh, wait, my childhood crush on Sue Perkins. You had to know I liked them butch.'

'Okay, okay,' I chuckle. 'Admittedly, I maybe missed the rainbow flags with that one. I guess I just always assumed sexual attraction was more hypothetical for you.'

Despite both being adults, despite being willing to talk about having sex with my friends in bars on the regular, despite having been physically caught in the act multiple times and laughing my way out of it, I find myself suddenly very grateful

106

for the separation between Dean and I right now. A flush is creeping its way up my spine to the base of my neck, and I'm desperately trying not to let on.

Thankfully, it seems as though Dean shares at least some of my awkwardness. She blows out a big breath, ousting all the air from her lungs, before answering.

'It is. At least, not until I know someone.'

'Oh, okay, so you're-'

'Demi. Yes. Shit, why is it so fucking weird to come out as an adult. I've seen you arse-naked. I'm pretty sure I have a memory of you peeing your pants.'

'What?! How is that relevant? And also when?' I am, impossibly, even more mortified by the surprising direction this conversation has taken.

'Oh, you were small. What I mean is that I know plenty of shit about you. I *know* you; this shouldn't be this weird.'

'Well, in future, I'd love it if we could leave my infant nudity and incontinence out of adult conversation unless entirely relevant to the point.'

'Right, sorry.'

'But, for the record, it's not just you. In the past two years, I've come out to literally hundreds of strangers, and not once have I felt as awkward about it as I did when visiting the little TESCOs by my parents' house, where I had to explain pronouns to Big Kenny.'

'Oh my god, how did he take it?' The question is equal parts fascination and trepidation. We've both known Big Kenny for twenty years. Back when we used to be allowed to walk to the shop hand-in-hand to buy a magazine and chocolate milk each for a sleepover.

'Pretty well, actually. It turns out he's got a cousin with a trans kid, although he got their pronouns muddled up a few times, so it was unclear what he was implying.'

'Sometimes gender is unclear. I mean, look at you.'

'Look at me?' I smirk.

'Well, you look so…classical boy and yet you're not.'

'Is that your way of subtly suggesting I might be a trans man, stopping by non-binary as a way station?'

'Jesus Christ! No! No, sorry, that is not what I meant.' The panic is clear in her voice, and I realise just how freaked out Dean is by the idea that I don't think she's on board with my gender.

'It's alright if that's what you are suggesting. You wouldn't be the first.'

'Fuck. Humanity is crap. That's such a terrible thing for you to be so blasé about.'

'I won't argue with that.'

'I just mean that gender defies clear outlines. It's fluid for some people but rigid for others. Is it a sliding scale, a graph, a Venn diagram?'

'Fuck me, you are a nerd. A gender Venn diagram.' I suppress my laughter to make it through the conversation. 'I guess you're right. It's all a muddle of words and feelings that mean one thing to some people and something else to others. To answer the unintended question. I'm not a boy. I'm just me. Femininity is attractive, but the word "she" makes my skin feel too tight on my body. "He" kinda leaves me indifferent. I don't hate it, but I'm not sure it's the most accurate. "They" is just the concise way to refer to me, I guess. Mostly I just identify as butch.'

'Butch?'

'Yes,' I grin. 'As long as I'm being perceived as butch,

everything else is kind of immaterial.'

There are a few moments of tranquillity as my words disperse towards the ceiling. I catch the distant sound of the kids hollering in the garden, and one of the twins arguing with my brother. It's nice, normal. It's kind of how I wish my life had always been: Dean and I hidden away together, our families near enough to feel present but not crowding our space, me knowing myself, Dean seeing it, sharing herself with me. I think, fleetingly, that this is the life I should have had if the world were better.

'You're so different now.' Dean says, turning on her side to face me again, and the casual beauty of her knocks the air out of me again. 'Not your gender. That part tracks. But you know yourself now; you're so much more confident and worldly. You fit yourself. Your personality... filled out. I like it.'

Without warning, I feel as if my heart might burst, scattering Normandy with thousands of pieces of Dexter confetti. I don't get a chance to process what that might mean because Rami is calling up the stairs for us to help with dinner, and I bury the feeling down to examine it later from my sleepless holiday chaise.

Chapter Twelve

Dean

Life at the Château is perfection. I have never understood the word blissful until this holiday came along.

Yes, the kids are rolling around on the grass, trying to leapfrog over one another's bodies like they're on the Total Wipe Out course, and every few hours, either set of parents gets too lovey-dovey and has to be yelled out to stop snogging, but, if I ignore my family, I am the most at peace I have ever been.

The last two days have included sangria and swimming, and I'm steps away from carving my name into one of the squashy loungers by the indoor pool, where I spend more time napping under my book than I do reading it. It's glorious.

The kidney-shaped pool is ensconced in a warm bubble of glass, complete with miniature palm trees. It curves completely around, more sunroom than greenhouse, making it the perfect temperature late into the night.

I'm almost entirely contented, almost. There's still that mild scratching guilt in the back of my mind.

I called Callie after dinner on Saturday and broke whatever

we had off. I did it alone, knowing that the girls would ask me why and Dex would look at me with that same frustrating sympathy that makes me wish I could go back to hating them. To say that she took it badly would be an exaggeration, but I also wouldn't describe it as going well.

There were no tears, no begging or wailing, just a strange, stilted silence from a generally chatty woman. She asked why, and I had no clue what to say. I still don't. It's not like there's someone else; that would be too simple. She didn't do anything wrong; I didn't do anything wrong either, although I kinda wish I did just to have something to point at and or blame. I just didn't care about Callie the way I should.

Which is what I told her. She said she got it, but I could practically hear the wounded puppy dog eyes she was making through the phone. Now, I silently bully myself about it while soaking in the sun or laughing with my extended family.

At present, the mums, Priti, Pom, Cami, Nora, Poppy, and I are all leisurely floating around the Olympic-sized swimming pool. An unofficial conclave of the girls gathered to help my sister contemplate her grand romance with David.

They've been together for three years, living with one another for two, and he's started dropping incredibly unsubtle hints about marriage in the last six months. I foresee an engagement ring by New Year's, but the room is divided.

'Twenty-five is too young to get married.' Pom states with her typical brand of self-righteous assertiveness. 'You want to know who you are before you sign up to spend forever with someone else.'

Mum clucks her tongue, and I can tell she's about five seconds away from whipping out my sister's government name.

'I don't know,' Nora adds, pulling her heart-shaped sunglasses down her nose to look around us. 'I don't think you ever truly stop developing as a person. So if you're sure you love David, you can say yes without rushing into wedding planning right away.'

Nora is nice. We aren't close because she pretty much started popping out kids as soon as she arrived on the scene, but that is the typical answer of a white woman. I know my family, and the second that one of us is engaged, both sets of grandparents will descend with expectations and family traditions.

Mum and Dad are very lax about faith. They do what my Mum jokingly calls 'the buffet tasting' of it all. Given that she comes from a Hindu family and he from a Muslim family, they met in the UK (the land of Christian-leaning atheists), and that neither of them believes much in anything, my childhood was a charming hodgepodge of half-practised faiths. We celebrate everything, but somehow I feel detached from all of it. The girls and I know history, we recognise traditions, but there's very little indication that we'll pass those on to our children if we have them.

It was a point of contention with my maternal grandparents when we were all younger. They don't visit often. Newcastle is a long train ride for two elderly people who refuse to drive, so we used to only regularly see them around Diwali, but I know they were pissed to find out we saw Dada and Dadu every week, and to find out we also celebrated Eid with them. I'm unsure if this was strictly a religious grievance or, more likely, an annoyance that Dad's parents lived closer and got to see us more often.

Regardless, you can bet that when the family engagements

start, the twins and I won't have the easy, breezy secular time Nora is imagining.

Judging by the way she starts trying to explain how hard it is to hold people off on wedding planning, Poppy feels the same.

She would know. Poppy and Archer might have three kids, but they aren't married. I was in my early teens when this drama went down, so I don't recall too many details, but I know that she comes from a strict catholic family, and they still aren't too happy about the absence of a ring.

'It's one thing to know you love someone and another thing entirely to get married, Pri. If you aren't ready for that step now or aren't ever, that doesn't make your love for David mean any less.'

'Wise words,' Mum says from the edge of the pool, splashing her feet in the teal water.

Pom and I exchange looks, recognising that, although Mum won't offer an opinion, she's weighing the conversation to indicate how she approves.

'You're not allowed to get married! You're our baby, Priti. If you get married, it means we-' Serena gesticulates a finger wildly between her chest and Mum's, 'are old. Are you calling us old?'

We all giggle at that.

'Speak for yourself.' Mum says indignantly. 'I'm still on the ingénue side of sixty.'

'No one would dare call you old,' Poppy says from her inflatable chair.

'Not to your faces anyway.' Pom and I quip in unison.

Serena whacks her arm through the water, affectionately smothering us with a tidal wave, but poor Cami gets taken down right along with us.

All three of us retaliate until the whole collection of women comes away, drenched, and screaming for a truce.

'Where was all your care for your babies when you just tried to drown us?' Pri cries, pulling her damp hair into a bun on the top of her head. 'Baby my arse!'

'Yeah,' Pom mirrors the action but with a French braid instead. 'What about Cami? She's the youngest. Isn't it time we pass that title down?'

'No, no.' Serena wraps an arm around her eldest grand-daughter's neck and squeezes her into a surprisingly effective headlock. 'Cami is my grandbaby. You girls are part of the original babies. Grandbabies get different rules; you all know that.'

It's strange to watch how Mum and Serena's lives have differed. They aren't a full year apart in age, a few years younger than their respective husbands, and remarkably similar, and yet Serena is a firmly established grandmother, with a veritable brood of children to dote on whilst mum's most reasonable grandchild-bearing prospect is...me? She shouldn't get her hopes up anytime soon.

At this rate, Priti might be the only one who produces any more Ashraf children. Pom and I are increasingly likely to become the weird old aunts from Practical Magic by the day.

'Marriage isn't the final boss of a relationship anyway,' I conclude, desperate for a conversation change. 'Look at Dexy.'

'It's Dexy again, now is it?' Pom hisses in my ear, low enough that only I hear, and I bat her away with my palm.

She ducks under the water to avoid the furthest reach of my hand, and I do my best to tune her smug smile out when she re-emerges.

'What do you mean?'

I'm very aware that the chattering crowd has fallen quiet. Every pair of eyes locked on me. As though they think I'm about to pull back the curtain on some grand secret.

The pressure of saying the right thing, making a good point, but not telling them something Dex would be uncomfortable with the full congregation knowing, squeezes in on me.

'Accha, listen. Dexy kept listening to what was expected of them; they'd been with Khloe a long time, and marriage felt like the enviable next step, but just because a relationship seems ready for marriage doesn't mean both people in it are or that it's the right choice for that love.'

'And you know this, how Miss I-never-intend-to-settle-down?' Priti asks.

'It's not that I never intend to settle down. I just don't have time for it.' My words come out with an unwarranted edge.

Pom joins the rabble, floating through on an inflatable flamingo.

'I think you're both focusing on the wrong part of it. Isn't it fucked up that we have to 'settle' at all?'

Mum rolls her lips and looks at Serena with a melodramatic frown. 'Re, you're going to have to let me in on some of that grandchild action. With these three, I might never get an heir.'

'An heir?!' the three of us repeat, indignantly.

Just like that, the tension dissipates, and everyone is laughing again. The Carpenter-Browns' in-laws move on to asking Cami about her boyfriend. We see pictures of a slightly scrawny white boy, his hair long and wildly curly, as he runs across a football pitch and hear about the teenage drama of him being her ex-best friend's new best friend's ex-boyfriend's cousin and how they had to hide their relationship in the third-period maths class they shared with them.

If I'm being honest, I lost the reasoning for the need to conceal the relationship somewhere in the trail of teens involved, but it's nice to see Cami open up, and teenage angst is reliably amusing.

She's showing us what she wore to her college farewell drinks, and, sure enough, in the background of a handful of photos is a blonde girl giving the happy graduated couple the filthiest side-eye I've seen in years.

We stay in the water until we're all nice and prunish, the glass-domed ceiling trapping us in a warm bubble of summer heat even as evening sets in. People slowly trickle out to shower or dry off or help with dinner until it's just me, parked back in my lounge chair, watching the sun decline overhead from the safety of inside.

It strikes me as strange that I have never been on a relaxing holiday. Camping trips used to be yearly, a handful of holidays across the country to visit family and a two-day coach tour of Brussels in year eight. It made me feel so worldly at the time. A hundred children crammed into two coaches that drove overnight, with a single night in a hotel and back again before the following evening. Even sleep deprivation couldn't stop me from feeling like a baller, the first family member to go abroad alone.

It never occurred to me that my family would surpass my travels with time. Priti and David go on European city breaks at least once a year to see different holiday markets or get away from the dreary British weather. Pom gets sent on all kinds of influencer trips now to sun-soaked resorts and grimy nightclubs in warmer climates.

My parents started taking holidays when the girls moved

out. Little trips to bask in their newfound freedom. It's embarrassing to admit how little I've seen of the world. I've been so focused on school—my BA, then my MA, then my PhD and spending all my time climbing the work ladder. I went from cashier to banker to training as an accountant during my holidays. There never seemed to be the opportunity to put that all on pause for a week and take myself to a different country to breathe. Shit, there never seemed to be the time to have drinks or make friends or have fun.

I'm trying to think of the last time I did something for myself that wasn't tinkering around with my truck. I love working on cars; it clears my brain. Locating the problem, examining it, knowing it has to have a clear solution, getting the right part, taking the old one out, replacing it with the new, and watching the machine gain new life again. It's beautiful. It's logical. It's thera-fucking-putic.

It's how I wish I could spend all of my time. But that isn't how the world works. I need a job, something that can make real money, something that can pull me out of poverty, whether it makes me happy or not. Accountancy does that, and with my PhD, I could progress to something bigger. Build a career.

That's what I've been telling myself anyway.

That's why I don't take holidays and I don't have time to relax. Except I'm exhausted, and I can't help but wonder how long I've been running on fumes without noticing.

Other people have time to take a break, to make friends, to find a partner if they want one. Most adults have a well-rounded life, boxes they check off and wants that they voice. I have none of that. I have work, school, and a family that begs me to open up to them. I had Callie, and I used her to scratch a sexual itch, and, do you know what? Not once was it worth it. That girl could not find my itch, even with clear and concise directions.

Fuck.

I stretch out my spine, letting my muscles pull and roll as I stand. I cocoon myself in the plush fabric of the towel and turn back towards the house.

I'm gonna need more alcohol to process these kinds of thoughts.

Chapter Thirteen

Dex

'It looks like Tangled,' is Parker's grand observation as we walk around the winding streets of Mont Saint-Michel.

'Actually,' Meggie's ears perk up, and I assume she's about to monologue on her favourite Disney movie, but she throws us a curveball. 'The kingdom of Corona was based on the commune of Mont Saint-Michel. As well as providing a key structural influence for Sleeping Beauty's castle.'

We look at our niece and then glance at each other, eyebrows inching towards our hairlines.

'When did you become an expert in castles?'

'And where did you learn that scary tour guide voice?' I follow up.

I don't catch what she says as she walks away, but I can feel the weight of her pre-teen exasperation and smirk at my brother.

'I think she's one educational year away from calling us plebs.'

'Thank god you're home. I need someone to share the burden of being the stupid uncle with.'

'Fuck off. You own the copyright to that title, no matter who's around.' We push at each other's shoulders playfully, blissfully unaware of the death glares we're getting from family and the wary looks of the French. 'Besides, if travel's her new thing, I'm coming to knock you off the throne of favourite.' He snorts. 'I am very well travelled, I'll have you know.' I say in my poshest voice.

'That's one way to put it. Back in my day, they used to call it getting around.'

I elbow his rib and receive a semi-violent hair ruffle that has Liam emerging from the woodwork to wrestle his way into it. Somehow, he has Parker in a headlock before I manage to turn around, and then we're all chained together in a rabble of arms and insults like we're kids again.

Behind our scuffle, I can hear the kids laughing and Nora begging us to stop embarrassing the family. We ignore them all, smacking each other with our available limbs in an attempt to break free from the older sibling's hold. I'm thrashing beneath Parker, who in turn is wiggling around trying to escape Liam, who in turn is saying a silent prayer that Archer's back is too funky to weigh in.

When we eventually scatter, I'm too busy staggering to see the firm smack on the forehead with a guidebook coming. I rub my head and watch, amused, as Mum works her way down the line of us.

'We're not puppies,' Parker gripes, quiet enough that I know he's testing his limits even as an adult.

'True. If you were puppies, you'd be better trained than that, and I'd have a little bottle to spritz you with when you're bad.' Mum replies stonily, sipping from her Evian bottle. 'You've just single-handedly made a scene in front of everyone who

120

lives here. So, unless you're looking to get demoted to the kids' table again, I'm begging you to behave.'

'Yes, mum.' Our shamefaced trio answers solemnly.

With a final damning look, one that used to speak of incoming apology chores and earlier bedtimes but now means something much scarier and more vague, Mum flounces off, looping her arm through Sabina's. The dads file after them, carrying Leon and Lois on their shoulders respectively, gracing us with lightly disappointed looks. Then the girls and kids file ahead, Nora glaring at her boyfriend like he's a gaudy Christmas jumper she'd rather avoid being reminded of.

'Nice work, dinlos.' Archer clips Liam around the ear, and they walk off together, leaving Parker and me trying to hold in the laughter.

We haven't always been close. He came out young and pretty much got accepted as one of the boys right away. The eight years between us felt much more prominent when I wanted to play with my brothers, and he wanted to be cool with the older boys. We never fought; the gap was too big to have that emotional bridge, we just didn't know how to communicate. His problems were always so much bigger than my childish ones. Then Parker hit his twenties, and I became a teen, and the world of similarities started to unfold between us. The older I got, the more of my brothers I saw in myself, the easier everything became.

We both get the giggles when we're in trouble, worse when we're in it together and have to physically fight the desire to make the other one laugh louder, thereby getting us both deeper in the shit. It's a tale as old as, well, the last ten years. Parker, my partner in crime, Dean, ready to stop me from doing time.

It's no surprise to me, then, that she is the only person trailing behind us. She's wearing a pink and orange sundress, perfectly white trainers, and a sly little smile as she meets my eye.

'She wasn't exaggerating, you know? The population of this commune is roughly thirty people,' she informs us, gesturing around at the sloping stone buildings that line either side of the street. 'You did just make a scene in front of the whole island.'

'Meggie got to you with the fun facts, too?'

She shrugs. 'What can I say, the kid's got a gift. But can you imagine only having thirty people around to talk to?'

Parker examines the people passing us by at their idle pace, the way they seem so at ease with one another. 'I don't know, it sounds kinda nice to me. Like one big family.'

'Yeah, I love you and all that, but I'm not wild about the idea of being stuck on an island completely separate from other people at high tide with you.'

'Clearly, you'd rather we exist through a phone screen at a couple of thousand miles distance.'

'Oi!' I blink at the sting of the words. They were said playfully, but the bitter truth to it feels like a slap to the cheek.

'I just mean,' Parker keeps his tone forcibly light, but I can see that he's registered the hurt the same as I have. 'It seems like a nice way to live. A quiet life. The same world, day in and day out, tourists, tides and everything else shut away at the end of the day. Nothing to interrupt your nights.'

'What's interrupting your nights, Park?' Dean asks with such honest curiosity that it disarms him.

'Oh, you know, pretty young things, work-fuelled night-mares. A recurring sex dream about Sissy Spacek that I've had since I turned twelve.'

'Ew.'

'Don't knock my girl.'

'That's not who the ew was for.'

'Have you ever thought about moving away from the city?' Dean pushes on, unwilling to let the one thread of honest conversation get bogged down by our jokes.

'And do what?' Parker says with a half smile. 'Move to the middle of nowhere?'

I stop, realising that maybe she is onto something here. Parker doesn't have a taste for city life. We've lived in one our whole lives. He moved from one small city to a big one for Uni and then back again, but more because he didn't seem to know what to do. He's always hated crowds, and he likes long drives. None of the things I value in a city call to him: cinemas, walkable venues, shops, convenience, or communities. He likes his personal space. He likes nature.

'There are loads of ways to live, not just in the city.' I'm thinking about the smaller European villages Hawa and I visited, where everyone said good morning to one another, or the farming community in rural Vermont, where all the kids skateboarded in the car park of the fairground or the local school.

'I'm not just going to move far away. My whole life is in Pompey. Work. Friends. My whole family too, or it was until you moved.'

Dean catches my eye, and I know she's thinking the same as me.

'You know that we'll still be here even if you move away, right? When I was moving around, you guys were still my family. We would come to visit.'

123

'Dexy, you can't drive. What are you talking about? You'd visit me, how?'

'You still haven't got a license?' Dean leans around Parker to let me get a peek at her appalled expression.

'Hey! I intend to live in walkable cities for the remainder of my natural life. I am all about that public transport, baby.' I toy with the end of my words, making a spectacle of myself again and making them laugh in the process. 'It's better for the world that way. It's eco-conscious, innit?'

Parker hoots in response at that and jogs forward a few spaces, spinning on his heels to walk backwards.

'Well, I can drive, so I'm not about to stay for Little Miss Mechanic's TED talk on its values. See you clowns later.' He turns again and speed-walks to catch up with Mum and Cami.

I watch him go, troubled by the conversation Parker so deftly slipped his way out of. It's evident that he's unhappy, settling for a convenient life rather than the one he wants. No use comes from stalling your life for the sake of other people; I know that better than most.

I tried to be the perfect daughter for mum, a cool but involved sibling, an easy-to-talk-to aunt, the perfect partner in the perfectly homo-normative life, no muss no fuss, the 'perfect' lesbian, not stereotypical but not too straight-passing. I spent so much time fretting about what everyone else wanted and whether I lived up to it that I didn't have time to listen to my brain screaming my own wants. I didn't know how to listen to it anymore, and I cut out the only person who knew how to give those things a voice.

Speaking of which, Dean is looking at me with that perfectly shaped eyebrow of hers raised.

'You can't be for real!'

'Hey. I have road phobia, and you know it.'

'You've never been behind the wheel of a car! You don't have any reason to be afraid.'

'Ah, but, see, if I got behind the wheel, then the rest of the world would have cause for fear.'

'You are so dramatic.'

We walk in shared silence for a while, listening to the sounds of our bickering families and the chatter of other tourists wandering past. I think she might lay into me more; I know she wants to, but to my surprise, nothing comes.

'It's nice to be able to laugh with you again,' she says instead. 'I wasn't expecting to have missed it that much.'

'Really? Forgive me because this is about to sound cheesy as hell, but I missed you every day.'

'You're right, that is the cheesiest thing I've ever heard.' She bumps her shoulder against mine and grins.

'No, but genuinely, I feel as though, for the past decade now, I've been walking around with my plug out.'

'I beg your pardon?' She looks horrified and confused by my words.

'Like when you fill the tub but the plug doesn't fit or you have a shitty replacement one, you know? And you keep running the water, doing what you're meant to be doing, but there's always something draining away. No matter how much water you run. You can't keep the tub steady and full; you're always fighting to catch up with the stuff that's slipped down the drain. It wasn't just you; it was identity and my confidence, but you were, are a big part of it.'

She nods, her eyes fixed on the outline of the Abbey just ahead of us. We're approaching the arched entrance, and the crowds of tourists are all cramming themselves into one long line.

'I slipped down your drain?'

'Metaphorically speaking.'

Until this point, we've had quite a bit of freedom to wander the ramparts, looking out at the horizon, and taking in the quaint cobbled streets without interfering with other people, but this is the first time since disembarking the ferry that the holiday has felt at all touristy.

The stairs are getting steeper, and I notice that Dad and Rami have gathered on the left side to let people pass the clump of our two families.

Dean and I make a beeline for them. It's a bustle of backpacks and bodies crushing against us as we move diagonally to the tide. A broad white man with a camera looped around his neck checks Dean's hip, sending her staggering sideways and mutters a complaint in German.

'Whoa, there.' Instinctively, my arm shoots out and wraps around her waist to keep her on her feet. The palm of my hand makes contact with the fleshy softness of her waist as I realise my mistake.

This ought to be normal. Just one friend helping another. Instead, I'm compelled to squeeze her close to me. She meets my eye, and I get the sense that she might be just as aware of the location of each of my fingers on her body as I am. Reluctantly, I pull away and flatten my expression into neutrality.

By the time we reach our families, I've regained my equilibrium and have nothing to hide. I sling my arm over Mum's shoulder in greeting, beaming at her and expecting her to grin back.

She doesn't.

She looks pale, and her hands are braced on her hips like

she's out of breath.

'Is everything okay?'

'Oh, you know, just too many stairs,' she jokes, sounding more pained than winded.

I flash a glance behind us. It was a lot of steep stair climbing, but this is the woman who voluntarily avoids using the lifts at work and forced us into a long walk every summer camping trip. Mum has always been the most active of us.

Patting her lightly on the back, I look around at our group. The kids are climbing over my brothers, but no one else seems to be struggling. Rami and Dad are distributing our tickets, but there's a worried look that flits between Sabina and Poppy that sets my peach fuzz on edge. I suddenly get the overwhelming feeling that I'm missing something critical.

No one elaborates, though, and Mum slowly lifts herself upright to take gentle sips from her water bottle as though nothing is off. The creeping unease dissipates. Maybe I'm just being overly cautious. Maybe my subconscious is having a weird reaction to loved ones' ageing. Maybe this is all completely commonplace, and sixty-year-old mums just have trouble with tons of stairs.

We continue the tour of the Abbey as if nothing is off. I carry kids on my shoulders, Pom gets shushed in the main hall, and we all stop to look out at the truly astounding view of the mainland and the encroaching sea.

It is stunning, but I have to admit, I'm relieved when we all pile out of the cars back at our holiday house. I'm starving and sweat-sticky, ready for an evening swim in the pool.

Archer and Liam disappear to put the kids to bed while Nora and Poppy giggle at each other and head in the direction of alcohol. Mum says something about needing to lie down, to which Sabina and Dad both agree. With Priti disappearing to call David (the boyfriend whom I feel less bad about forgetting, given his generally forgettable name), that leaves only a handful of us unattended in the massive Château, so I aim to be the first in the pool for a shot at the least-deflated inflatable.

I scamper upstairs at lightspeed, looking for my swim trunks and not thinking to knock before busting through the door to my little attic room.

It's then that I remember the room isn't just mine. I remember very quickly because, to my surprise, I am greeted by an entirely topless Dean as I stand, blinking, dazzled by the gloriousness of her tits and their unexpected appearance.

Chapter Fourteen

Dean

I scream.

They scream. Reflexively, I throw the closest thing I have at Dex. Unfortunately for me, that thing is my bikini top. It lands over their face, one large cup covering only their right eye like a comical eyepatch.

'Shut the door!' I yell, immediately bringing my hands up to hold my breasts.

They kick it closed with their heel, not bothering to avert their eyes or move with the door to give me some privacy.

'You're naked.'

'Half-naked! You're wearing my top as a hat.'

'Only because you chucked it at me,' they protest.

'I panicked.' I snipe, still clutching my chest helplessly.

Dex seems to come back to themself in that moment, their eyes instinctively squishing shut as they pull the bikini from its landing spot and hold it out with one dangling hand.

They use their spare hand as a clamp over their eyes and turn around for triple good measure, giving me space to put it on.

I take the offering gratefully and release the weight of my boobs back down a fraction too sharply.

'I'm sorry. I didn't think to knock. I hadn't seen you come up the stairs already.' They explain, muffled by their back to me.

Until now, we have avoided the uncomfortable obstacles of sharing a room pretty neatly by being hyper-aware of one another's whereabouts.

Dex surfaces surprisingly early, sneaking out to use our tiny upstairs bathroom and shower, taking their clothes with them. I wait until I hear them creep back in and take a seat on their makeshift bed before I say good morning and begin my routine. Then I usually turn in first, brushing my teeth and peeing before they've started to climb the many stairs so that I'm safely in bed and scrolling my phone as they return in pyjamas.

Honestly, the whole thing is surprisingly comfortable. We chat before sleep, both staring up at the ceiling. Sometimes, we reminisce, other times, they tell me about their skate-boarding adventures and the different techniques of it across the world. It has kind of felt like one big sleepover, and I'm pleasantly astonished at how I've missed the easy friendship.

Now, though, it feels distinctly different. I am reminded that adults do not have sleepovers for this very reason. An adult sleepover is something altogether different and usually involves a certain level of nudity. A level I've just brought it to.

'It's not your fault,' I say, trying hard not to let the burning embarrassment in my cheeks creep to my throat. 'I was in a rush. I wanted to get to the pool before Pom steals that damn Flamingo again.'

'Great minds. I'm pretty sure it's the only pool toy the kids haven't managed to pop yet.'

I grimace, recognising that this means two things: Dex will also be changing, and there is no avoiding mentioning what they just saw. We should clear the air around it if we're going to be heading down to the pool together.

I hastily slot the clips of the top in place and make sure everything is secure and supported appropriately before letting them know I'm done.

Dex spins around, nodding, and I'm at least gratified to find that their white skin is unmistakably flushed, even with their new tan. At least it isn't just me who feels silly.

'It looks better on you than it did me,' they say with a slow smile.

'Alright then,' I pat my hands awkwardly against the top of my thighs in a penguin motion. 'Let's get this over with.'

'What?'

'You know…let's address the elephant in the room.'

'Huh?

'This! What just happened! These!' I gesticulate madly down at my cleavage before I have the good sense to stop myself. 'Let's at least make a joke about it so we don't feel weird.'

'You want me to make a joke about your boobs?' They question cautiously.

'Yes! Tell me one is bigger than the other,' (the right one), 'or that they're comically big.' (they are). 'Clear the air!' I urge them.

'They're perfect.' Dex replies without hesitation.

We stare at each other for a second. From this angle, with the window behind me, every part of them appears to be alight

131

with a golden aura. Their gingery hair is almost copper, their tanned skin speckled with freckles, even their shirt is a soft yellow knit buttoned contraption that they've slung over a white vest.

Only their eyes contradict the golden sunset glow, still a fathomless blue-green that I can't look away from.

I should say something! They should say something! Although, on second thought, I'm slightly afraid that if Dexy opens their mouth, they'll say something else that will surprise me. I should be the one to speak first. That would be good. I just need to work out what to say.

It would be easier if I wasn't caught in Dex's wide eyes, watching the dying sunlight sparkle in the whites of them. Shit, have they always looked like that? How does anyone get anything done with them around? I'm beginning to sympathise with all the fleets of silly women who volunteered to be their holiday flings. It might be nice to get flung.

Fuck. I have got to pull it together. That was a really weird thought.

'Well,' I cough, struggling to regain any semblance of my old composure. 'Thank you. That was unnecessarily nice.'

My skin feels alive under their observation, prickling lightly in response to the roving line of their oceanic stare. There's something indeterminable in their expression that I haven't seen before. I wish I knew what it meant. After all this time apart, I still recognise so many of Dex's emotions as they are written across the animated planes of their face, but this one is a mystery. A phenomenon in my studies.

There's a hint of hunger to it, as though they can't consume the image of me standing before them fast enough.

'Sorry.' Dex appears to break free of their trance then,

clearing their throat and moving towards the growing crap pile that is their emptied-out suitcase. 'I'd do you a fair trade, you know tit for...well tit, but I'm already wearing the sports bra I planned to swim in.' They chuckle lightly, but the static energy in the room remains disconcertingly alive.

'Give me something else then.' I sit down on the edge of my bed before I can think better of it and register, belatedly, just how suggestive that sounds. 'Tell me a secret or something. Trade me nakedness for emotional vulnerability.'

Their body is bent in half, stooping to pick up swim shorts straight out of a 2000s teen surfer movie, but I can hear the smile in their response.

'I suppose I can get on board with that.' They walk back to face the bed, standing over me in a way that traps all the air in my lungs. My chest feels seconds away from exploding. 'What do you want to know?'

Great question. The only problem is that I hadn't thought that far ahead.

'Did you ever come close to falling in love with any of the girls you met on holiday?'

It sounded like a perfectly innocuous question in my head. The kind of thing two friends discuss over drinks, but we aren't drinking alcohol, they've just seen me shirtless, and we haven't made our way back to that type of friendship yet. I'm prepared to accept that I am the one leaning into the weird vibe between us right now. Is it wrong that I kind of enjoy it?

They're grinning again, that wide Heath Ledger smile that flaunts their oversized teeth and highlights the smile line indenting their cheeks. For a flash, I pity those silly girls who only got Dex for a week or a month because that's a smile I could see a thousand times every day and not grow tired of.

133

'You don't know how to make it easy on a guy, do you?'

'You're a guy now?'

'Sometimes. Guy, dude, boy, bitch. They're all kinda gender neutral, don't you think?'

I tip my head in assessing agreement. This is the Dexy I remember from my teen years: the unassuming philosopher, the learned stoner. They have always been a master of taking something commonplace, that you might never have given a second glance, and inspecting it from unique angles. I've seen them play the stupid card more times than I can count, and yet Dex Carpenter-Brown is one of the most emotionally astute people I've ever had the pleasure of interacting with.

As if to prove my point, they answer my original question with beautiful intricacy.

'I fall in and out of love pretty easily. If you look hard enough, there's something beautiful in everyone. Maybe it's physical, a perfect pair of tits, or more obviously pretty eyes. They might fit your type or kinda resemble a childhood crush. Some people are kind or keen to share their brains with you. Lots of people look for love in the stereotypes. The butterflies that take up residence in your stomach, or the excitement when they text you.

'It's easy enough to get swept away in how they make you feel about yourself, what they do to you, even. I think that's what people talk about when they say they love someone, but those things are easy. They come and go like a tide. You can't always make someone feel butterflies by flirting with them, not if you spend the rest of your lives together. Those things don't mean love. They indicate a crush.

'Everyone I've dated recently... it was textbook. Butterflies and giggles and tingling touches. They enjoyed the way their body responded to me, and I liked making them feel that way. So when I say I find love easily, it's because it's not the act of love.

'I loved parts of those girls, they loved what I did to them, but we weren't *in* love. Being *in* love with someone is a state, something you are in together. It requires the act of love, waking up every day and loving them and staying as the crush ebbs and flows. At least, that's what I have to believe. I loved all of those girls…sometimes it was fleeting, but I never came close to being in love. Does that make any sense?' Dex gets awkward towards the end, their hand coming up to scrub at the back of their neck, playing with the freshly shaved hair there.

I'm left immensely frustrated both by the way they so succinctly summarised thoughts it would have taken me years to gather together and that they have enough mass in their biceps to look like fucking butch Adonis while feeling insecure.

'Sorry, that was probably drivel.' They chew on the inside of their cheek, and I know I'll have to think of something semi-coherent to say to stop them from overthinking. 'I guess I've had time to think about love and not a whole lot of people asking for my opinion on it.'

'No, it was shockingly spot on, loverboy.' I don't mean for the nickname to sound as flirty as it does. I contemplate apologising for it, but seeing their smile, I choose not to. 'I know what you mean.'

'Callie?'

Now it's my turn to cover my eyes because, honestly, that's not who I was thinking of.

'I never thought about Callie enough to find something

135

lovable in her.' I might as well be honest about it with Dex; at least, it's not as if they'll stick around long enough to tell anyone. They're probably counting down the days until they fly away again to some exotic location. 'Maybe that makes me cruel. I'm sure she was plenty lovable, but I barely paid any attention. She didn't make me feel…anything.'

'Nothing?' Dex sits beside me on the duvet, and the waves of heat that radiate from their body make my thigh prickle at our proximity.

'No butterflies, no giddiness, no…anything. No one I've ever dated has made me feel any of those.'

'Well, surely they've made you feel something. You've come at least, there's some love to be found in sex.'

Ah. The bitter truth of the matter. That secret shame I've been taught to hide away as a card-carrying queer fifth-wave feminist.

'No one else has ever been able to make me finish.'

I shake my head, sure that the embarrassment of it all has gone straight to my cheeks.

'Never?' Dex looks as though the bottom has fallen off of their world, land and sea spilling out all over the place, rushing at one another and shifting everything they know to be true.

'I mean, I'm fine on my own. Everything…functions if that's what you're asking. It's just with other people that I have trouble.' A frown has formed between their brows, and it's so comically unnatural that I can't begin to interpret it.

'And you're sure you're not entirely ace?' They follow up. It's a perfectly natural question, one my doctor asked, my therapist in university, and even my gynaecologist when I broached the topic.

'Oh no, I like sex. I want to come. I just want it to be with someone I know and trust first. Picture a drawbridge.' I try to explain.

'A drawbridge?'

'Yes!' I recall the island today, the way the bridge lay over the remains of an old moat. 'A drawbridge. I'm on one side, my potential partner on the other, and there's a body of water between us, deep and vast and entirely unknown. I can't begin to imagine wanting them sexually or how we'd be together until we have a way to connect to each other.'

'Okay,' they're staring at the floorboards, nodding like a dog on a dashboard to let me know they're still listening. 'So once the connection is built, the drawbridge is down, you can start to want them?'

'Precisely!'

'And with Callie, you wanted to, but it was no good?'

'Eh.' I wish I had a simple answer, but I fear the problem is more in-depth than I'm willing to get. 'With everyone else, it felt like they wanted to get off first and then deal with me. I've always taken a long time; it can be tricky. So I got the sense they didn't care whether I was satisfied or not. Callie…tried, at least. She asked how it was and if I came, until eventually, it got awkward to keep saying no. So I lied.'

'You lied?' Dex's head snaps up, and they're boring a hole in my skull with the strength of their stare.

'It's not her fault I'm hard work!'

'So you lied to protect her ego?'

'Millions of women do it every minute, Dex. It's not as if this is a revolutionary response to bad sex.'

'It was bad sex?' They lock their eyes onto mine, and it's clear they think they've caught me on something.

When I look back and assess the words I just said and the

ease with which I admitted them, I'm not so sure they're wrong.

'What, no. Not bad, just not good. I might be the one who's bad at it.'

'Dean,' they say with startling self-assuredness. 'I promise you that, as someone with a vagina it is incredibly hard to be bad at sex.'

'Not impossible, though,' I counter.

'True. You can be stiff, tense, or not in the mood. Those things do make for bad sex, but they aren't necessarily the fault of the person feeling them.'

Throughout our conversation, we've both shifted our weight so that we could face one another. Dex still has one leg on the ground, the other propped up with their heel on their knee, while I'm cross-legged, my hands in my lap.

I watch, mesmerised, as Dex talks with their hands and then brings them down to rest reassuringly on my knees. The contact makes my skin vibrate, a thousand tiny fireworks at the point of contact.

'When did you first know you were interested in sex?' They ask, unwittingly opening the floodgates on a memory I've repressed for years. Giggling teenagers, white-winter afternoon sun all around us, a childish game of tickling and play-fighting that splintered my world in two. The time before, when everything was hazy and easy, and the times after, when I rapidly understood what feeling was brewing inside of me. *Loverboy*.

'I don't remember.' It's a lie, but a necessary one.

'Okay, well, what would make sex good for you?'

The question is so absurd that I'm utterly unsure what to do with it. How am I meant to know that? I know what I like the idea of. I understand how to satisfy myself, but translating that to a two-person act is like asking me to quote the Dutch dictionary. The words exist in my internal language, one that I don't have the foggiest notion of how to voice.

After what must be a prolonged silence of me panicking and blushing furiously, Dex brushes their thumb across the tender flesh where my thighs meet my knee and lowers their voice to a husky whisper. It brings me back to the present. I wonder how many people they have comforted like this, and if it always makes the recipient's blood turn to lava in their veins.

'It's okay not to have an answer, De.'

'But I bet you have a response. I'm sure you know what makes sex good for you.'

'Well, I mean, yeah, but I'm a different person. I think about sex, honestly, more often than I should. It, uh, motivates me is probably the polite way to put it.'

I press my lips together, not at all reassured by Dex's admission. Of course, they know what to do; they're an adult. An adult with a healthy, potentially overactive sex drive. I wouldn't know how often is too often to want it. Is there a hard limit on that?

Groaning, I drop my head into my hands.

'See! I didn't know that it was possible to think about it too much. How do you find the time? My sex drive is broken—no!' I correct myself. 'No, not my sex drive! Or not just that. My brain. My brain is shot. Kaput! No good; throw it out and get a new one. It doesn't know how to receive and transmit desire properly.'

Dex raises their hands, catching my face in the curve of their palms so that I'm forced to be still. Like this, I have no choice but to watch their features, the creases at the outer edge of their eyes, the slight crinkle of their nose that tells me, despite being worried, my little speech tickled them. The splayed lines of their bare lashes as their eyes flick down to my lips and then back up again.

They've always radiated an excessive warmth, not sweaty or clammy but undeniably warm. When we were pre-teens and deep in the Twilight stage of our development (it was a pretty substantial phase for me, unfortunately. Much merchandise was purchased and many birthdays were spent making friends watch the movies over again) we used to joke that they were a werewolf; an oversized puppy, ready to function as a human furnace.

It's strange the speed with which these old jokes and memories pop up in my brain. Ten minutes ago, I would never have thought of that; now I'm flashing back to nights when I made them top and tail with me in the bed just so that I didn't wake up sweating. Stranger still is the fact that the flashbacks aren't entirely unwelcome. After all the time I spent resenting my connection to Dex, I might actually enjoy reminiscing about our friendship.

I'm so distracted by their face and the ghost of the old Dex I can see in their adult features that I've temporarily deluded myself into forgetting my current crisis.

'I need you to listen to me. You are not broken. I can't tell you about the inner workings of your brain and what it may or may not transmit. As you'll recall, Dr. Reynolds begged me to drop biology when I got the lowest marks in school history. But I can tell you with 100 per cent certainty that even if all of those things are true, it does not mean that your brain is broken. Everyone functions differently; there's nothing wrong with it. You just have to find something that helps you achieve your goals.'

Beneath their warm grip, my cheeks are slightly squished so that I feel like a cartoon chipmunk when I move them to speak.

'When did you get so smart?'

It comes out sharper than I intend it to, more of a barb than the light joke I aimed for. I can feel the moment that Dex closes up. Usually, it might not matter, but school was always hard for Dex.

They're not wrong about their biology mark. They also failed chemistry, geography, drama, and history. An impressively mixed bag of subjects to struggle with. They were diagnosed with dyslexia and dyspraxia at a surprisingly young age, accounting for their atrocious handwriting and spatial awareness. Maths, physics, philosophy, and languages were no problem, but certain things tripped them up. It wasn't until university that a friend suggested they might have autism and ADHD, and, honestly, I've been kicking myself about it ever since.

Imagine the Dex that might have been if they'd been given the support they needed from the start. It makes so much sense that the subjects they didn't care about just fell by the wayside of their mind, never to be picked up and made sense of.

The more I watch them, the clearer it is to see the inner workings of Dex. How they pause to watch for someone's reaction, matching words with expressions, their ever-pliable nature, rarely having a strong opinion to give until they're in safe company, the fidgeting limbs and fast-moving mouth.

A conversation with Dex can sometimes feel like running a

ten-minute mile, them bouncing from topic to topic with endless enthusiasm while you struggle to see how they managed to put those two thoughts together, words pouring out of their mouth without pause or hesitation, passing me by before I've properly considered them.

I recognise exactly why my words cut them. Me, with my across-the-board A's in school. Our families compared us a lot back then. I was the knife that other people used to cut them, and I've just done it again.

They go to pull their hands away, and I stop them with my own. There are two sets of palms on top of my cheeks now; it's warm and weird, but I don't want to let them leave this moment feeling bad.

'I didn't mean that. Not how it sounded, at least. I meant that your advice surprised me. You have always been smart. I'm just crabby that you make a better adult than I do. I'm sorry.'

They take a second, watching the words come out of my mouth and then meet my eye.

It's strangely intense despite the strange double hand hold, but their features open up again, the pain seeming to disperse.

'We should head back down to the pool before Pom steals the good floaty.'

I know that they're right, but I feel kind of sad about stepping away from this. It's hard to say why, a knotted mess of emotions I can't begin to piece apart, but suddenly sharing Dex with the world feels impossible.

As they drop their hands from my face, I'm jolted by the absence of their warmth, like stepping out of the sun on a spring day and realising it was the only thing keeping you from freezing.

I blink furiously, trying to find some echo of my previous self, the Daena from before this muddle of emotions.

'Promise that we'll never speak about the humiliation of you walking in on me topless ever again?' I say sternly.

'Cross my heart.' They grin.

Chapter Fifteen

Dex

I am a big fat liar.

A repeat, criminal offender of breaking promises. Okay, that's a tad melodramatic. It's not all promises. I'm usually very good at only agreeing to promises I confidently intend to keep. It's just one promise in particular, but I break it at least a dozen times before the night is over.

I have been, however inadvertently, thinking about walking in on Dean shirtless ever since it happened. I don't mean to. I try not to, but the thought circles in my mind every time it goes quiet.

As I hold a semi-deflated lime floaty steady for Dean to sit in, I marvel at the outline of her hips and wonder if the skin on them is ever so slightly paler like it was under her shirt.

When Nora and Poppy return with huge jugs of margaritas, I refrain from making the obvious joke (I have some sense of chivalry), but holding the thought back brings my mind to Dean, and I have to drink to drown how wrong that is.

I should not be having these thoughts. Dean specifically made me swear never to think about it again. Well, I suppose she only said speak, but if I'm being real with you, my brain is doing a lot more than speaking; it's screaming. Yelling. Shrieking. *I saw Daena Ashraf topless! I saw Dean's tits and they were perfect! I saw my long-time best friend, semi-estranged, without a shirt on, and I liked it!* I'm not sure it's ever been this fucking loud in my brain.

This is, I imagine, how teenage boys felt in the old days when they snatched their first glimpse of a boob in Nuts or Playboy or whatever. It feels like I got away with something illegal, as though I shouldn't have the knowledge that Dean's nipples are a glorious dark brown and perfectly pert.

Oh my god, I need to be stopped!

Shockingly, consuming vicious amounts of alcohol does not fix the problem. If anything, it makes it worse. When Dean gets out of the pool to take her glass from them, I can't help but notice the way her wet bikini clings to her. When she wraps a towel around her and snuggles into it, it's adorable, and I'm too reassured by the knowledge that I still know what the curve of her breast looks like to be sad about it. When she starts to get tipsy and giggles at something my sister-in-law says, I can't tear my eyes away from her smile; the sound of her laugh shoots straight through me. Fuck. It's bad.

The more I drink, the less subtle I get until Pomona is watching me with that signature Ashraf eyebrow arch, challenging me. Still, I cannot stop.

I know that it's wrong. This is not who I am. I delete everyone's nudes the second we're done, physically and mentally. I recognise that consent, once, is not a standing order to be played on repeat for my enjoyment. My 'spank bank' is purely fictitious, scenarios and hypotheticals that have no place in real life and, when it fails, I have no shame

145

in turning to porn. I'm a goddamn grown-up! And yet, no single mental image has fascinated me this much ever before. It's borderline euphoric.

I float through the night, buoyed by the fact that when I sleep, Dean will be close by. When we finally turn in for the night, each drunk as a skunk and me, remarkably giddy on the night's events, I playfully smack her arse to hurry up.

It's stupid, thoughtless and any other night, probably not a terrible idea. We were once those friends, touching each other's bodies without weirdness or repercussions, but it's hard to pinpoint when that stopped. But it's potentially the best thing I've ever done; I'm entranced by the way Dean's arse shakes at the gentle contact and absolutely taken out by the small yelp of surprise as she scurries up the stairs ahead of me.

There, watching her take the steep curving attic staircase at a canter, with her furiously shushing me, I am helpless to do anything but watch. When she reaches the top step and finds me waiting below, Dean manages an impressive simultaneous frown and smile and silently urges me towards her with her hands.

I take them two at a time, unable to disobey the action, knowing I'm running towards danger.

Every possible warning sign is there. They are written in large, bold letters, in dyslexic-friendly font on massive fuck-off big, red flags, warning me to slow down before I get hurt.

Those red flags look very pretty right now. The second prettiest thing in our shared little room.

We've never had to get ready for bed at the same time, so I let her go first and slip into my pyjamas hastily while she's not around. I crack the window open because, at the top of this château, the hot air refuses to ease off, and I lean out, letting the tepid night air sober me up a bit. If there was any hope that sobriety would make me see sense, it dies a rapid death when Dean re-enters, her thick thighs on full display in tiny shorts.

Seriously, someone needs to put me down. I am worse than any man. No, that's not quite true. I'm staring, slack-jawed, but most of the fantasies currently playing out in my brain involve lavishing the soft, dimpled skin of Dean's thighs with kisses, letting those kisses trail up to her stomach. Or potentially her resting those legs on me, folded up on the sofa, and me being allowed to let my hands run idly over and up them, rubbing away the day's aches.

Shit. I need to get ready for bed before I say something honest and mortifyingly horny aloud.

I'm carried through brushing my teeth by helium-fueled thoughts. Floating along on my little flights of fancy. It's nothing, I reassure myself. Temporary insanity. I've had a dozen too many drinks and not enough sun and certainly not enough private time to get off. Yes! That's it, I'm horny and drunk and these thoughts will all be gone in the morning.

I tuck myself into the comfort of that notion, letting the melodic sound of Dean telling me about her life lull me into a much-needed slumber.

When I wake up in the morning after a night of Dean-themed dreams, I have no choice but to admit that this is a problem. I might be an adult, but now I'm an adult with an adult-sized crush on my best friend.

Fuck.

147

Chapter Sixteen

Dean

We head to Paris tomorrow, and I'm all too aware that it will likely mean the end of my proximity to Dex.

A week ago, there was no world in which I could imagine comfortably sharing a bedroom with them. Now, though, I'm trying to rationalise the sinking feeling in my gut, the strange sadness I feel at the thought of sleeping solo, without our placid nighttime conversations. All day, I watched them spin in the pool, thinking that I might never get to see this Dex again. The lazy holiday Dex, running around the garden in pursuit of nieces and nephews, teaching Cami how to skate on the cement patio, falling asleep floating around the pool. There is no way to know when they'll come home again, and the chances of us doing another super-sized sixtieth trip are slim to none unless we all unexpectedly win the lottery.

This might be the last time I see Dex like this. I'm not sure why that makes the inner corners of my eyes ache, but it does. Maybe it's the knowledge that holiday Dex has existed in this form for a while now, and I've just been denied the privilege of seeing them. They have, after all, been hundreds of girls' holiday Romeo all over the world in this exact iteration of themselves. Not that that's what they are or have ever been to me. We aren't—I mean, they don't see me as…It's not romantic.

Dex and I will never be romantic.

But a perverse little part of me wonders whether we could be something else.

We are sitting on my bed at the end of a long day of doing nothing, a pair of tittering children swapping secrets and playing red hands. I'm fairly sure that any buzz we had from drinking this afternoon has worn off by now, but it hasn't dipped our mood.

It all feels oddly familiar, like a bigger, better version of our childhood sleepovers. If you went back in time and asked teenage Dean where she saw herself in fifteen years, I'm pretty sure this is exactly what I would have described.

Tinny nostalgia music is playing from Dex's phone; we've moved on from Britney to Hannah Montana. We haven't stopped laughing since we sat down, and I can tell as each hour passes because the ache in my cheeks gets stronger the longer we talk.

Sure, literally no other part of my life is how thirteen-year-old Dean would have described it. I don't make big money, I don't own a house or have a Pomeranian trimmed to look like a tiny bear and certainly couldn't describe myself as having a healthy social or romantic life. But this moment, sitting playing with a fully realised adult Dex on my bed, listening to songs we loved growing up, is something pre-teen me understood and could imagine in the future.

I'm glad that I got to prove her right even once.

'You're telling me that you never had a crush on Zac Efron?' Dex says, disbelieving.

I scrunch up my nose, feeling my glasses shift, but don't look away from their hands.

'Nope. I guess he was cute in a boyish way, but I genuinely did just like the music.'

Somehow, Dex is managing to trounce me without glancing down at where our hands hover over one another.

'God. My life would have been so much easier if-' they yank their hands back, narrowly avoiding my attack and barely missing a conversational beat. 'Someone had just explained to me the difference between wanting to be with someone and wanting to be them.'

'Troy Bolton?' I ask, thinking of the multiple pencil cases, bags and posters that used to decorate Dex's bedroom.

'Naturally. He just had this effortless boy-next-door charm going for him.'

'It's very lesbian coded.' I agree. And I'm wondering if they are thinking what I'm thinking. If Dex sees that they carry that same boy-next-door perfection. They can party with the boys but still help an old lady across the road with her shopping, all while being back in time to whisk someone away on the sweet date they planned. If Dex had known who they were sooner, they would have been a walking high school cliche. They already practically were, but looking like they do now, well, no girl would have stood a chance.

'Now that I think about it, the majority of your icons were pretty butch coded.'

'Go on?'

'Clark Kent. Steve Rogers. Hercules.'

'Are you calling me a goody-two-shoes, Ashraf?'

'No, it's not quite that. Because they all have the vibe that they would break the rules if they believed it was the morally

150

right thing to do. It's more like the Autistic All-American Boy.' I venture.

'I'm British!'

'You know what I mean. All-British Boy sounds like you might be kinda racist. So, just take the compliment. They're all buff and caring and deeply whipped by a confident woman.'

They pull their mouth wide in consideration and dip their head to the right to acknowledge their agreement, and finally, I sneak up on them.

My palms make instant, stinging contact with theirs. In response, Dex lets out a maniacal chuckle. They take so much glee in my beating them that you'd think they'd won the whole game, but I'm too busy glaring down at my traitorous hands.

'Shit, I don't remember this game hurting that much.'

'Oh crap, is it bad?' Dex sits up slightly straighter, eyes darting across my face with genuine concern.

'No, I'm just being a pussy about it.'

'Show me,' they say, and there's a firmness about it I can't disobey.

I gently offer out my fist, watching as they catch it with their proffered hands. All of Dex's usually languid movements seem unbelievably graceful right now. They slowly twist my arm so that my fist is facing skyward and tenderly unfurl my fingers to expose the raw red skin of my palm.

Ever so lightly, Dex's thumbs run over the thick flesh on either side of my hand, checking for pain, and I wince. Despite my gaze being locked on our hands, theirs must be on my face because they bend their body, lowering themself to place the most delicate kiss in the centre of my hand. As they move, their eyes stay fixed on me, lowering into my sight line and catching me completely off guard.

They stay there, lips pressed to my palm for only a fraction of a second, but it feels as though the world has frozen. Every external noise fades away, and time moves like treacle in an hourglass. My skin feels zapped under their touch, and I can't parse out whether it's because of the slap or their kiss.

Their kiss. Dex just kissed me. Or kissed my hand, at least!

I blink in disbelief, breaking our frozen moment of privacy from the universe. Dex moves back to an upright position, and I suddenly feel like I'm seventeen again, understanding want for the first time ever.

It comes over me exactly as strong as that first moment of discovery, pinned down to a sofa. I am hungry for them, starved even. As though I cannot live another minute without knowing what their lips feel like on other parts of my body.

But I do. I have to. I pull my eyes away from Dex's mouth. *Shit, have I been staring at it this whole time?* I need to get a grip on reality again.

'Dean?'

'Dex?'

'How's the hand?'

I clear my throat and deliberately do not look at the incriminating evidence that is my still skyward palm.

'Right as rain.'

They nod. We sit. Nothing happens other than the galloping beat of my heart. I can feel them readying themselves to wrap up. They are milliseconds away from pulling their body away from this bed, from this moment, from me. If they do, it'll be ruined: a card tower crashing down, never to be erected the same way.

'Dex?'

'Dean.'

'Tell me a secret.' It's halfway between a plea and a command. I expect them to laugh. They don't. Instead, their reply is surprisingly sombre.

'Sometimes, I think I agreed to get married as a form of self-punishment.'

'Why?' It's so serious, so undeniably sad that it feels at odds with Dex's whole personality.

'Because then, if I was unhappy with my life, it was because I was with someone who didn't truly love me. Who I didn't want to spend forever with, and not because I was hiding who I was.'

'Fuck. That's-'

'Depressing?'

'Honest.' I say, not contradicting them but offering an alternative.

A beat passes, and I worry they might pull away again, but to my relief, Dex slips their palm into my still outstretched one where it's propped on my knee.

'Your turn.'

'You want me to tell you a secret?'

'Please.' Another command plea, and now I understand why they couldn't defy it. The words rocket through me, and I know what I want to say before I've evaluated it.

'I'm scared about the sex stuff. Not because being able to come is the point of sex, but because I enjoy it. I'm scared because I know that I want someone to make that connection, and then I want them to be able to make me come. I'm scared it will never happen. That I'm broken inside. I don't believe anyone will be able to.'

Once I've unleashed the secret, I am a thousand times lighter. I didn't know how badly I needed to acknowledge that fear

153

until I see it written out in the air before me, as though my words emerge in the smoky physicality of Alice's Caterpillar.

It's bizarre and maybe a bit bonkers, but I fight the desire to laugh. Dex's pupils are practically vibrating, quivering back and forth across my face. I don't recognise this expression; I can't begin to read it. A challenge, maybe. Curiosity perhaps. But it's tinged with something new.

'Dean.' I nod. 'I'm going to suggest something, and it's going to sound mad, but just think about it. Okay?'

A prickle of fear creeps up my spine; what could be so serious that they think I'll react badly? Do they think that there is something wrong with me? Have they changed their mind? Did my secret cross some invisible line I hadn't known existed?

'Let me try.'

'Try to what?'

They open their mouth, hesitate and close it again, expelling just the tiniest bit of air. Dex's free hand fidgets, and I'm too busy analysing it to look at their face when they explain.

'Let me try to make you come. I bet it would work.' The world freezes again.

'You bet?'

'If you want, that is. No pressure, obviously. If you don't find me attractive or don't want to ruin us with that, I will totally understand, and I'll never mention it again. No harm, no foul.' My neck snaps upright, and I take in the anxious set of their features. Dex's words are coming in a rushed, faux-nonchalant tone that I don't buy for a minute.

'It's just, look, not to brag or anything, but I know what I'm doing. We have an emotional connection, even if it isn't romantic, and, honestly, that might be for the best. It'll take

154

the pressure off you to feel like you have to perform. If it doesn't work, my ego won't be bruised.'

'You'd do that for me?'

They're running their hand anxiously over the back of their neck again, and I'm momentarily dazed by the curve of their muscles again. They've relaxed a fraction, their wide grin coming back onto the page, and I repress the craving to eat my words and just scream yes.

'It's not completely selfless. Without being a total douchebag, or a disgusting creep, you are undeniably one of the hottest women I have ever seen. And if I somehow didn't notice before, my little slip-up yesterday made it abundantly clear that I am, in at least some way, attracted to you.'

The words aren't distinctly romantic or particularly sexual, but the raw earnestness of them, the earnestness that I associate so plainly with Dex, creates heat between my thighs.

'Again, you don't have to. I won't take it personally. It's a wild suggestion; I get it. I just figured you wouldn't feel the need to lie to me, I'd like to and we could-'

My body answers for me. Darting forward, I take the bet. I hold their face in my hands and stop them from chattering their way out of it with a kiss.

Chapter Seventeen

Dex

HOLY.

FUCKING.

SHIT.

Dean took the bet.

Chapter Eighteen

Dean

I'm about to have sex with Dexter Carpenter-Brown.

That's all I can think.

I wish that I could do something seductive or sexy, maybe change into lingerie or light a candle, but we're both already mostly in our underwear. Our dried swimsuits don't leave a lot to the imagination, and I suddenly hate my past self for not having picked something sexier.

I've heard Dex's stories. They've been to topless beaches and declined invites to sex parties. Their idea of seduction and mine are not on the same level, yet they're pressing me back into the bed as if we might somehow match.

When I got ready to sleep with Callie, I did a full-body shave and made sure I moisturised every visible part of me. We'd fuck with the lights off, maybe just my standing lamp in the corner of the room illuminating us, and very rarely in any position other than her on top. It was never bad. Usually, it felt pretty good, but between her muffled grunts and my uncertainty, I never came away feeling sexy.

With Dex, the environment is immediately different. Their

hips roll into me every time our lips reposition against each other, and I'm shocked to find myself answering with moans and an arching back.

I want them!

The revelation is way more astounding than it should be. But I want them, and my body is responding to them. It's amazingly novel.

The room grew dark around our little game earlier, and, despite the late European summer sunset, we are now making out, lit only by the streams of moonlight coming through the open window.

A small voice in the back of my head screams that we should close the blinds, but I silence it as I remember there's no one around to see in.

There are no neighbours for miles, and we're two flights of steep stairs above our families. As far as sexual privacy goes, this is far better than anything I've ever had back home, living with my sister or uni flatmates in houses with perpetually thin walls.

I press my back against the mattress, letting Dex kneel over me, supporting their weight on one forearm while their left hand roams over my hips and waist.

We're kissing as though we can survive on shared oxygen, passing it back and forth between us with no intention of ever breaking to gulp in fresh air. Every time one of us pulls our lips back ever so slightly, the other is there to catch them again. It's fun, and I wonder if this is how making out is supposed to feel, not just a necessary and slightly boring prerequisite for sex.

Every slight action I take elicits a new and luscious reaction from Dex. When I suck lightly on their bottom lip, they press

158

harder against me, giving my hands more of them to feel. As I flick the tip of my tongue against theirs, they open wider. Each new step gives me more access to Dex than I ever dreamed of.

Eventually, I stop feeling as though this moment is delicately sculpted glass that will break if I cherish it too hard. I get comfortable with my wanting. I bite ever so gently on their bottom lip. Revelling in my reward as they give a low reverberating moan that turns my insides to warm, gooey honey.

My knees drop open, letting Dex between them, and I hook my ankles behind their back.

Another groan, a roll of their hips. Suddenly, I'm the one moaning. It's small, more of a purr, but it shocks me.

I have never been vocal about sex. A yes, maybe, a few swear words, the odd direction when someone was radically lost, but no moaning. It's oddly freeing. For years, I've wondered how incredibly loud women didn't feel self-conscious during sex. Surely, dirty talk would feel silly, right? But I get it now. I see the urge, and I let the last remaining scraps of my embarrassment disperse.

I lose myself to the desire pooling inside me.

As if they can sense my shoulders relaxing, Dex brings their hand up to untie the knot of my bikini and watches, rapt, as it falls away. My breasts drop free.

There's that same hunger in their expression again, the one I couldn't place, and it all starts to make sense as they move their mouth to my nipples.

They start by licking the peaked skin of each one once, then twice and then doubling back to circle the crest with the tip of their tongue. By the time they suck the full bud of my nipple into their mouth, I'm humming with pleasure. Every tender movement echoes on my clit, and I have to press my core against them, seeking friction, just to hold back from touching myself.

Dex treats undressing me as a task that cannot be rushed. They run their hands across the chub of my ribcage, fingers splayed wide as if they've never seen a stomach before. Then they move to my waist, a perfectly non-sexual body part and yet as Dex squeezes my edges, still toying with my nipple, it's as though I might scream in desperation.

My hips are next on the docket, warm palms tracing my curves with a firm grip. I can't shake the sensation that I am safe in these hands.

These are capable hands, small but wide, strong, unfaltering. Dex makes quick work of my bottoms, slipping them down my thighs and then pulling their whole body back to ease them off of each ankle. The sudden loss of pressure against me is unbearable. I want to beg them to come back, but they're busy lavishing my legs with the same attention that they put upon the rest of my body. They're moving back in, hands mirrored on each leg, working up my thighs, and I spread wide for them.

It's shorts and swimsuit season, so I'm shaved to a precise crop that I usually wouldn't bother with. I can see Dex appreciating my work, though. I watch as their eyes examine my cunt; admiring. Their fingers run once down my core, and I can hear how wet I am. Another thing that I would usually be embarrassed about, but to my relief and surprise, Dex groans in approval.

As if responding to their noise, my hips buck, pushing their gently stroking index finger between my lips. They manoeuvre themself so that their face is level with my own, mouth capturing me in another breath-snatching kiss, and I melt into them as their fingers tease at my clit. They run little circuits, dancing around the swollen flesh and back towards my entrance. Each time they complete a circuit, I get wetter and increasingly wanton. I crave contact, I need something to move against, I'm desperate for—Oh!

They've delivered. One finger is neatly curled inside me, and their thumb has honed in on the apex of my clitoris. I sigh with relief, head tipping backwards, breaking our kiss for the first time.

Dex chuckles; it's low and gravelly, and I might hit them for it if I weren't utterly devastated by how good it feels to have them inside of me. In a breathy exhale, I tell them as much.

We move together, the bed squeaking ever so softly with each undulating movement. I rotate my hip towards them experimentally, testing my body's limits, gasping as their finger extends within me.

They brush their thumb against the swell of sensitive skin, and curse words come to my tongue unbidden. Dex laughs again, but I know that it's a joke we share, one that we are building together.

'You feel so good around me.' They mutter directly into my mouth, and I devour the words. I eat them whole, not bothering to chew, and come away full of them.

Literally…because they've pushed another finger inside of me.

I can feel my walls stretching, the muscles more relaxed than they typically are. Dex works with me, curved fingers flexing as they move in and out until I gather up the spine to ask for what I want.

'More,' I whimper. 'I need more of you.'

I don't need to ask twice or add a please. Dex answers my call deftly, a third digit slipping in and opening me up. I am delightfully full. I'm rocking against them, enjoying the sensation of being crowded with them.

Dex pulls back from kissing me to glance down and lets out a low, private groan.

'Fuck.' It's so appreciative it almost feels like direct praise. I preen at the curse meant only for me, sweeping my hips to push them further in.

Dex brings their tongue back to my nipple, teasing it in parallel with my clit, and it's... I'm—I don't have a word for it. They work so succinctly, never fumbling finger or tongue, and every flick of either leaves me panting for more.

'Don't stop.' I command to the ceiling. 'Just like that.'

It's rudimentary dirty talk. Directions 101, and yet it is by far the bossiest I've ever allowed myself to be with a partner.

Dex obeys, and I bring my hands up to the curve of their head, running my fingers through their shorn hair. Even the prickling brush of their stubble against my palms drives me wild.

They haven't let up on my clit, and their fingers are still pumping in and out of me in time with the beating of my heart. It all feels so in sync; my muscles begin to tighten and tense. A flash of worry crosses my mind that maybe this is the moment, the second it all falls apart. I'm about to stiffen as I always do, switch off. Unable to finish.

But Dex's free hand is on my shoulder. They're holding me to them. It's as though that small action keeps my brain in my body.

They carry on, and, to my surprise, I stay present. My cries begin to come out faster and more pleading. *Yes*, and *fuck*, and

162

oh, don't stop. Things I've never dreamt of saying aloud. My muscles get taut, and just as I'm preparing to have to tell them to stop, to give up, I feel it. My gut clenches first, my arms and thighs next. It's a rolling wave, crashing over me before I can register it. I'm coming.

Fuck. I'm coming.

It's unclear if I said that last part aloud. The whole world feels foggy. My muscles are spasming, my clit feels as if it has a mind of its own and I'm tightening around Dex's fingers.

They still don't stop. They move back up to kiss my lips, giving me my air back as I ride it out. As the last pulse of pleasure rocks my body, I tap their shoulder, and they, ever so delicately, pull their hand out.

'Fuck, Dex.' I manage to press the words into their cheek-bone with my lips. 'That was-' I struggle to find an apt description.

'Incredible.' I think they're being egotistical, and they'd deserve a pass on it after that performance, in all fairness, but there's something reverent in their tone. They aren't offering a suggested end to my sentence; they're affirming my feelings with their own.

I curl into their chest, arms wrapping around their waist as we both wait for our breathing to level out.

It should feel strange, pressed up against my oldest friend, our bodies rising and falling to the same rhythm, knowing that they have just witnessed me in a way that no one else ever has. I should feel embarrassed by my breasts pouring onto their stomach with nothing to contain them. It probably ought to be awkward that I'm completely naked and Dex remains clad in their sports bra, open button-down and swim shorts and yet none of that bothers me. It registers but doesn't phase me.

I just finished. With another person.

A core tenet I've been living by has completely crumbled. Every excuse I've ever made up for not fully enjoying sex is now null and void. I like sex. Love it. That wasn't arduous or tiring. No one was mad at how long it took me. It was... incredible.

Dex is right.

Time returns to me in fragments. I catch the subtle shift of streaming moonlight through the window, the distinct ticking of the hallway clock and realise that we may have taken longer than expected. Sex with Callie was fast, not in the single-digit minutes but certainly never longer than thirty. Maybe I just wasn't giving myself enough time, maybe it takes me thirty minutes to get relaxed enough to enjoy it. But that doesn't track with what just happened.

From the very first moment, Dex touched me with intention, their hands cradling my waist and ribs, I was comfortable. More than comfortable, I was turned on. The hours passed as seconds. I luxuriated in the feeling of what Dex did to me.

To confuse matters further, I feel as though I could do it all again.

My breath is no longer ragged, and the soft stroking of Dex's hand on my back has moved from reassuring little circular motions to long exploratory drags. It's enough to ignite a fire in my stomach again.

'I can't believe that just happened.' I crane my neck to meet their eye.

'Us or the orgasm.'

'Both. Neither.' I shake my head and try to hide the creeping start of my smile. 'It's not nearly as weird as I expected it to be. Of course, you would wind up knowing my body better than anyone else. The suggestion felt wild at first, but now that I consider it properly, it makes total sense. The orgasm part, well, let's just say I'm more than pleasantly surprised to have lost that bet.'

'Wanna test the limits of my ability to be right?' They whisper with a decidedly cheeky grin.

'What are you suggesting?'

'That I could make you come again, quicker, probably this time.'

The itch to play at being outraged is so strong, and yet it ultimately loses out to my eagerness.

'I've never had multiple orgasms, even alone.'

'You've never had me.'

'I'm not sure it can be done.'

'Wanna bet?' They extend their free hand for me to agree, and as I do, they use it to coax me up and over them. With one leg on either side, I am straddling Dex, and they look reverent.

'Are you sure this is how you want to spend your night? We could be here awhile.' I warn them.

Nodding, Dex runs their hand from my thighs to my hip. 'Way better than sleep.'

'I'll remind you of that in the car tomorrow when you're begging for caffeine.'

'Seems only fair given all the begging you're about to be doing.'

Gobsmacked is not a strong enough word to describe my astonished response to this. I've known Dex to have a dirty mind, always the first to whisper a crude joke in my ear in school or laugh at something childishly tangential to sex, but I've never heard them say something downright filthy before. It's playful, so I know they were anticipating my flabbergasted

165

reaction, but serious enough that I wholeheartedly believe the intention.

'First though,' I manage some sense of seriousness and pluck lightly at their swim shorts and the open shirt. 'These have to go. It doesn't seem very fair for me to be entirely naked, with you, the butch version of fully clothed.'

I wait for them to nod in agreement and raise my body enough to help them pull the shorts off while Dex shucks off their shirt.

Now is probably a good time to point out that my limited sexual experiences have not included trans people. Not for any particular reason other than a lack of interest in me on their behalf and my poor game, respectively.

I've slept with masc-presenting lesbians. Masc, in the mullet haircut having and boyfriend jeans wearing way, I have come to learn is distinctly different from butch.

So, staring at the gloriousness of Dex Carpenter-Brown laid out beneath me, I am hyper-aware of doing or saying the wrong thing. Dex is butch and trans, and despite years of separation, I know they have a complex set of feelings about their own body.

My hesitation must be clear because Dex pulls me down toward them and gives me one quick, reassuring kiss.

'I'm gonna keep my bra on, okay, and I'd prefer if you didn't touch me.'

A small bubble of disappointment emerges within me, rising and falling like one of those globs in a lava lamp. 'Anywhere or there?'

They pause, seeming to weigh up the options. 'Just let me focus on making you feel good for now. My arm, neck, hips, all of that is good though.'

I try my best to hide that blob of disappointment, not having realised how curiously excited I was to return the favour to Dex.

'This bet is about making you come after all.' They say with a smile and another kiss.

And they're right. In all the pleasure, I've lost sight of what's happening between us. This isn't the start of a relationship, neither of us is catching feelings, this is the conclusion of a bet, an extension of the hypothesis, if you will. Dex isn't going to come away from this telling me I broke their understanding of the world, I'm not reinventing the wheel sexually. This is one friend helping another, albeit in a slightly unusual way.

'Now,' their hands are on my tits as we've been talking, and I hold back an undignified whine. 'I want you to ride my face.'

Has anyone ever said no to that statement? I wouldn't know because this is my first time ever being asked.

'I beg your pardon.'

They smile again, and I'm still fighting that moan.

'You heard me, princess. Sit on my face.'

'What if I crush you,' I say, gesturing down at my considerable body mass, my wide thighs.

'Then I die doing something I love, and you can tell the world of my legendary cunnilingus skills. It'll be the exact opposite of the Elvis on the toilet myth.'

'Can you not talk about Elvis right now?'

'Fair enough.' They shrug. 'But seriously, you won't crush me. Put your knees on each side of my head; then you can either hold onto the headboard for support or rest your weight on the backs of your heels.'

They're playing with me still, those nimble fingers coaxing me closer towards gormless incompetence. Desperately curious and, well, just plain desperate, I comply with their instructions.

I kneel above their mouth, sort of hovering in a surprisingly comfortable position and sigh as they finally pull their hands away from my tits.

'You look so fucking gorgeous,' Dex hums appreciatively and, even though I find it hard to believe, I don't protest.

They've moved their hands to my waist, repositioning me ever so slightly and then their tongue is between my legs, slowly teasing my slit open.

I gasp at the sudden contact and feel my body melt into the sensation of their mouth on me. It's more gentle than their fingers had been, moving in slow, unwavering lines.

Dex is methodical, picking up that same rhythmic pace that drove me wild the first time, drawing a line between my entrance and my clit and then circling the tender apex.

I've sunk my hands into their hair before I know it, urging them on. Each new lap leaves me jagged and raw. I can barely stand it, and yet I'm certain I'd wither if they stopped. My nails dig lightly into their skull as I give in to the pleading.

'Please, Dex, please, I need more.' They were right. I am the one begging tonight.

'Whatever you want, princess,' I catch them murmur before they bring their focus onto my clit.

They drag their tongue around it, moving in tight circles before stroking across it.

'Oh, fuck, yes.' They do it again, and I urge them on. 'Please, just like that.' I implore them.

Another swipe of their tongue once, twice more, until I abandon my remaining inhibitions entirely and bring my index finger and thumb up to pinch my nipples greedily. I'm rough with myself, and Dex takes their directions directly from me, sucking on my clit with more force than before.

'Fuck me, please. Don't you dare fucking stop,' I beseech them as my hips bare down and I grind against their face. I might be worried if Dex didn't groan obligingly.

Their hands have moved to my arse, cradling it, urging me forward as I ride them, hips bucking furiously in search of that friction.

We stay locked together for what feels like forever, each new ministration of Dex's tongue leading me to entreat them for more, to bring me further, fuck me harder. In turn, every appeal that falls from my lips seems to stoke the fire in them and earns me a range of hungry growls, moans, and hums that vibrate against my pussy delightfully.

I sense the familiar shudder and core-wrenching jackhammer motion of an orgasm overtake me. My body feels laid bare, a million exposed nerves readjusting to the world.

The words tumbling out of my mouth have slipped into nonsense, and as I make one last circular motion with my hips, I feel as though someone hollowed me out of all my worries and doubts and left a gelatinous puddle of satisfaction in my place.

Those strong hands that I've been watching so keenly these last few days manoeuvre me off of them and into their waiting arms. They press a kiss to my forehead, sloppy and ever so delicate, but I don't care. I don't have enough bones in my body to consider moving off of them or to be worried that their legs will fall asleep with me cocooned on them like this. Instead, I interlace my fingers with theirs as my eyelids succumb to the oncoming heaviness of night.

'You did so well, princess, rest up.'

Chapter Nineteen

Dex

When you've spent the last two years of your life waking up in new and beautiful locations, you start to feel as though there are no astounding sights left. You've woken up next to iconic landmarks of all kinds. Mountains, waterfalls, skyscrapers, deserts, beaches, forests, stunning crystalline waters, all of it waiting for you before you've had your morning coffee, and you stop being surprised by the beauty of it all.

Waking up millimetres from Dean's face, the slope of her nose, free of glasses, the curve of her cheek as it squashes up against the pillow, is the first time I've felt awe in a long time. It's bizarre because I've woken up beside De a thousand times throughout my life, but never like this. Those were childhood innocence, drifting off to sleep while cuddling up to watch stupid YouTube videos or a movie. This is post-sex Dean, still crawling out of the trenches of slumber.

I've been awake for a good ten minutes, too afraid to move, just watching her pupils dart around behind closed lids, the remnants of her mascara giving her impossibly full lashes a sexy, messy look. Hell, all of her is subject to that gorgeous dishevelment. Her hair is chaotic, with wild, unruly curls that I had to smooth down to stop from inhaling them while she slept. She's still curled in my lap even though I managed to position us so that I was lying flat. Her leg is splayed atop me at a crooked angle, so it's more akin to being squeezed by a koala than anything else.

The hallway clock is counting down the seconds until this tranquillity is interrupted. I know that it can't possibly last. Dean's alarm will go off at any minute now, breaking the spell and dragging us back to reality. We'll be whisked away from the privacy of our shared room to some slightly less fancy Parisian hotel where I will, no doubt, be sleeping next to my brother's grubby feet. I should be excited for Paris. I was not twelve hours ago. But whatever just happened, whatever this is, unalterably shifted something in me.

I don't remember a world without Dean. It's never existed for me. When we weren't talking, she still popped into my mind unsolicited at least once a day. I took photos I thought I might never be able to show her, kept an album of them, wrote jokes in my notes app just so they wouldn't slip away, I even started sending memes I thought she'd enjoy to myself, just to give my brain's need for her an outlet. Dean's friendship is one of the core foundations of my life. I've constructed my worldview around it. Last night loosened that brick. It's not gone, it's not broken, but it doesn't sit the same. 'Friend' no longer fits seamlessly.

Never before have I held Daena in my arms, naked and peaceful, watching sleep drift away from her as daylight calls. It's stupid and naive, but I sort of don't want to put things back to the way they were.

What am I talking about? Fuck!

I may have just made a calamitous mistake. Not the sleeping with my newly reaffirmed best friend, nothing that good can be a mistake, but the *sleeping* part of it. I should have gone back to my ridiculous mountain-shaped chaise. The back pain would have been worth it, and, sure, it's nice to have a duvet cover the whole of my body for the first time in days, but I should never have *slept* with Dean. Now I know how it feels to wake up with her. I am forever changed by the way her rogue straggling curls catch the early morning light, turning from their usual deep walnut to a luminescent golden brown, as though laced through with gold leaf.

Dean's skin is impossibly soft beneath my fingertips, and I clench my hand into a fist to stop stroking a slow, reassuring line down her side.

OH MY GOD! Pull it together Dex!

If I could move without waking Dean, I'd have my head in my hands, trying to knock some sense back into myself. What on earth am I thinking? Dean doesn't want to date me. I'm flighty and avoidant and completely bleeding, lost in life. I have no career, no clear goals; I don't own an eighth pair of pants for fuck's sake. She's smart, driven, sexy and, most importantly, she wants someone who can provide her with a better life.

That's all she's ever wanted. To have wealth and make a name for herself.

There has never been anyone less equipped to provide her with that than me at present. Just because I can make her orgasm does not mean I can keep Dean completely satisfied in all areas of life.

I take a second, closing my eyes, inhaling, exhaling.

There is no way around it. Nothing to be done. I need to

172

let this dream go. It's a new dream, fresh; it should be easy enough to dig it up at the root, chuck it out and never see it surface again.

Dean's alarm starts ringing, and I watch as she blinks her way into clarity. Her wide brown eyes latch immediately onto mine, and it's like someone's tying a noose around my heart that squeezes it tighter with every passing breath.

'Good morning,' I manage to sound semi-suave and not like I'm having a complete freak-out. At least I hope I do.

'That happened?' Dean croaks, and I am momentarily ruined by the foolish hope that she might feel the same I do. If I'm outstandingly lucky, in a way no Carpenter-Brown has ever been known to be, Dean might wake up foggy with sleep and believing that she dreamed it all just as I did.

Which would at least mean that she feels something about me. That us together is categorised as dreamlike in her mind as opposed to nightmare material. I could work with that.

'I need a million more years of sleep.' She says, prising herself off of me to silence the alarm. 'Oh shit, we need to get packing.'

And just like that, I'm reminded that Dean is far too good for me. She hasn't mistaken last night for a dream; she's just surprised to find me holding her when we should be up and getting ready to leave.

I avert my eyes, both to stop them from ogling Dean as she gets dressed and to hide the pricking of embarrassment at their inner corners. God, it's so ridiculous. I knew what last night was: a bet, nothing more. I set the terms.

Seeing no other recourse to deal with this carnivorous feeling, I locate my own phone and send Hawa a singular message. A distress signal.

down bad. send marbles, appear to have temporarily lost them. requesting immediate aid.

* * *

When Dean and I finally emerge downstairs, bags packed and in my hands, the vibes are real fucking weird.

'You don't have to do that, you know,' Dean is trying to wrestle her suitcase out of my grip.

'Oh, whisht up. It's good for my wavering masculinity. Helps me feel all chivalrous and shit.'

That provokes a sharp caw of a laugh from her, and it lands in the dead air of the kitchen area like a lead balloon. All the adults are standing around, leaning against the kitchen island or the cabinets, with Mum sitting on a grandiose dining room chair in the middle, her leg propped on a second one.

'Are you good?' I drop the bags and my smile simultaneously. The atmosphere screams everyone is not good.

I glance around, and no one will make eye contact with me. It's a billion degrees outside, but I abruptly feel chilled. I walk towards Mum and Dad, his hand resting on the back of her chair.

'What's going on?'

'Oh, Dexy, honey, it's nothing to worry about.' Mum pats my cheek as I crouch beside her. It's a familiar action, but oddly disjointed in the current setting.

'Mum, come on!' Liam says indignantly.

I whip my head around to look at Liam, his arms folded across his chest, mouth set in an uncharacteristically stern line.

Liam is not the angry brother. Liam has never been the

angry brother. He's always been aloof, composed, firm, but funny. But now Archer is silent, shaking his head and turning away, and Liam is rolling his eyes. I feel as though I've stepped into an alternative universe where everything is swapped.

'Just tell her-them already.'

'Tell me what?' It's difficult not to sound like a petulant child with this kind of conversation happening about me as though I'm not present.

'It's not your decision, Liam.' Dad warns in that steely tone he's rarely had cause to trot out since our teen years.

'There doesn't seem much point hiding it now.' Parker says with a shrug.

'Hiding what?' I'm hoping someone will cave and answer my question. Parker is usually my reliably weak link, but he's stalwartly avoiding my glare.

'It's not as if you're going to be able to explain away the holiday being cancelled.'

'Pomona!' Sabina and Rami chide at the same time, and I hit with the horrifying realisation that everyone here knows something I don't. Everyone here *has* known that something for a while, long enough to tell the Ashrafs. Long enough to decide to exclude me from the decision-making.

I shoot a wary glance at Dean, dreading what I'll find there. I look for some confirmation that she knows what's happening here, that she conspired with my family to keep me out of it, but find tender confusion instead.

'I'm not hiding anything,' Mum protests. 'I just don't think there's any reason to make a big fuss about it.'

'You know what's making a fuss.' I snap, getting to my feet and looking at the whole mortified collection of them. 'This. This is the definition of making a fuss. In fact, I believe it's officially a scene. So, if you would all be so kind, I believe I'm in desperate need of an explanation.'

No one answers me. I expel air in a short, sharp huff of disbelief and rage, which Sabrina takes as the cue to usher her family into another room. Nora disappears with them, excusing herself to check on the kids, until I'm left with just my parents, Poppy and my brothers.

'Great family meeting, guys. Anyone feel like reading me the minutes?'

'Dex, chill.' Archer warns me. There's enough of an age difference between us that I've always sort of taken his word as gospel, undeniable law. I'm just frustrated enough that that doesn't matter.

'No, seriously, I'm just wondering how there's some great secret that everyone knows but me. Everyone, including the girls. And still, no one wants to tell me what's happening.'

'What do you want, Dex? An apology? It's not like you were exactly available to us while you were off gallivanting all over the world.' The jab comes from Parker, and I'm so shocked by the cut of the words that I don't have a comeback.

'Can everyone please just take a second and cool off?' Dad holds a hand between me and Parker. I bite the insides of my cheeks to stop my anger from flaring.

Turning to face my mum, I give Parker the finger and try to pretend that they aren't all here.

'What's going on? Why are we cancelling the holiday?'

Mum straightens her shoulders and finally meets my eyes. I've never thought we look particularly similar, but I know because people have told me all the time that I have her eyes. So when she stares at me, and I see a shimmer of the waterworks she's hiding back, I recognise embarrassment in them.

Whatever everyone else's motives were, Mum truly did want to avoid the scene that just happened. The public airing of family shame.

'This is all so silly. So much drama over nothing.'

'It's not nothing.' Liam interrupts and receives a jab in the arm for it from Archer.

'Mum, what's happening?' Fear creeps into my voice, making it hitch slightly. A million worst-case scenarios circle through my mind.

'It's not dying or anything. I've just been having a few hip problems.'

'Hip problems?'

'It's nothing serious. Standard, just age and well, reckless youth.' My mind flashes back to yesterday, Mum pausing on the stairs on Mont Saint Michel, looking peaky and exhausted. 'I've got surgery scheduled for next month.'

'Surgery? How long has this been going on?' The NHS isn't speedy about that kind of thing, which means this issue is not new.

'Two years.' Archer answers before Mum can evade the question. I am stunned.

'Two years?' I wasn't what you might call a routine caller of my parents, but we spoke at least once a month. I told them what country I was in, with whom, and what my plan was, if any. They told me about the family and gave me life updates. Hell, I once spent a forty-minute call with Dad bitching about Janet from work and how she always uses the last of the tea and coffee but puts the pots back and pretends it wasn't her. Diabolical work behaviour, truly, but not record-breaking news. Certainly not worthy enough to forget about major health issues. Which begs the question, 'Why didn't you say anything?'

'It didn't seem worth worrying you. You would have wanted to help, and there's nothing you could do about it. I'm fine and the boys have been so good, so helpful.'

I shake my head in confusion. Nothing I could do? But my brothers were some crackpot team of medical geniuses helping her with what? Bullshit.

'So you all kept it from me instead?'

'What did you want us to do?' Archer asks earnestly.

'It wasn't like we were going to ruin your elaborate holiday. Anyway, mum told us not to.'

'It wasn't a holiday!' I've finally had enough of the derision in my brother's tone, and I don't hold back when I bite at Parker. 'That's my life. It might not look the same as yours, stuck in one place, but I'd love it if everyone could stop diminishing it. Just because I wasn't physically here does not give you the right to write me out of this family.'

'No one is writing you out of the family.' Dad interjects calmly.

'No,' Parker picks up for him. 'You did that all on your own. You kept us at arm's length, ignored us and then bolted.'

'Parker!'

'No, let him talk,' I urge them. 'It's time that people stop holding back the truth.'

'Jesus,' Liam sighs. 'For the record, this is why I didn't want to hide it.'

'Well, at least someone trusted me with the truth.' I mutter bitterly.

'December! I mean Dex.' Dad corrects himself, but the presence of my dead name does the job. All the emotion drains from me. My anger is quenched, I'm left hollow and sad. Every time my dead name is used, it feels like being dowsed in ice-cold water.

'No one was hiding anything. I didn't think you needed to know Dex. I had everything I needed here. It's a hip injury. It's normal.'

'If it's normal, then why are you cancelling the rest of the trip?' Parker asks.

'Fucking hell Parker can you shut your mouth for a second.' Archer says in his terse tone.

'Arch.' Poppy rubs his arm in what I know is a gentle warning.

'Sorry.' He huffs.

Mum stands, using Dad to leverage herself up.

'We are cancelling the holiday because I'm a stupid old woman. Is that what everyone would like to hear? Does that make it all better? I thought I was up for this trip. I hoped I would be able to go about my life normally, but I was wrong. I pushed myself too hard yesterday, and now I can't walk too well,' she looks at me to explain that last part. 'Certainly not well enough to go touristing it up around Paris. Your father and I offered for everyone to go on without me, but you chose to all come home and postpone. So yes, children, this is a normal and unfortunate part of ageing. It wasn't because we didn't trust Dex, it wasn't personal, I wasn't protecting them and choosing to subject you others to suffer. I just didn't want to feel old and pitiful. Is that a crime?'

We all look around at one another, thoroughly chastised. We return to uncomfortable silence for a moment before giving a chorus of 'Sorry, mum'.

It's incredibly tense as Archer goes to grab the kids and

make sure they have their things, and Mum apologises to me personally for the cancellation of the trip, as though I haven't had enough travelling to last a lifetime.

'It's fine, Mum, let's just get you home, okay? Then you can start filling me in on all the details I missed.' She smiles at me with that slightly exhausted, eye-heavy smile parents are so adept at, and I know she's not going to give me the full story if I ask for it.

Behind us, Dad claps his hands together and rubs them so they make an audible scratching noise.

'Well, look on the bright side,' he jokes. 'We get to ride the ferry again!'

Chapter Twenty

Dean

If last week felt like a slow, luxurious interlude in my life, this week is an anomalous limbo space. I went from blissfully ignoring all of my problems with copious amounts of sangria in a pool to thinking about them twenty-four-seven without distraction.

The worst part, I returned from the trip with more problems than I left with. That's not normal! That's not how holidays are supposed to work! I'm no expert, but I can confidently say that most people return rejuvenated and replenished.

Granted, I was supposed to have an additional week to get some more of that replenishment in, but who am I kidding? Another week in close proximity to Dex. That wouldn't have accomplished much other than making my mess bigger and maybe a couple of additional orgasms.

I'm glad Serena is taking the time she needs to rest. Truthfully, I hadn't realised how bad it was until the little family explosion at the Château. Here I've been cursing Dexy's name and considering them this careless chauvinistic prodigal child who didn't want to return home to help their ailing mum before her surgery, all the while they were none the wiser about what was happening back home.

I mean, it's not as if Serena's hip problems impacted that much that I could see until the trip. It would have been stupid for them to come home to try and help, but I know Dex. They would have. That much was clear from the utter devastation on their face the whole ride home. That carefree, happy-go-lucky attitude they tote around was entirely sucked dry. Not a single joke during the two-hour car ride, and then they sat alone the whole duration of the ferry outside in the misty sea drizzle, just watching the land draw further and further away from them.

Which is why it is so totally and completely selfish of me to be semi-obsessing over what happened between us on the last night. I want to tell someone, to talk to them about it, but the only person who can know about it is Dex, and they have way more important things to deal with than my overthinking brain.

I'm starting to get the impression that Pom and Priti were right. I should have more friends who aren't my sisters. If I tell the twins, it'll be seconds before my sex life is full-on family fodder.

No, thank you.

Aside from that, the only other person whom I would usually text is Callie, and that's just a step too cruel even for me.

So, between avoiding spending one-on-one time with my sisters lest I let something slip and having no other friends to speak of that I haven't yet slept with, I've been spending the majority of my time under my soulmate, Hedy.

I feel no shame in referring to Hedy as my one true love.

From the first second I laid eyes on her, I knew we had something special. She might be old and cranky, but my girl has never let me down; she just needs a tender hand.

The way I see it, if men are allowed to be in love with bikes and boats, then no one should have any problem with me pouring my affection into a 1963 Chevy SideStep. She's a beauty, with her flatbed trunk and boxy hood; it was love at first sight. Before sight even. I fell in love with the idea of her.

Two years ago, I hit a new emotional low.

I had been rejected by my first-choice PhD program, leaving me no option but to move out of my cute, and admittedly overpriced, Manchester flat and come home. In doing so, I abandoned any social life I'd dreamt of maintaining, and I couldn't find the rhythm of who I had been before. Any faith I carried as a child had lapsed. Sometime during my undergrad, I even stopped fasting during Ramadan, with no family around to celebrate with, it felt easier to just forgo the holiday. It was weird to try and start again in adulthood. I couldn't find work here, and every time I turned a corner, I thought I was going to bump into Khloe or one of her family and have to hear the nasty things they said about me all over again.

I don't believe in sugar-coating things, but for the sake of my own sanity, let's say it was bad with a capital B and a side helping of antidepressants. But modern medicine worked its wonders, I got the help I needed, was accepted into the local three-year PhD course, and, of course, I found Hedy listed on Marketplace.

She was rusted; practically no salvageable parts remained of her original interior, but the exterior body was in good structural shape. I made Dad drive me the three hours to pick her up under the guise that I would just see if she was a viable purchase, but the truth was, if there was any hope of reviving her, Hedy was coming home with me. Honestly, the guy selling looked pretty relieved to be rid of her, the imbecile, and only charged me £150 because he thought I'd use her for scrap metal. We hooked her up to the back of Dad's Toyota and carried my baby the whole way home to Archer's shop.

I'd call it a steal, but in the years since, I've probably spent every spare penny I could find on her, so she turned out to be a pricey date. Hedy lived the first nine months of her life almost permanently parked at Brown Owl Motors. I owe Archer and Kyle a debt of eternal gratitude for letting me rebuild her there. It wasn't as though they had to, but they helped me source parts at low cost.

Ideally, her initial stay would have been a one-and-done kind of visit, alas, my girl is tricky. If we're not at Brown Owl once a month fixing something, it's a miracle.

Last year, I finally got the cash together to pay them to refinish and detail her, you know, the neat bit I can't be bothered with, and now she's a gorgeous bubble gum pink. The kid Arch hired to do Saturday work in place of Parker offered to pinstripe her in exchange for letting his friend take pictures with Hedy to post online, which was a deal I couldn't refuse.

So, I invite you to imagine Hedy, named in deference to screen icon and scientific hero Hedy Lamar, the pink pickup truck of my dreams, with elegant white pin striping decorating her sides and smooth peach interior leather in the seats. She is truly a lesbian beauty, which is why she is my soulmate and the matter is settled.

Today, though, Hedy's throwing a bit of a fit.

A light reverberating knock lets me know someone is waiting for me up top, and, sighing, I scoot my body out from underneath her.

'What's the damage, Doc? Is our girl in for the long haul or just a whistle-stop visit? ' Archer has his overalls flapped down so that he's mostly just in a tank top. Like this, with his muscly arms flexed and folded over his chest, he reminds me disconcertingly of his youngest sibling. It's both an unwelcome reminder of Dex and strangely intriguing to see some echo of how they might age.

I wipe my greasy hands on my dungarees and stretch out my neck. 'Well, we were right. That horrible grinding noise is the transfer case; there's a nice little pool of liquid underneath it to prove it.'

'Bollocks.'

'You're telling me. I'd wager that the replacement case we put in a couple of years ago had more miles on it than we were led to believe. I'll probably have to look at getting a new one, but for now, she should be good to drive, I just might have some trouble shifting gears.'

'She won't sound pretty.'

'There are worse things in the world.' I pat Hedy's hood affectionately. 'Got anything else around here for me to tinker with?' I ask, desperate for any task that keeps my mind busy.

It's not atypical for me to kill time by helping out at Brown Owl. I've been doing it since Archer took over floor operations in my teens, and he first taught me how to diagnose a weird clunking noise. Nothing in the garage ever held any appeal for Dex, despite two of their brothers going into their Dad's family business, but for me, it's where my brain comes alive. Problems have solutions, broken things can be put back together again, and replacements found. It's not easy work; it's physically draining, but it's rewarding to watch things come together again and to know you did well.

'Free manual labour? I won't say no if you're offering.'

I while away the afternoon helping Lochlan fix up a car that failed its MOT. He's not too shabby for a sixteen-year-old. Given that he seems to have begged Kyle for every available hour they'll give him over the summer, I thought he might want to go on to become a mechanic, but he doesn't sound too sure.

'I don't know, man, I mean, I enjoy it, but I feel so,' he holds the wing mirror he's refitting in one hand and waves the other in a frantic jazz hand motion instead of finishing the sentence.

'You've only just finished your GCSEs; you don't need to rush.' I tell him.

'Yeah, but I need cash.'

'You need to finish school.'

'No, well, yeah, but I mean after that. I have bills to pay; I've gotta make sure my siblings eat.'

'Hark at you, man of the house.' The joke makes him beam, and I wonder if Kyle and Archer hired him because he reminds them of a young Parker. That's not to imply that all transmen are the same, but they're both pale and fidgety with this mischievous energy you can't help but love. Less a golden retriever than a corgi who thinks it's twice the size it is.

There should be no need for a teenage boy to work multiple part-time jobs to keep his family afloat or worry about supporting them after school. I'd love to know where the fuck this kid's parents are, but Park warned me not to push the matter when they hired him, so I opted for gentle coaxing instead.

'I get it, though; you want to make money, have a career that supports you. You're just young, you don't need to sell your dreams away.'

'When did you know you wanted to be an accountant?'

I pause, my wrench halted in mid-air.

There should be an answer to this question, right? I should know it, but if there is, I don't want to give it.

The truth is, when I was about Lochlan's age, I googled 'Jobs that pay well', and Accountant was the first one that came up that wasn't involved in the medical field. That's not helpful. That's exactly the opposite advice I'm trying to give this kid. Which begs the question, why am I living it? He isn't my child or my employee. This isn't a do as I say, not as I do scenario. It's just embarrassing.

Surely I can just come up with a lie. I don't need to tell him exactly how I decided to be one, I could just tell him what I enjoy about my job.

Crap, do I even like being an accountant? I like the money. I like that I find the work easy, but I don't enjoy any of it.

Oh my god. This is mortifying. Far too long has passed since his question, and I'm not sure how to recover from this social situation without unpacking my impending quarter-life crisis on a teenager. Luckily for me, I don't have to.

The all-too-familiar sound of skateboard wheels bumping along the stone slats of Brown Owl announces Dex's arrival, and, as if that weren't enough, they caw to the ceiling like Peter Pan. It's a sound I heard a thousand times in my teens and, before I can think better of it, I smile.

Pulling right up beside Lochlan, Dex slaps his hand in greeting before dismounting and leaping off to ruffle his coiffed hair. It baffles me how easily people take to Dex. I can't fathom when they've found the time to get close with this kid in the fortnight since they got back, and yet they greet each other like old friends. It momentarily displaces my panic at their arrival.

'Ashraf, I should have known that you were hiding out here.' They say as the hair ruffle turns into a noogie.

'I'm not hiding!'

'You're not answering my texts.'

'That's just called common sense,' Archer calls from the office doorway. 'Now, free my employee.'

Dex promptly drops Lochlan, and the pair stagger apart laughing.

It's nice to see Dex now and not feel resentment. However, the lust replacing it is slightly problematic.

Until now, my updated image of them has been based purely on photos and clips I scrolled past on social media or that my sister passive-aggressively pinned on the fridge. I had no context for the way their short hair swishes as they move or how thick and muscular their thighs would have gotten in the time since they left. On holiday, it was abundantly apparent that they stopped shaving, their toned legs are peppered with fine fuzz and their underarms the same. It shouldn't be sexy. Hairy men always kind of freaked me out, but Dex isn't a man.

Sodding hell, I need to pull myself together. If I could slap myself right now, I would.

'This is perfect, though, because now I can kill two birds with one stone.' They keep talking, beckoning Archer over with a wave. 'So I was thinking, since Mum's birthday trip ended kinda climatically, we could make it up to her.'

'Make it up to her how?' Archer looks sceptical, his arms still folded over his chest as he inspects Dex.

'That's the best part, we could do it this weekend and, thanks to a friend of mine, it'll be pretty much free. I've organised us all a camping trip this weekend. Same as we used to have.'

'A camping trip?' Archer and I parrot simultaneously.

'How is that going to keep Mum's hip rested?'

'What do you mean you've organised it?'

'Both good questions.' They wave their index fingers palm up at us, and if I didn't know any better, I'd say Dex is stoned. Actually, I know them incredibly well, and I'm certain they're stoned, which is all we can expect, letting Parker and Dex live together. 'Bear with me.'

Chapter Twenty-One

Dex

'Ta-da!' Despite my best efforts to make the arrival of the camper van dramatic and appealing, it still comes off as somewhat of an anti-climax. My arms are spread wide, in the style of Will Smith in that meme, as nineteen people blink back at me. 'Everyone already had the weekend off from work, so I called in a favour with my friend. We have seven pitches and a camper van spot.'

I finish my little speech in a cheerful tone, even though I have yet to witness an ounce of enthusiasm from anyone. This plan felt more exciting when I was stoned.

When just enough time has passed to make it weird, Mum pipes up.

'That's very thoughtful of you, honey.' She's up and walking today, albeit a little stiffly on the right side. 'It'll be nice to spend time with everyone again.'

'As if we don't do that every week.' Pom snorts. I'd be hurt, but that's just how she is. The girl has got more walls than a prison, but she's a secret softy behind it all.

'It'll be great. Just like the camping trip we had when we

were younger!' I enthuse.

'My favourite part of those trips was when we stopped having to go on them.'

'Pom!' Priti looks appalled.

'Oh, don't pretend you didn't feel the same. You used to fake period cramps to avoid the hikes and stream The Kissing Booth movies on your phone.'

If it's at all possible, Priti's perfectly puckered mouth has stretched further in outrage. I won't lie, losing Priti stings, but there are still plenty of people to win over on the idea.

'There won't be any long walks this time, per Dr. Scars-brook's recommendations, just short walks to and from the lake. A lake we can swim in...' I try to make it sound as tempting as possible.

'Not quite the Château pool, is it?' Dean adds.

'I have floaties and a rubber dinghy for the kids and copious amounts of alcohol for the adults.'

'I'm in.' Liam says with a smile.

'I thought we kinda had to be, given that we drove out here already?' Cami says, looking distinctly unimpressed.

'Excellent point, darling niece of mine.' I drop my hands and stare the grumbling remainder of the families down. 'You're all basically stuck here, whether you like it or not. So, unless it's currently your sixtieth birthday and you have hip problems or are the spouse of the birthday lady, pick a tent and make yourself at home.'

The disgruntled mass disperses, and I show Mum and Dad around the camper van I borrowed for them. It's pretty thoroughly decked out if I do say so myself, it has one of those fancy built-in bathroom shower things and a fully operational mini fridge.

I leave them to unpack their bags and assess the tent situation. Of the seven tents, two were family-sized multi-room contraptions, three were just large rooms, and there was one two-man and a single sleeper pop-up. I sort of expected to find myself left alone with my unpopularity in the one-man tent, but, to my immense relief, Parker had already set the thing up and is sticking his feet out of it.

Nora and Liam have things under control as Lois and Leon run around them in circles, while Poppy uses her impressive parenting skills to enlist Archer with an army of tiny helpers. Even the nieces are coping well, with Martha calling out instructions and Meggie and Cami obeying dutifully.

The only exception to this is the twins, who appear to be mid-argument, debating which of them will start setting up their tent. If I were to place a bet, it would be on Priti cracking first, but Pom appearing to do it correctly later. To the side, watching this little showdown, Dean is sitting cross-legged, giggling to herself. I walk over and pop a squat.

'How long do you think before they realise it's a pop-up?' She points at the manual for their tent in front of us, which suggests a single cord pull will erect it. 'I'm giving it a solid thirty minutes.'

'Are you sure you're up for losing another bet to me?'

I've spoken before, I can consider the implication of my wisecracking, and I wish I could clamp my hand over my mouth to stop more stupidity gushing out.

We haven't acknowledged what went down in France since it happened. Now is not the time to bring it up casually in front of our entire collective families. Especially since, as I look around and do the maths, I realise that the two-man tent Dean is sitting beside is meant for us.

CHAPTER TWENTY-ONE

Balls.

'Just because we're sharing a bed or tent, I guess, again, does not give you permission to get all flirty with me, Dexter.' She says with playful judgment.

Is it wrong that her faux seriousness is turning me on? Probably. No, definitely. Dean just made it very clear. What happened between us changes nothing. We aren't going to catch feelings or have a repeat incident.

'Noted.' I stand and examine the bag. 'So are you going to help me with this or-'

'I'm just a poor weak girl,' Dean puts on a terrible country accent and holds the back of her hand to her head melodramatically. This is not the first time she's pulled the damsel-in-distress act to get out of something she doesn't want to do. It's a signature Dean move. 'So helpless. I can't lift anything. I couldn't possibly assemble a tent. I need a big strong butch to help me.'

I'm too busy laughing to challenge her laziness, so I unzip it and get cracking, pausing only to dip down next to Dean and whisper in her ear.

'You're taking the title princess incredibly literally, I see.' I let my lips brush against the shell of her ear before pulling away entirely.

If she wants to be treated like a princess, I can make that happen. We both know it, and I have no shame in making that point over again.

* * *

By the time Pom and Priti are finished setting up their tent, darkness has descended, and my brothers are living their best grill dad lives, barbecuing various types of meat. Liam and Rami are manning the Halal barbecue, while Archer and Parker appear to be roasting anything and everything that's ever walked.

Dean looks revolted as she pokes her pescatarian grill, shaking the halloumi and blackened veggies. Her nose is all wrinkled up, and her plump lips are downturned.

'How can you eat that?' She glares at my hot dog, and I move my hand as if to reflexively shield it from the force of her disgust.

'Hey,' I waft her concerns away with my beer. 'Eyes on your own food. You don't see me judging your squeaky cheese.'

'Squeaky cheese?'

'Yes. Cooked halloumi squeaks when you chew it. It's like gnawing on rubber.'

'It does not!'

'Well, if we hear a mouse, I won't panic because I know where the noise will be coming from.'

'We're in the middle of a fucking field. There are hundreds of mice around us. We're practically sleeping in their home.'

Beside me, in her comically small camping chair, Martha freezes.

'Hundreds of mice?' Her eyes are blown wide as she processes the words.

When you're six and three-quarters, mice are apparently a big concern, right up there with venomous snakes, surprise spelling tests and quicksand.

'Don't listen to the mean lady,' I shoot Dean a mock scowl. 'She's just grumpy because she has an iron deficiency.'

Priti scoots into a seat beside me, snagging a piece of cheese from her sister's barbecue. It squeaks as she talks. 'So where are you heading next?'

'Hm?'

'Well, you've been travelling pretty much non-stop, what's your plan after this weekend?'

It was a fair question. After all, that is exactly how I have lived my life for the past two years, applying for the next visa before I was done at the current location. It makes perfect sense that I would resume my globe-trotting the second Mum's birthday celebrations conclude.

'I don't have much on the cards, honestly. I've been treating my friend's flat in Brooklyn as a home base, but couch-surfing only works for a couple of weeks at a time, so I can't head back there and just hang around until I find something.' Which was, I wasn't going to admit, pretty much exactly how I'd found travel opportunities the last few times.

It's always nice to spend time with Hawa; we are very different people with closely aligned brains, but I resent being a burden on her. Brooklyn is Hawa's home; she has a real career there, dates, friends, all the hallmarks of a life. It's incredibly kind of her to offer to house me in my layovers, but I don't want to hold her back. She's six years older than me and dating this hot non-binary teacher, the one who got us invited on our Hamptons trip. I know she wants to settle down. Not necessarily kids, but maybe a small dog and a bigger apartment that doesn't function as a way station for her directionally confused friends.

The last thing I want is to take advantage of the generosity my friends offer me.

'I've gotten pretty lucky with the pro skater title; it doesn't make a ton of money, but it's kept me afloat and booked me a few flights.' I'm skimming over the shabby reality here. I refuse to divulge the honest truth that I've been poorer than a church mouse for the last nine months.

There are two types of 'pro skaters': the kind that compete and win titles, and the ones that got the 'pro' in their name by posting online. There's nothing wrong with either route; in fact, many people hold both titles. But, historically, skateboarding has had a problem with women. So when people look down upon those of us who make a name by posting online, they are often overlooking the systemic misogynoir and classism that prevents women, POC, trans, disabled people, and poorer skaters from participating in competitions that would allow them to win money and make a name for themselves the 'respectable' way.

I decided, very early, that I wanted to be the latter and not the former kind. For starters, there were next to no competitions in our area that had a girls' division and those that did treated them as a politically correct demand that they had to adhere to rather than something anyone cared about. I started posting videos of my skating online when I was fourteen and have gathered a happy little community of followers. It's nothing wild by influencer standards, but enough that when brands hear I'm in certain countries, they offer to fly me somewhere free of charge to attend an event or be interviewed. If it weren't for the marginalised skaters that came before me, I wouldn't have been able to say yes to any of that.

Sure, the brand might fly me somewhere and pay me in swag, but how was I going to eat, or where would I stay while there? Because Hawa doesn't subscribe to social media, she keeps all of her friends in a Rolodex, real old school, with their location and numbers. So when I started seeing offers, she'd call up a friend in the area and ask them if they were okay to house me for a week or a month, and I'd bounce around from there from friend to friend. Eventually, I started adding to her Rolodex.

That's when Hawa and I started something we've been jokingly calling the 'Skater Girls' Network', a community of marginalised skaters across the world willing to help each other out. Each time one of us travelled, we took down our new friends' contact details, logged them, and asked if they were alright with us passing that along to other friends in need. It's worked out pretty well for us, and we haven't stopped expanding it, but I can't begin to explain all of this without touching on the riskier parts of it that might make my family worry.

'A friend of mine runs this campsite, so I might double back and crash here for a while to give her a hand this summer. Make some extra cash, breathe in that British summertime.'

'You're friend runs the campsite?' Parker asks from across the circle.

I nod, biting down and then try to talk around my hot dog. 'Mia. She used to be one of those, like, van-life people, that's where the camper came from, but she stopped here in the pandemic and took over a couple of years ago when the owners were looking to retire.'

Priti looks horrified, and I can't tell if it's because I chew as I talk or at the idea of living in a van full-time. Parker is nodding pensively, though, and I can tell he wants to ask more about it.

'Oh, nice. It's never occurred to me that people live in a place like this in the off-season.'

'I'll introduce you to Mia tomorrow if you want. She'll

197

probably show you the farm they run too if we ask nicely.'

'Do you know anyone who lives a regular life?' Priti's eyes are trained on her plastic plate as she speaks, watching as Dean throws veggies at her.

'I know you guys.' I shrug. 'Honestly, I've never thought of it that way. My world isn't divided into the people who work corporate jobs and those who build a different life. I've known Mia since she worked in a Debenhams HR department and wore pencil skirts to work. People change, lives are transitory, and wants fluid.'

'Deep man.' Parker says sarcastically.

'Hey, not to be all hippy-dippy about it, and it's rough sometimes, but the 'ideal' life we saw as kids just doesn't work for everyone. Lots of my friends don't plan to get married or have kids, or they want one of those or both, but not in the order that's acceptable. It's hard—not to mention, fucking expensive.'

'Sometimes I think about the fact that our parents had four kids by my age. Four! In this economy, can you imagine it?'

From the low drawl of his words, the way the vowels round out and skate in the gutter of his mouth, I can tell my brother's had a joint or two already.

'I do think I want that life. At least settling down some day.' I say. Then, because I can sense the jokes coming, I add, 'No big wedding though. One was enough for me.'

The group laughs good-naturedly, and I can tell I've taken some of the sting out of the topic. If any of them still felt awkward acknowledging it, it's past now. Only Dean watches my reactions. Behind her glasses, her eyes are trained on my hands, watching my fingers move as I speak.

I try not to let it fluster me.

'Personally, I just can't see myself in the corporate world. Every single office job I've ever had felt as though it was specially designed to make my AuDHD self want to scream.'

Everyone nods thoughtfully, and just as it looks as if Priti might keep talking, Martha opens her mouth.

'I'm going to be a vet!' She offers unprompted.

'You would be an excellent vet,' I say, holding her plate up to catch the ketchup currently sloughing off her hot dog.

She has the bun in the centre of her fist and squeezes it a tad too hard as her eyes meet mine and she stage-whispers.

'Vets don't have to work with mice, do they?'

Parker dips his chin to hide his grin, and I have to bite down on my own. I don't dare meet Priti's or Dean's eyes, knowing they'll both give me the giggles.

'No. There are special kinds of vets for mice.' I manage with a semi-straight face.

'Okay, good.' She resumes her munching, and I focus on the plate to stifle my laughter.

It has luminous pink and blue dots on a white background and a million tiny serrated scratches and nicks from a lifetime of picnics and ill-begotten camping meals. I'm pretty sure we've had the same camping plates and cutlery since Archer was a kid: a large set of twelve polka-dot plates and bowls with horrendous neon green knives and forks—just another one of those familiar things that warms my heart to find unchanged.

We stay like that, everyone chattering and eating until the last vestiges of the sun sink below the horizon. It's almost as if I never left, old family jokes come out, two of the kids show us their gymnastics routine and Parker and I take a drink every time they check if we are still watching, Archer and Liam insist on only walking to the treeline to pee rather than using the bathroom and the mums heckle them and the parents get so wine drunk that Rami cannot comprehend my explanation of how to make a s'more.

'You've got to toast the marshmallow and then whack it in between the biscuits before it cools off,' I reiterate for the third time, demonstrating with one that I promptly pass off to Cami.

'But then it gets all oozy,' Rami protests, his nose wrinkled up the same way Dean's does when she gets grossed out.

'Aree baba! That's the point, Dad! You want it to melt it all together.' Pom rolls her eyes while Priti mutters something about not being able to take parents anywhere.

Beside him, Sabina and my Dad are pissing themselves with laughter. Sabina is slumped low in her chair, toasting her Croc-ed feet by the bonfire, her wine glass held aloft. Mum is in an acutely more upright position but equally as wankered. I'm beginning to think that Priti has the right idea. In my time away, the parents have regressed to teenage-level mischief.

'Were they always this bad?' I turn to Dean when I run out of ways to explain the act of s'more making. 'Or did they get worse while I was away?'

'Oh, they definitely got worse.' She's watching her mum with narrowed eyes. 'It's a combination of kid-free childishness and old-age cantankerousness that's almost impossible to reverse-parent.'

'That's exactly it!' I'm relieved that someone has managed to put what I'm feeling into words. 'Between this,' I wave my hands in the general direction of their chaos, 'and refusing to tell me about Mum's hip, it's as if I've become one-quarter of an unwitting caretaking unit with my siblings. I don't remember them being this much work to corral and communicate with.'

Dean sighs, still not taking her eyes off her mother, but I feel her energy shift.

'Sure, you do, Dexy. It was different then, but it's the same problem.'

'What do you mean?'

'You ran away from your wedding, for fuck's sake. That's a communication problem at its worst. You stayed in an unhappy relationship for years; you hid your identity. I'm not saying any of this to make you feel bad. It's normal. We're all guilty of keeping our worst parts, our darkest moments, from our parents. It's that damned Empirical stiff upper lip training us not to voice our feelings to our loved ones. You hid all of those parts of yourself because it was hard to talk about them with people who had preconceived notions of the person you were. I won't ever know exactly what that felt like for you, but I can empathise with it.'

'Bloody hell, have you ever thought about being a therapist?'

'You couldn't afford me.'

'Fair enough. So, can I get one freebie?'

She shrugs. 'I'm sure you can pay me back somehow.'

Blood rushes through my veins, and I come over feeling flushed...from the fire, I'm sure.

'Why is it different now? What changed?'

'You did. They did. We all aged, the parents included. You went away and learnt how to be Dex, how to let people see you, how to be happy. You came back stronger, more honest and a better communicator for it. Maybe now it's their turn to conceal some of their darker feelings. You just have to be there for them while they work out how to—ah!' Dean stands, waving her hands at her mother. 'Ma, no! Move your feet away from the fire. Ma!' And sure enough, Sabina's plastic Crocs have begun to melt in the proximity of the fire.

Sabina reacts slowly, cursing and stamping the offending foot against the grass. Beside her, Mum cackles with laughter, and my dad, oblivious, sets fire to his marshmallow.

Dean takes her seat with a cluck of her tongue and glares at me.

'Remind me to murder you later for bringing us all camping.'

'You're welcome.' I grin back just as the rain starts.

Chapter Twenty-Two

Dean

By the time everything has been safely set away for the night, the rain is torrential. I've got the last of the food locked in Priti's car to stop any particularly adventurous deer from getting it in the night as Nora shepherds the last of the kids back from the bathrooms. We shoot each other a haphazard wave goodnight, and I'm suddenly incredibly jealous of her wellies.

It never occurred to me to pack for extreme weather. My coat doesn't have a hood!

I turn around to the dying embers of the bonfire, ready to take my disappointment on myself for not checking the weather out on Dex for daring to pick a weekend with rain, but they've moved. I note the bin bags tied over the camping chairs, the tarpaulin over the kids' toys and the surrounding grass to stop it from descending into a complete mudslide and survey it, impressed.

A shadow moves in my peripheral vision, and before I can jolt away, I'm being shielded from the rain by an obscenely large beach umbrella.

'M'lady.' Dex says with a joking tip of their chin. 'Can't have my damsel getting damp-eth?'

The laugh that comes from my mouth startles even me. 'Why thank you, good...sir?'

Dex chews on the thought, the cogs visibly turning in their brain, and it's so delightfully easy to read that I wish I could memorise every inch of their face as they think.

'You can call me sir.' They say and then screw up their face upon finishing the sentence. 'That came out much more sexual than I intended it to. What I meant is that, sir is good from you. Nope, still sounds sexual. I'm not opposed to sir, gender-wise, I guess is the point.'

'But you're not a man?' I double-check, just to be sure I'm not missing signals they're putting down.

'Not a man. Boy, or boi with an I maybe, but not a man. Sorry, it's confusing, I know.'

'Don't apologise. It actually kinda all makes sense when I see you now. Like I see you respond to these words and the new pronouns, and it fits better than anything did before.'

Neither of us follows my statement with anything. It doesn't need it. Instead, we just take one another in. We're both soaked through, my plaits are dripping onto my chest, and I'm sure I look like a drowned rat. Dex, to my immense relief, looks equally saturated. Their ginger hair is plastered to their forehead, along with the fabric of their hoodie. The light denim of their jeans peeks out, darker around the centre of their thighs and shins, where it must be pressed flush with their skin, and their vans are covered in mud beyond the point of recovery.

'Want to head to the bathrooms together before we attempt to get in our tent without letting in Tilly?'

'Who is Tilly?'

'The storm currently raining on my perfectly planned camping trip.'

'Ah.' I say, not having known we were in the midst of a storm.

'She was supposed to hold off another two days before heading for the south. Total bollocks.' They shake their head.

'Clearly, she couldn't wait. Let me just run and grab my toiletries kit from my bag.' I step in the direction of our tent, but in their free hand, the one not holding the umbrella I'm sheltered under, they extend my toiletries bag.

'How did you manage that?'

'I had to grab the umbrella anyway and figured I might as well save one of us the effort of leaving their soggy shoes out in the rain for two minutes as we rummaged around the tent.'

I look down again, taking in the destruction of their vans with new comprehension. It was impressive before when I thought they had just been trudging around cleaning up with the rest of us, but I'm strangely touched to know they subjected themselves to puddles forming in their shoes for the sake of my toiletries.

The longing to mention my gratitude wars with the fear that doing so will break the spell of this moment. I mean, Dex was being kind, thinking of me, saving me the effort of trying to rescue my stuff from the tent without soaking both of our possessions, but they didn't do it solely for me. It must have just been convenient.

My heart warms, all the same, a bright glowing heat that keeps the chill of the rain away.

Unsure what to make of any of that, I head in the direction of the toilet block with Dex mirroring my every step.

We're quiet for most of the journey, focused on not slipping on the liquid ground underfoot. The rain is lashing down around us, pummelling into the umbrella and riveting off its sides so that Dex and I exist in a bubble of protection. Our private world is unaffected by Tilly. In the time it takes us to both pee and brush our teeth, the ground has turned to marshland.

Dex scoots behind me, their hand coming lightly to rest on my lower back as they take their place next to me in the narrow door frame. It's the tiniest motion. Only a fraction of a second and flicker of heat, and yet I feel it burrow inside me. It's familiar and easy, and I wish they would leave their hand there.

We stand, safe in the bathroom doorway, staring out. Apparently, despite the national predilection for it, heavy rain is all it takes to make Brits turn in early for the night. It's not yet ten, but not a single soul is around to be seen. It's as if we are completely alone.

'This is going to sound mental,' Dex is watching the rain fall, head tilted up as if the view of it mid-descent is different from the one on impact. 'But I kind of missed the rain.'

'You missed the rain?' I question. 'You went to a billion beautiful countries, toured around most people's dream destinations, and you missed the rain.'

'British rain specifically. It's different, meaner maybe?'

'It's mean.'

'Maybe not mean, but it's purposeful. It gets you wet like it's got something to prove, spiteful almost. Even the light rain manages to soak people here.'

'So you think that British rain has a vendetta of some kind.'

'Yes.' They laugh.

'Weirdly, that makes total sense. I can think of several things the universe might want to punish the British Empire for.'

'And we would deserve it. Ten thousand years of vengeful rain for attempting to conquer lands we had no business being on.'

'A lifetime of shitty summers for fathering white supremacy.'

'And still having the gall to keep a monarchy like they're cute little mascots.'

We both laugh at the familiar dark tinge our conversation has taken. This is how we work best: playing with each other, catching the other person's thoughts and adding to them.

Their shoulders shake, and the action flicks water around sporadically, catching me in the process.

'You look like a wet dog.' I wheeze.

'Well, you look like you just went swimming in your jeans.' They're beaming at me, brushing the water droplets they shook off of my cheek with their thumb. It's a strangely intimate action, the pad of their thumb grazing lightly against my skin and lingering just a second longer than necessary.

'I feel as if I just went swimming in my jeans.' I admit. Their left hand still hasn't moved, and I'm frozen, waiting for them to do something.

'You look beautiful, though. Even waterlogged.' Dex's eyes are wide, their smile dimming slightly as they glance down to look at my lips and back up again. It almost looks as though they might kiss me until the distant sounds of screaming children bound towards us.

Dex flinches back, clearing their throat.

'You want to make a break for it?'

We dash back towards our tent, the umbrella still locked in their hand as we both cling to it for support. In our haste, my foot skids in the mud, giving a great squelch as I try to pull it free. Dex stops, holding the umbrella one-handed over my head as they lean down to help.

It's funny. Deliriously so, and as I finally break out of the mud, our heads collide. They pull back as I lean in, both of us too busy giggling to notice what the other is doing. We both give a low exclamation and rub our heads, standing face to face.

With nothing but stars to light their face, Dex looks almost ethereal. The strange beauty of their wide-set eyes and the sharp squareness of their jaw, like something you might find in a painting.

I can't tell what they're thinking, but their eyes are locked on my lips, and I know, in a way I can't explain, that they're about to kiss me.

Which is exactly when the damp wind rushes at us. It blows the pelting rain sideways at us as it catches the lip of the umbrella, turning it inside out.

Whatever tension built is torn apart by laughter and necessity. The infectious giggles from earlier persist. I feel like a schoolgirl again as we run for cover and struggle with the zip, shushing one another and shoving our bodies through the gap.

We've got just enough room for one large airbed, our two sleeping bags laid out on top of it, and a single foot's worth of space on either edge for our belongings.

I get in first, slipping my shoes off onto a plastic bag Dex hands me and then ushering them in after me. With two people, outerwear still dripping on plastic flooring, it's a squeeze. Our knees are touching, wet denim chafing unpleasantly.

CHAPTER TWENTY-TWO

'What now?' I ask, lost in a seemingly normal social scenario.

'Take off your clothes.' Their voice is low, barely above a whisper, and, although I'm not sure they mean for the command to be sexy, it thrills me all the same.

Thoughtlessly, I obey. I unzip my jacket, shucking it off, and then meet their eyes. The connection there is a spark, as if I've just pressed my damp skin against an electrical socket. I want more.

Not letting my eyes waver, I grab the hem of my shirt and pull it over my head. I stay trained on them, not letting my emotions show, as I stretch my arms behind my back and unclasp my bra. It's just as sodden as all my other clothes and gets tossed aside carelessly.

Right now, my brain doesn't have room for practicality. I only have space for one thing, and it's Dex. Dex, who is looking at me like they might devour me at a moment's notice. Dex, who is pulling off their hoodie, unbuttoning their trousers in tandem with me.

There is no looking away. No averting our eyes. This moment is isolated from everything else, a photo encapsulating the moment of attraction. I am suspended by the lust in Dex's eyes; it surpasses being palpable and verges on becoming a taste lavishing itself on my tongue.

'Fuck,' they whisper the word like a prayer, intended only for themself and a higher power to hear.

'Dex.' I swallow my fear.

'Dean?'

'Please fuck me again.'

My words make them melt. A groan of relief escapes them as they pull me onto the airbed.

'I thought you'd never ask.'

Dex looms over me, and I realise, to my shock, that they are shirtless. Two neat strips of tape cover each of their breasts, holding them up and aside, smoothing the shape into almost-pecs.

I run my hand over the newly flattened skin, marvelling at how soft they are and the stark tan lines from their swimsuit. The length of my arm keeps us separated, leaving them to watch me drink them in.

'You are gorgeous.' I say, not sure what kind of compliment will speak to their gender correctly. And then I travel my hands over the curve of their shoulders and loop around their neck, beckoning them down to kiss me.

Dex obliges. Their lips are soft, satiny against my own. The push and pull of their applied pressure boiling the blood in my veins. Dex's hand comes to settle on my chin, firm and just a little forceful. It's nice. They rest their thumb on my chin dimple and use that to tilt my head to the side, exposing the length of my neck. I gasp as they move their kisses from my mouth to my neck. A slow, precise trail, devoting just as much attention to each new inch of skin as though I were hallowed ground.

When their lips reach the base of my throat, they open wider and latch on to suck at the skin. The rain descending on the top of the tent is blissfully loud, cocooning us in our own private moment.

Having had a slightly lacklustre sex life, love bites are not something I have experience with. I never truly considered it, but conceptually, I thought they might hurt, pinch, maybe. It's nothing like that at all. It's a gradual squeezing sensation that builds with each prolonged second of its application.

It pulls a moan from my lips as Dex's disconnects with a smacking sound. They kiss the reddened skin and then let their tongue run one single line from the fresh hickey to my earlobe, sucking on it gently.

I whimper at the contact, dragging my nails down their back, urging Dex onward. I want more. If this is what they can do just by kissing me, I cannot fathom how good the sex would be tonight. My one night of experience isn't enough to produce a solid visual image; instead, a thousand filthy suggestions burst to life in my imagination.

They take my scratching as instructions and kiss their way to my nipples. I remember this feeling from the other night, and yet no memory can compare to the sense of restitution I feel as their tongue glides over my raised nipple. It's as though this belongs to me; their mouth ought to have been mine from the very first moment it made contact with my skin last week. Every second spent away from me was theft. With it restored, I release a keening moan.

If my underwear weren't already drenched from the rain, Dex's mouth on me would be enough to soak them thoroughly.

The edges of their teeth play with my nipples, drawing them into their mouth before relinquishing them to be sucked. It's one sharp spike of pain accompanied by immediate comfort and caretaking, and it leaves me breathless for more. It's a kind of feeling I wouldn't have been able to express a desire for prior to experiencing it, and it causes me to wonder just how much I have to learn about my sexual interests.

They move to my other nipple, tongue teasing at its peak before letting their teeth nip gently at it, and I cradle their head in my hands.

'Yes, Dex.' I rake my hands through their hair, delighting in the soft dampness of it as they groan into me.

The sound of their need is enough to make me spread my legs, dropping my knees to the mattress as-

The edges of our tent shake aggressively, purposeful motions that could only be caused by a human hand holding its support beams.

We both freeze, waiting to see if it's a stranger stumbling past or one of our party. I'm filled with sudden, immobilising dread that my moans were audible to the tents around us. I was too focused on the gratification of Dex's mouth on me to consider curbing my volume.

The shaking comes again in a short burst, and then the unmistakable sound of Parker's voice.

'Hey, guys. Open up.'

In a feat of impressive and detestable restraint, Dex pulls away from my tits with one last reluctant look and heads to the zip of the tent. They open it just wide enough for their face and promptly stick it out.

'What's up, man?' I hear them say.

'There's been a slight problem with my tent.'

Dex groans, low and deep, not the kind that I just witnessed, but in frustration.

'You touched the edge?' They ask him, and I put the problem together. The one-person tent Parker was so pleased to nab was single skin, which means that the second anything touched the side of it, all the water pooling on the outside would start to seep through.

'It's like laying in a fucking water feature. Can I bunk in with you guys for tonight?'

'Why don't you sleep in the car?' Dex tries.

'I lost my keys. They must have been in one of the camping

chair pockets, but I can't find them now.

'Bugger.' I hear Dex mutter. 'Yeah, just give us like two minutes to get into our PJs.'

I whip my body up and snatch up the nearest dry hoodie and sleep shorts from on top of my bag as Dex retracts their head from the hole and zips it back up.

I'm sorry, they mouth, reaching for a fresh shirt and boxers.

I shrug, trying desperately not to let my sexual frustration show. Dex seems to sense it, though, because they catch my frantic hand mid-motion and bow their head to plant a kiss on its top side.

'Hurry up.' Parker whinges. 'It's a fucking swamp out here.'

'Alright, don't get your knickers in a twist.' Dex snaps. 'I'm getting there.'

The zip pulls up in one quick motion, and a very soggy Parker steps into our tent, spraying us both with excess rain as he shirks his shoes off and crashes onto the air mattress.

'Christ, it's snug in here.' He squinnies, oblivious to the fact that only moments before this tent was our personal paradise.

The look on Dex's face is so far past done that it's comical.

'Budge up,' they whack their brother on the side so that they can press their body in on the edge of the tent.

I wind up restlessly watching the roof of our tent, separated from Dex by the already slumbering form of their idiotic older brother.

I've always thought that blue balls were a fictitious diagnosis used by men to guilt their partners into gratifying them sexually, yet, at this moment, I'm considering the validity of sexual vexation as a cause of a breakdown.

It's made all the worse by the realisation that the hoodie I've snuggled up in isn't mine. It's blue and torn at the cuffs, the same as every jumper Dex has ever owned. The citrus and sweat smell of them encases me, and unable to avoid it, I opt to just indulge for the night.

I stay like that, the sleeves of their hoodie holding me, listening to the snores of Parker mix with the splattering of rain around us for hours, debating whether I've just wrecked the longest friendship I've ever had and, if I did, why didn't I at least get to touch Dex once in the process.

Chapter Twenty-Three

Dex

Early mornings at campsites are a no man's land of time and social expectation. You emerge from your sticky, condensation-ridden tent with a wonky spine and a poor night's sleep to walk half a mile to the nearest toilet. There, you'll witness kids singing to their parents outside bathroom stalls, older couples doing their washing up, and inevitably, someone showering without the proper footwear to publicly do so.

You'll return to your campsite to find at least one parent barbecuing a full selection of meats, children eating dry handfuls of cereal from tiny boxes, and grown adults rationing lukewarm milk for tea in plastic mugs like there's a national dairy shortage. Chairs will be dragged out from under pools of water and propped on waterlogged ground so that people can perch to eat. Someone across the way will be playing a game of Velcro catch whilst the family next to them disassembles their full set-up with a screaming toddler and a dad yelling about needing to get on the road. All before seven in the morning.

That's what waits for the early risers. Those of us who cannot sleep through various tiny feet tripping over their guide ropes and tugging our tent sideways or full-volume conversation from people over the age of fifty. Some rise in the late morning, blissfully unaware that everyone else has already lived half of their day, but their perspective remains an elusive mystery to me thus far in my life.

This morning is much the same as any camping morning: entirely chaotic and unpredictable.

Once I extricate myself from the depths of a gradually sinking air mattress, I surface into a veritable quagmire. The ground is more puddle and muddy bog than grass. Our camping chairs have all tipped over in the night, drenched in dirt and the wet remnants of their protective bin bags. Liam and Sabina's cars are entrenched in a foot of slush that looks as though it'll be a bitch to get out of and Parker's tent is entirely absent and replaced by an enormous lake.

I blink in the bright morning light, looking around, befuddled and catch sight of my parents and Rami and Sabina, all sheltering behind the van's presence with their hoods up. Rami catches the confusion in my eye and points his index finger skyward. I look up, and sure enough, there is Parker's tent twisting around in the distance, caught up in gale-force winds. It's being thrown around like a loose ornament in a snow globe, innocent and unable to stop the violence it's continually subjected to.

'Well, shit.' I whistle by way of greeting. 'That's a first.'

My dad shakes his head firmly and extends a mug of tepid tea my way. 'It's not the first tent we've lost, and it won't be the last. Summer of 02.' He informs me. 'Your mum decided it would be a grand idea to go camping in the middle of a national weather advisory.'

'Damn, okay.' My eyes pop in surprise, unaware that we were seasoned vets at fly-away tents.

'It'll come down soon, I reckon. Probably somewhere near the river. Then we'll assess the damage.' Rami's eyes are still locked on it.

'How long has it been up there?'

'Oh, only about five minutes.' Mum says with a sigh. 'I said we ought to secure it down, but someone wanted to have his tea first. Said it would still be there by the time he'd caffeinated.'

Dad shrugs. 'I've been known to be wrong. It's a risk I'm willing to take.'

'Am I the first one up?'

'Good, lord no. The under-ten portion of your nieces and nephews have been up since the sky was dark. So I'd drink that quick if I were you before you get roped into a game of tag.'

I groan. It's much too early for games, and I'm a morning person.

Sabina pats my shoulder sympathetically. 'Rough night, kiddo?'

I scrub my hand over my face and make a blergh noise.

'That air mattress sucked.' I offer as explanation.

'Ah, that's the old age talking. It's all downhill from here.'

The truth is, I'm running on a total of two hours of sleep. I couldn't pull my mind away from Dean and the way she looked at me as she told me to fuck her. There's no way I can admit that aloud to both of our parents, though, so I just toughen up and pretend it's the crappy back support that kept me from a restful night.

217

Right on cue, Archer and Poppy return with a horde of children. Half of them are freshly showered and thoroughly overexcited for the early hour, the other half are plagued by bedhead and, in Lois' case, are blinking at me as if they might still be on the verge of sleep.

'Morning.' Archer claps me on the back.

'You're up early for someone without children,' his partner laughs.

'I'm amazed that anyone can sleep through Parker's snoring. I've met quieter bulldozers.'

'So that's where he got to. I wondered if he'd been blown away with the tent.'

'Nope,' I roll my eyes. 'The moron decided to squish in between Dean and I last night. Spent the night using me as a bleeding teddy bear.'

A loud gasp sounds, and then, the children squeal in delight.

'Uncle Parker's tent is coming down!' Martha says, in the loudest voice one can manage before officially screaming. 'Can we go catch it?'

I watch the silent conversation take place between Poppy and Archer, the battle of not wanting to fight the kid's desire but having just showered some of them and knowing, with firm certainty, that chasing a blown-away tent in a storm will be muddy work.

The familiar droop of resignation falls over my brother's face, and I recognise that whichever specific side of the argument he was on, Poppy came out trumps.

'Alright,' Arch sighs. 'Let's go-'

'I'll go with them if you want?' I offer before I can second-guess myself.

'You want to go and chase down a tent at seven in the

morning?' Poppy quirks an eyebrow at me.

'Don't look a gift horse in the mouth, babe. Just let them go.'

'I can think of worse ways to wake up.' I smile at the kids. 'Come on then, let's go get it before it lands on someone's breakfast.'

It turns out that capturing a rogue tent from the sky takes one adult and four children roughly an hour to track down and safely dispose of. The zip was snagged shut, so Roscoe and Leon stamped on the support beams while Lois and I pulled at the fabric. The whole thing was coated in mud and grotty-looking rainwater, so we return to our camp, bedraggled adventurers after a long, unsuccessful quest.

I throw my body into the dirt, accepting that everything I'm wearing will need to be soaked in bleach to have a hope of coming away clean and wave my hands at the exhausted brood of children trudging back through the mud.

'I give you four tuckered-out hooligans. You're welcome.'

Thinking on his feet, my Dad produces four bin bags and lays them on the ground like beach towels for the kids to lie next to me. As if to prove my statement, they all take to their bags relatively silently, with only Roscoe narrating our journey without pausing to breathe.

I close my eyes, letting the early morning sun warm my skin, its brightness colouring my subconscious red, and breathe slowly. Despite my present debilitation, it was nice to spend that time with the kids. They have all changed so much since I left and developed their pint-sized personalities; I feel guilty for missing it. It's one thing to hear about their interests on a FaceTime call, but it only goes so far. I miss getting to interact with them, to play and have an active role in the way they grow up.

It's a sobering reminder that I have decisions to make when we get home. I need a life path, something ahead of me that I can point my energy at. It's been amazing to travel these last few years, to get to understand myself in so many different contexts and to exist without steady work. I'm aware that those things are a privilege, but they've had their drawbacks. I want to work; I want to care about what I do. I'd like to own more than two pairs of shoes and have a regular bed I fall asleep in. I'd even enjoy babysitting, getting tired of my family and longing for space again.

I don't want to blink and feel surprised by the wrinkles appearing on my brothers' faces, the greys overtaking my parents' temples.

I think the point I'm reaching is getting clearer. I might want to move home again or somewhere near it. If I accept that, though, it means facing the fact that I might want to rebuild a life here, not the restrictive, hidden one I lived before, but something new, something that honestly reflects me.

There's a tap on my shoulder, and I crack one eye open to see the shadow of my mother looming above me.

'Shift over.' She instructs me, bending carefully at the hip, to place a soft foam mat down between her and the sodden grass. I follow, offering out a hand to help her lower herself to the ground one knee at a time.

Once she's settled beside me, I return to staring at the cloudy sky.

'You look cream-crackered, honey.'

The phrase is so different from anything I've heard over the past few years that it startles a snort out of me. Trust my mum to dredge out the Cockney rhyming slang when she feels a mother-child talk coming on. I am utterly wiped out, dead on my feet, and I'm starting to think I have been for a while.

'Yeah, it's been a long couple of years.' I track the crawling progress of the clouds overhead, watching the bruise-coloured one creep across the blue morning sky. It's a uniquely British weather; beautiful but liable to give way to horrid at a moment's notice.

'Penny for your thoughts.' Mum ventures after the appropriate amount of silent cloud consideration.

I chuckle. 'I've never understood that statement. Is it offering or invoicing? Is that where therapists got the idea for their gig? Pay them a penny and they'll listen to your thoughts.'

'If that therapist of yours is only listening to your thoughts and not offering any professional expertise, it might be time for a new one.' My mum clucks her tongue. 'Now are you gonna deflect more or genuinely get around to answering my question?'

This is exactly how my parents have always been with emotional issues. They sense them in the same way sniffer dogs catch a whiff of a bag of weed. Dad is attuned but never wants to pry, and Mum is unwilling to give up until she's gotten to the bottom of it and given you a good dose of her opinion.

It used to drive me mad. Imagine being a teenager in a world where you're never allowed to just be moody without supplying a good reason. I didn't want to hear my mum's thoughts on all my problems; sometimes, I wanted to sit with them awhile, and as the youngest and the only 'girl', I was subject to an excess of intense parental attention. The time at home that they had previously had to split between the four of us focused solely on me for the last eight years of my life with them.

I chafed against it constantly and had the kind of screaming matches with my mother that I never saw any of my brothers have. It made me feel like a dick most of the time. Dean, Pom, and Priti didn't do that with Sabina. They never yelled, just quietly bickered for days until one or all of them apologised.

But Mum and I fought often throughout my teen years. Every time she poked at my emotional wounds and offered opinions, I resisted and ignored her until we wound up shouting.

I've been informed, in the years since I gained a therapist, that this fraught relationship with my mum is part of the reason I bottled up my gender identity for so long.

Parker came out young, only a few years after Mum turned up in his life, never really having to be raised as a girl. My mum was very proud to have three sons; she loved them all dearly and just as fiercely as if they'd been born to her, but she felt an affinity to my girlhood. It didn't get me special treatment or extra love, but just by being a girl, I was connected to her differently from my brothers.

Neither Sabina nor my mum are your typical 'girly' girls. They are both feminine but with their own flair. I very rarely see my mum in heels or a dress, despite her meticulously maintained blonde highlights and manicured nails. Sabina is more fluid and comfort-based, opting for knitwear and bright colours regardless of cut. As kids, we were lectured on the white supremacist misogyny of Barbie's ideal image of womanhood, taught to idolise women who broke through the glass ceiling, to defy expectations of what a girl could be and do.

I thought that I was embodying those things as a skater

girl, someone who oscillated between femme and masculine expressions easily without cutting my hair or refraining from makeup. Turns out I was just living to appease someone else.

Mum's relentlessness when it came to my emotional vulnerability was an extension of that. When she insisted on telling me her opinion, she was, subconsciously, living through me, and I was letting her. She offered opinions on my life as if it were her own because neither of us had learnt to separate our self-perception from the other's.

It messed me up, but then that's the lot; everyone's parents screw them up a bit. I got off lightly, all things considered.

All I can do is manage myself, remember who I am and how I see myself and meet my mum with that. (Pennies well spent, I'd argue.)

So that's exactly how I compose myself to let my mum in.

I take a deep breath, don't look away from the cloud, but let my shoulders relax so she knows I'm being receptive.

'I'm thinking of what to do next, life-wise. I'm considering moving back home.'

'Really?' I can hear the self-discipline in her voice as she controls her glee.

'I'm not sure. It's all still very hypothetical. But I'm tired of moving around and not having a home, my own stuff, a doctor, even. And,' I sigh. 'I'm broke. Like proper broke. No-money-in-the-bank-after-my-phone-bill-type-of-skint.'

'Well,' the weight of Mum's sigh feels similar to my own. 'If you want to move back in with us, you know you're always welcome. You can apply for jobs and—'

'Yeah, maybe. I might see if Park is willing to hold the room for a month or so until I can get the rent together and move in with him. No offence, I just don't fancy being twenty-seven and living with my parents if I can avoid it.'

'I think that's a great idea if it works out.'

I nod. Not sure what to follow up her comment with.

'When you left,' she continues, and I steel myself for a wedding jab. The kind of guilt-inducing comment I got a lot when I first started calling them again. 'I thought it was a ridiculous move-'

'It was stupid and I'm-'

'Let me finish.' She chides.

I raise my hands in apology and indicate for her to go on.

'It was rash and ill-thought-out. You wasted money on a wedding you abandoned. I still don't really understand what happened with Khloe, and maybe one day you'll tell me, but at the time, I thought you were running away from something real. You had nothing to your name, and while you might still have nothing financially, you have gained a sense of self again. I can see how much happier you are now.'

The quaver of Mum's voice surprises me.

'Dex, these last few years, you've grown into a person I'm proud of. You aren't always perfect and you can be a pain in the arse, but that just means you're one of us.'

'Thanks, mum.' I say, trying to hide the curving edges of my smile.

'So, what are you planning to do for work? You haven't exactly been beefing up that resume while you were travelling.'

My eye twitches at the faint jab of her words. It's not worth explaining that, yes, social media is a genuine source of work and applicable in many areas, because she won't get it, and frankly, I'm not convinced I should start saying that before I put it into practice.

'I haven't made it that far yet. But I will. Right now, I'm just getting my head around the idea of staying still for a while. Checking that it's right for me.'

'That's a good plan, honey. Don't rush things. No need to make any hasty decisions. Is there anything else, anyone else, perhaps that's making this decision tricky?'

I groan, unable to hold in the tandem flecks of annoyance and amusement. I should have known this wasn't a magnanimous parental chat. My mum is too damn nosy for it to be just that.

What is unclear is whether she's talking generally or about Dean. If she knows about my feelings for Dean, I'm in for a lecture. She's bound to have thoughts on how I should handle that, *if* I should be allowed that, without fucking up our conjoined family lives. She'll wager her approval and make me justify it, detail by excruciatingly personal detail, and I'm not ready to tell my mum about making out with my best friend yet.

On the other hand, I can't imagine who she could possibly think the other person was. It's not as if I've spent any time with other girls since coming home. Dean all but banished that thought from my mind.

She must take my silence as evidence of something because she starts to ramble.

'I know that you've been hesitant to plant roots anywhere, and it's wonderful that you've gotten to see so much of the world. I used to dream of travelling with Sab; I'd look at her postcards and wonder if she had the right idea and if I had made the mistake of settling down so early. Don't get me wrong, I love you kids, it's just I could have used some more time to get to know myself before I became a mum.'

This is a lot of honesty, and it all catches me unawares. I've never heard my mum talk about this kind of doubt. She always speaks of her past self as if she were so self-assured. It's hard to imagine any vulnerability there.

'Watching you turn your back on stability, working out that it was the wrong thing for you at that moment, and focusing on you. Well, I couldn't be prouder. I'm not saying it was the ideal time or place, coming down to the wedding day crunch, but the important thing is that you got out safely.

I've been so incredibly awed by your bravery these last few years. But it's been nice to know that you're not alone, that you have Hawa.'

'Mum.'

'I know, I know you don't need to hear the lecture, but I worry. America is far and—'

'Mum!'

'Yes?'

'I'm not dating Hawa.' It's so bizarre that it makes me laugh. 'We're just friends.'

'You're not dating?'

'No! She has a partner.'

'That doesn't mean anything in this day and age.'

'Okay, well, for starters, I'm monogamous. But more importantly, Hawa is like a sister to me. I love her *platonically*. She'll be in my life forever, regardless of where either of us lives, but I cannot imagine thinking of her like that.'

'Well then, I just don't get it. You've looked sort of lovesick this past fortnight.' Mum shakes her head. 'What's keeping you away?'

Sitting up and folding my forearm over my knees, I consider my words very closely. I'm not ready to mention Dean, but I remember what she said last night. It's my turn to be the

226

adult with parents. Let them see all of me.

'I never felt free to be me here. I love Portsmouth; I'm happy being a part of this family and being so close to the girls. I love the sea and being able to see the kids grow up, but for a long time, I was diminishing myself to fit in.

There's not exactly a thriving queer community. It's not small by any means, but it's tight. I didn't have a place in it for a lot of reasons, but I know how to be myself now, how to socialise in a way that makes me comfortable, that allows me to be honest. I guess part of me is scared that if I return things will magically go back to the way they were before.'

Mum throws her arm over my shoulder, ignoring the mud that coats my back and tips me toward her.

'Oh, my baby. No one can ever take you away from yourself. You might get lost for a bit, but you know better now. You're too strong for that to happen again.'

Maybe it's silly, but her words make me a little choked up. I distinctly don't meet her eye as she rubs my shoulder affectionately. It might be harder to hide, had the heavens not picked this precise moment to unleash a torrent of rain down on us.

Chapter Twenty-Four

Dean

The decision to cut our little woodland excursions short is unanimous.

We pull down the tents in coat-soaking showers, and I watch as the Carpenter-Browns with kids pack up their things and disperse immediately. The parents are all riding with Priti; their muddy supplies chucked in the back of Hedy for me to bring back to them.

I get that not everyone appreciates my baby. I'll admit, she is objectively not the best truck, and as cars go, she's far from reliable, but none of that is what's important to me. I've dreamed of this exact truck for nearly two decades, and I work hard to keep her up and running. She's a tough old broad, creaky and made up but not without her flaws; an inspiration for my future.

Pom, currently camped out in her passenger seat, clearly does not care how long it'll take me to clean the orange leather interior. She's too busy bitching about her wet hair and banging it against the headrest with each passing second.

By the time I've waved Priti and the parents off, the only car that remains is Parker's. The process of him getting ready to leave was relatively simple, what with his tent having blown away before he woke up, but Dex is nowhere to be seen.

'You guys heading home in a second?' I ask when he moves towards the now vacated camper van.

'Nah. Dexy has rented the van from their friend for another night, so we're gonna stick the rain out and chill.'

'Nice.' I say, thinking the exact opposite.

'Besides, Mia has offered for them to help on the site for a bit, so they might stick around for a couple of weeks and make a bit of floating cash. I'll probably stay as long as Arch can spare me from the shop.' He chuckles and then turns to face me with that Carpenter-Brown smile that's so damn infectious. 'Hey, you don't wanna take my shifts, do you?'

He's joking, but weirdly, I wish I could say yes. I would much prefer to spend tomorrow and Tuesday working on cars with Archer and Kyle rather than in my beige cubicle under artificial lighting. I smile, laugh politely like I'm supposed to and suppress the impulse to agree.

'Dex is staying here?' Trying to distract my mind from its erratic wants, I focus on what Parker left unsaid.

If Dex is staying on the campsite with their friend, helping out for a few weeks, it means that they're going back to their regular ways. They might not bother to come home and see everyone before jetting off again. This week, it's a campsite in the New Forest, next week, it's Prague or Peru or wherever they're sending skateboarding influencers these days.

For some reason, it's as though I've swallowed a rock as I reckon with the thought. It wedges itself in my throat, and I gulp it down, pushing until it lodges itself in my chest, weighing on my heart. If Dex never comes back, we will never get a chance to revisit last night. Not to finish it, but to at least talk it through.

It dawns on me all too slowly that they probably realised this.

Without seeing me again, they won't have to let me down easily or hurt my feelings in any visible way. I see it now, how they'll just slip away, shirking their responsibilities once more, running away from the mess they made in just two short weeks.

The stone sinks to my stomach, its weight grounding my feet to the floor.

As if summoned by my thoughts, Dex comes skipping up, their hair water-logged again, a stunning granola blonde in tow. She looks like something out of a Western movie; her hair is the colour of wheat, and she's wearing high-cut shorts, red cowboy boots and a peasant shirt that is practically plastered to her bare chest. It is shockingly braless and deliberately visible in this weather.

It's the sort of unapologetic self-confidence I want to admire. She looks amazing with or without the bra, but the second I notice the hoodie she's wearing, whose hoodie she's wearing, I hate her.

I feel foolish. Just another girl in a worldwide conquest. A blank space to fill the time while Dex was home. Less than twelve hours have passed, and already, some other girl is wearing their hoodie.

It's ridiculous. I'm ridiculous.

I wish I could say I stay strong, my cold, hard exterior returning quickly enough to conceal my pain. It would be a lie.

Have you ever sat in the corner of a class you aren't good

at, faced with a word problem that stumped you? You're in your regular seat, you usually understand at least half of what is said by the teacher, and only an hour ago, you were at lunch laughing with your friends and having a pretty good day. Maybe you didn't want to come to this class, but you weren't expecting to have your self-esteem completely obliterated. Yet there you are, blinking back tears, staring down at an unsolvable problem. It makes no sense; you're trying to find its solution, applying all the knowledge you've learnt from the teacher, but you can't make any answer make sense. You know the wrong ones when you write them out, but haven't found your way to the right one, and now, you've run out of solutions. You are exasperated and exhausted, and to make matters worse, everyone around you is flying through it, not stuck on this one silly problem that's halted the progress of your life. You can't do anything about it. The teacher hasn't gotten to you yet to answer questions, and you refuse to publicly admit that you're stupid, so you do nothing. You've wasted so much time on this one question that the rest of them feel like a wash. You've already fallen behind everyone else, but you have to just turn the page and pretend that you aren't crumbling under the pressure of your private shame. Completely lost, maybe a solitary tear dripping on the page, as you can't help but wallow in your self-pity.

That is how I am feeling. Humiliated in front of only myself, confidence demolished, and forced to pretend that I'm not fighting back tears at the thought of being so foolish.

I've always had a great knack for self-loathing, but I'm taking it to a new level right now. My self-loathing isn't just reserved for me. It's a burning supernova bound for collision, and Dex is a stray object trapped in its trajectory. If I'm being devastated, I'm taking them down in the crash.

They're still bounding towards us, blissfully ignorant of the hatred they've just reignited in me.

'Oh, cool, you're still here!' They grin at me. 'Dean, this is my friend Mia, who runs the site, Mia, this is Dean, she's-'

'Just leaving.' I cut them off. I angle my head away so that I can't see the way the smile tumbles off of Dex's wet face.

'Cool name,' Mia nods, unperturbed by my rudeness.

'Thanks.'

'And you must be Parker, right?'

Parker and Mia chat engagingly about the farm; he's immediately more excited than I have seen him in years, and I can't tell if it's because of the stunning woman or the wildlife. Probably both.

'You sure you and Pom don't want to stay and dry off a bit?' Dex asks, shifting their posture towards me, their shoulder shielding us from Parker and Mia's conversation to create the illusion of privacy. It does nothing to soothe me. I can still see the worn blue fabric of their hoodie covering her head. I still know that Dex's attention has moved on to its next flavour of the week lover.

Bitterly, I wonder if they found time to fuck her already while I was saying goodbye to our parents. It would be just like them.

'No thanks, I have things to get back to, unlike some people.' There might have been a way to administer those words like a joke, but I do it with every ounce of contempt I can muster.

It has the desired effect. Dex's auburn eyebrows crumple together as they try to catch my eye.

'Okay, ouch,' they half-heartedly chuckle. 'Well, I guess I'll see you—'

232

'Don't worry about it, Dexy.'

'What?'

'You're going to go back to doing your thing. Hopping around from place to place, woman to woman. You don't need to do the little speech-'

'What little speech?' They sound confused, and I remind myself that this is how people get away with crushing girls' hearts like grapes to make wine. They play innocent, naive, someone who would never purposefully hurt you.

'The one where you tell me it was fun, but you don't do repeat visits. I get it. It was a bet. You won. No hard feelings.'

'Dean, that's not-'

'This is just what you do. You run away when things get weird or hard.' I glance over at the other two and drop to a whisper. 'Last night was a mistake anyway. A slip-up.'

Their eyes are locked on my face, dancing around, trying to get my attention. I stay steadfastly focused on my shoes, refusing to give them the privilege of my attention.

'Do you genuinely believe those things?'

'It was a mistake.' I try my best to sound cold and firm and not to let the emotional quaver of my voice creep in. 'You're flighty. Irresponsible. It's just who you are.' I'm not sure I believe those two, but I've said them aloud now, and I can't take them back.

'I don't understand where this is coming from. We were good. I apologised. We've been good!'

'It's not coming from anywhere. I'm just stopping before you feel the need to make a big deal of something that meant nothing.' I protest.

'Okay, hey, take a beat. Do you want to stop before you say something you'll regret?' Dex uses a calm, distant tone, and it grates on me.

How dare they be so relaxed when I've just taken shots at their character! How dare they not care that I've told them everything between us was a mistake! It was a lie, or at least an overreaction, on my part, but seeing them this unbothered by it hurts more than I could ever have anticipated.

'This isn't new. You bolt the second life gets real.' Instead of retracting my knife, I gouge the wound wider.

'That's rich.' They scoff, and I'm rewarded with the flicker of annoyance that underlines their words.

Finally, I've had some emotional impact on them.

'What is that supposed to mean?' My voice trembles as my anger flares.

They fold their arms over their chest and double-check that Parker and Mia remain unaware of our tiff.

'Your life wouldn't know real if it came and bonked it on the head. Everything about your life is meticulously curated so that it stays at arm's length. A job you don't like. Friends you never engage with. Romantic partners you aren't interested in. You don't give your real opinions on anything. You hold back. You always hold back.'

That is the final straw for me. I can't stand here and let them rip me to shreds when Dex has already done enough emotional damage for a lifetime. I already feel too small for this kind of talk.

Their words hurt, and maybe, another time, I might be able to admit that some small part of them is accurate, but not right now.

'Who needs friends like you anyway?' I mutter just loud enough for them to catch, and to my relief, my sister rolls down Hedy's window to whine.

'De, move it, I'm freezing my tits off here!'

I take that as my exit signal and turn to wave a curt goodbye to Mia and Parker, ignoring as Dex calls out to me one final time.

Chapter Twenty-Five

Dex

Summer doesn't so much slip as skitter away from me like a many-legged critter I am failing to capture. Before I know it, the long, light summer nights are skulking back into shadows, bringing a brisk chill with them.

It's surprisingly nice to watch the seasons change from the safe consistency of one window. The full-blooming tree outside Parker's spare bedroom begins to wilt a little, its leaves ripening in colour until they blend in with the early sunset behind them, the warm russet and umber hues of a fox. It's comforting to track its progress parallel to mine, seeing the evidence that staying still doesn't have to mean staying the same.

'Tell me again what it is that you do?' Hawa feigns ignorance from the phone in my hand.

'I'm an insurance viability claim advisor.'

This is not the first time we've had this conversation. The wheres and whys of my current role get most of my friends hung up, but it pays decently and leaves me enough free time to work towards something enjoyable, so I'm stomaching my way through it.

'Those are just words jumbled up to make a title. That's not what you do.'

'I sort through old files for claims that never went anywhere and bring them up so my company can pass them onto other insurance companies, who will then call to hassle them about a possible claim they will inevitably not want to make. Is that what you want to hear?'

'So you just facilitate cold calls.'

'That's precisely what I do. They pay me to rummage around in a labyrinth of filing cabinets, supply a weekly report of contacts, and dispose of the rubbish. It's not exactly ethical, but it's no worse than any other office job.' I chug the last of my Coke can and lean back on the bed.

'Do you even have an office?'

'No, but I have the basement, and no one else wants to come down there because it's dusty, and I have a desk and a swivel chair, which is kind of like having an office.'

'Only you would find this job and not hate it.'

'No more about my boring butt, show me the ring!'

Graciously, Hawa obliges, hovering the back of her left hand in front of the camera to show off her whopper of a rock.

'Good god, I didn't know teachers made that kinda money in the States.'

'They do not,' my friend is practically glowing with pride. It's nice to see her so visibly happy from afar; my insides feel like they are, in some small part, basking in the excess warmth of her glow. 'Iman is calling it an *investment* in their future.'

'Can't fault that logic.'

I only know Iman in passing. They met while I was in Canada, the winter before last, and didn't start living together until I headed home, so the only quality time we spent together was sharing a wing of that Hampton's mansion back in June. We have that strange mutual fondness you gain when you both love the same person in different but no less wonderful ways.

'What are we thinking? Spring wedding, summer, destination?'

'Dude, relax. My mother doesn't know yet; I am not ready to make any plans before I've done the numbers.'

In response to that nonsense, I make a fart noise. 'Bo-ring. Call me back when you find your sense of fun again.'

'If you don't stop being such a little bitch about this, I'm going to have to find another butch of honour.' Hawa holds my gaze, and I just know that she was holding that little nugget in to use when I pissed her off.

She was right to, obviously, because it makes me shriek with glee. I've never been a part of a wedding before, at least not in an accessory sense. Poppy and Arch still haven't made it down the aisle despite putting a ring on it more than a decade ago, Nora and Liam have no plans to, and, despite being relatively popular most of my life, I've never had any friends close enough to offer me so much as an usher position. Well, with one notable exception, but the thought of Dean and weddings in the same sentence makes my stomach twist itself up.

My reaction might have been a fraction too loud, though, because Parker peeks his head through the door in alarm.

'You good?'

'Oh, shit, yeah.' I smile and turn the phone to face him so that Hawa can flash the ring once more.

'Bloody Nora, that's a big diamond,' he says in response.

238

'Thank you, cutie,' Hawa singsongs back down the phone.

When we first met, it took Hawa all of about three seconds to comment on how hot she thought my siblings were. I mean, across-the-board markings and what she would say if she saw them in a bar. She was a particularly big fan of Parker. I believe the words she used, despite my gagging, were 'he's got a rough and tumble look I'd take for a ride'. Needless to say, I've done my best to keep them apart ever since.

It doesn't exactly help that Parker finally realised who Hawa is two months ago. I get that she doesn't look the same as the lanky, awkward 'boy' who used to be reblogged repeatedly on Parker's Tumblr and pinned to his wall as a teen.

Once he realised why she looked so familiar, their friendship appeared to be destiny, whether I attempt to keep them apart or not.

'If you're not dying and you have a spare minute, can I pry you away to help carry some boxes down to the car?' He asks in an unusually polite tone.

I know my brother, and this is not how we interact, so either something is wrong, or Parker needs a favour, either way, I'm too curious for my own good. I sign off with Hawa, promising that I'll call her soon so we can make more business plans and I can hassle her about weddings before trotting into his room.

The walls are strangely bare; the shelves filled only with dusty knick-knacks and books, I assume Park has no intention of taking. At the foot of the bed are six large boxes labelled clothes, crochet, and miscellaneous shit.

'You got to work quick.' I survey the remaining things he has to pack, impressed.

It's only been three weeks since Parker announced his grand plan to move into that old decked-out van of Mia's and help

239

her run the farm in the campsite's off-season, and he's mostly already moved out.

He does, in theory, still legally live with me. His room will stay empty to house his furniture, and he'll pay half the rent for a couple of months to test his plan before jumping head-first. I can't complain; a two-bedroom flat to myself for a discounted fee is nothing to scoff at, but truth be told, I don't think he's coming back.

As we share the weight of one of the book boxes and head down to the car, I try to cut to the chase.

Parker has been doing what he calls a 'slow move' where he takes one car full of things up to the farm at a time, every few days, and I'm beginning to wonder whether there's more to that than meets the eye.

'How much room is there in this van? You've got a ton of stuff for a quote-unquote temporary situation, my guy.'

'Mia's offered to put some of it in the main house for me while I get settled.'

'So you think you'll like it there long-term?'

He clears his throat and smiles. 'It's good work.'

'Sure. It's just about the work.'

'Dexy?'

'Mm-hmm?'

'Do you think that there's any chance Mia might like to go out with me?'

I snort, shifting the sharp edge of the cardboard box in my grip before my fingers go completely numb.

'The girl is housing you, feeding you, and employing you.'

'So?'

'I think there's more than a chance, dipshit.'

The corner of my brother's mouth tips skyward, in the

smallest indication of a smile, as if he is trying to keep it private.

This doesn't come as a complete surprise to me, given that he hasn't stopped talking about Mia since I introduced them four months ago.

It's easy to see how they could work. Parker is laid back and introverted, Mia is the same kind of happy-go-lucky person, but she's much more extroverted. I have never seen her hold her tongue when someone needs to be set straight or see someone floundering socially and not extend the offer of friendship.

I'm not saying that their getting together is inevitable, but I see the potential there and knowing my brother, if he's been getting the slightest vibe, it probably means that Mia has been dropping some heavy-handed hints. He's always erred on the side of overly cautious and self-doubting.

We finish loading the boxes into the car, and I see Park to the driver's seat to wave him off.

'So, I spilt mine, but when are you going to tell me what the deal is with you and Dean?' The nosy git asks, switching on the engine and looking up at me expectantly.

I know I'm fucked the second defensiveness tinges my words. 'Nothing's going on. Why do you ask?'

'You guys were inseparable for days while we were camping and in France, and then, nothing, as far as I can tell, you haven't spoken unless you were forced to since. Not to mention that this is the longest Dean's gone without visiting Brown Owl since she learnt how to fix a carburettor.'

'We're not avoiding each other.' At least, I'm not. The truth is, I can't recall whether those two weeks in July came across as us being inseparable or not. In my memories, every moment

Dean and I spent apart felt arduously long. I wanted to talk to her, to be with her when she wasn't doing anything interesting. The brain power it took to keep myself from touching her back then was so fatiguing that even now I am aware of it's ache. It's very possible that our families picked up on some part of that.

As for now, we only talk when we have to. I've tried to apologise a couple of times, to catch her alone and have a conversation, but Dean always finds a way to dip out of it. I got the memo after a few months. Dean wants nothing to do with me after the fight.

'Sure thing. Whatever you have to tell yourself, buddy.' Parker laughs, and I tap the edge of his car door, indicating that he should get on the road.

He takes the hint and pulls away, still subtly smiling to himself. I take the opportunity to yell at him.

'You're a dick.'

He waves magnanimously in response, like the queen.

I'll be overanalysing my interactions with Dean for the rest of the night now, and he knows it. Every time I think we're fine, that I'm content with our new distant friendship, someone talks about her or tells me about this funny thing she told them over the weekend, and I'm lanced through with jealousy.

I wish I could point at someone else here and blame them, but that would be a lie. What I said hurt Dean, and as much as what she said hurt me, it was at least partially accurate. So all I can do is take her words to heart and show her that I'm not flighty or irresponsible. Prove that I am worthy of her friendship again.

Chapter Twenty-Six

Dean

Nothing is more humbling than realising that even your elderly grandparent has Friday night plans when you don't.

Actually, I tell a lie, it's marginally worse to be so reliably date-less that said grandmother can ask you to dog-sit on Fireworks Night at a moment's notice when she has a party to attend, and you were just going to get an early night.

This is the kind of social mortification having sisters should preclude me from, but Pom had a fancy influencer event to attend in London, and Priti had to go and get engaged. She offered to bail on plans with David and his friends to spend the night with me, which is painfully pitiful. I mean, it was sweet, and I appreciate the sentiment, but it's a fucking bleak statement about my social prospects that my little sister felt she had to offer that.

So, instead, here I am, hurrying down the dark autumn roads towards Dadu's house to spend the night cuddled up with four justifiably neurotic rescue dogs who hate fireworks more than postmen, running late because my beautiful, temperamental truck crapped out on me again.

It's chillier than I expected; my thin anorak keeps the drizzly rain at bay, but not doing much about the wind.

I should have known that Hedy wouldn't make the journey; she's been stuttering for weeks, waiting for me to work on her. I just can't face the boys at Brown Owl right now. Ever since Parker officially moved, Archer has been asking to 'talk' to me, and I don't have it in me at the moment. I got away with it for a while, using uni, then Diwali, and finally Halloween as an excuse, but it's November now, and I've officially run out of reasons to be too busy.

I was hoping that Hedy would make it to the holidays at least, that way, I would have enough time to prepare to let him down, but no such luck.

As I slot my key into Dadu's door, my fingers frozen, my mind is lost in debate with itself. I slip off my shoes and follow the distant rumble of playful barks. Dadu said that her 'gentleman caller' would be collecting her at three, so I'm just relieving the regular dog-sitter she's been hiring for the last few months. It's never once occurred to me to ask who she pays to look after the puppies when she goes out on her dates—honestly, I try to think about her dates as little as possible—so turning into the crowded living room to find Dex buried under a pile of fluff catches me off-guard.

'Oh!' Tom Bones, an elderly cesky terrier, comes charging in my direction, he's sprightly for his old age, nuzzling his snout into my thigh. I rub the top of his scraggly head. 'Hi.'

Dex looks just as surprised at my arrival as I am seeing them, which is strangely reassuring. At least both of us are on the back foot here.

They are starfished out on the carpet, with Madogna's wrinkly shar-pei body weighing down on them, and they try to scramble to their feet at my arrival but have to haul her off themself first. It's not an easy task; she's a hefty girl and comes away looking mightily peeved by their disruption to her rest.

'Hey! I didn't know. Dadu didn't say that you were the night sitter.'

'Yeah. That's me. Sorry, I'm late. Hedy's engine was giving me trouble.'

'Ah, shit. It wasn't on the road, right?'

'No. She's safe; didn't make it out of the parking space.' I confirm.

Dex nods, and we lull into an awkward silence. It's discordant with the unstoppable babble we were once capable of. Even when I thought I hated Dex, we were never quiet. We argued, we sparked, and even in anger, we laughed. It's only been this way since the fight at the campsite. We both said harsh things, words we may not have meant, but neither of us apologised or mentioned it ever again. Instead, we just became this, this odd awkwardness.

I hate it. I'm bad at it. It makes my palms sweat.

'Well, I'll just nip to the loo, and then I'll get out of your hair.' Dex bends down to pat Cilla on the head before walking to the downstairs toilet.

Throwing my bag down on the armchair, I meet Barkbra's eyes. She's always been my favourite of Dadu's rescue dogs. The very first one, she transitioned from foster to family member, and she's always remained a diva. Barkbra Steisand is a black and white papillion, her wide ears, fluffy coat, and impeccable posture make her feel like she lives up to her title. Most of the other dogs lay on dog beds or the large sofa Dadu claims to have brought for guests, but which is conspicuously always covered in too many dogs to sit on, but Barkbra has a plush red velvet cushion that Dada used to use for his back. It's very rigid and has these preposterous yellow tassels attached to each corner that only add to her dignified air.

It makes her strangely comforting to confess to and carries the same vibe as talking your thoughts aloud to an old portrait in a museum.

'Don't look at me like that.' I whisper. 'It's not my fault that it's weird, at least not *only* my fault.' She looks unimpressed. Her large black pupils fixed steadily on mine. 'What am I supposed to do, ask them about their evening?' Barkbra blinks at me, her expression unchanging. 'I'd rather not hear about whatever girl they're dating this week. What?' She stares me down. 'Just because I haven't heard about them dating around doesn't mean they aren't. It's Dexy, for fuck's sake. That's who they are.' I get a stern, reprimanding glare from the dog. 'Oh, alright. That was mean, but it wasn't entirely untrue, and you know it.' If we had a staring contest, I'd lose in seconds. 'Oh fine, I'll be polite, okay? Is that better?'

Barkbra eases her stance, relaxing onto her extended front paws.

'Did you say something?' Dex calls.

'Uh, yes.' I try to come up with something to deflect away from the bonkers-sounding truth of arguing with a dog. 'I asked if you are doing anything fun tonight?' I shoot the dog a look and mutter, 'Are you happy now?' out of the corner of my mouth.

They come back into the room, Cilla trailing faithfully at their heels, and I chuckle at the thought of her following them to the bathroom like an attendant.

'Nah, no big plans. I'll probably just walk home, catch the

fireworks that way and then watch TV till I fall asleep. Living that old person life.'

'You're crazy, Wildcat.' I say solemnly.

The joke has its intended impact, and their awkwardness cracks into that easy smile I love.

'What about you, nothing calling your name more than these four rascals?'

I shake my head. 'Embarrassingly, at eighty-six, Dadu has a more active nightlife than I do.'

'That's nothing to be ashamed about, that lady's got game.'

I'm so horrified by the idea of Dex ogling my grandmother that I can't do anything but slap them on the shoulder.

'Dexter Carpenter-Brown, you best not have been making eyes at Dadu!'

'I didn't mean it like that! God, no!' They give an inadvertent shiver, which eases my mind. 'I was saying that she's a player. I saw tonight's date; he was young. I mean, we're still talking pension and early bird dinners here, but my guy was no more than early seventies.'

'Damn Dadu,' I contort my mouth in an appreciative frown, equal parts impressed and revolted.

'And the guy who always comes on Wednesdays to take her to local theatre matinees, he's older but big with the cash.'

'There's another guy!' I'm appalled.

'Oh, there's more than two. Homegirl has got a busy roster.'

'First of all, Dadu is not your homegirl. Secondly, I cannot believe she's the social butterfly of the over-seventies scene. And lastly, but not least-ly, I am astounded that you know Dadu's life better than I do!'

'Well, I see her twice a week, three times if it's the second week of the month.' Dexy pauses to expand. 'She has bridge

247

club on the second Saturday of every month.'

'And you look after the dogs?' I attempt not to let my surprise show.

'Yeah.'

'And you're happy doing that?'

'Well, yeah.'

'And you don't have plans of your own that it interferes with?'

They nod, rolling their tongue in the divot of their cheek. 'I see what's happening here.'

'What? You see what?' I'm off put by the way they've managed to turn this around. One second I was leading the investigation, and now my defences are up and the tables turned.

'You're shocked that everything you said back in July wasn't true. That I avoid responsibility. That I can't be there to support the people I love. That I avoid blame and can't be dependable. You're trying to work out where I'm fitting in my weed-smoking, responsibility-shirking and Lothario-making ways around my busy schedule of work, skateboarding, and dog-sitting.'

'I am not!' I protest, though we both know full well that I am.

'Are too.'

'Dex!'

'Dean?'

'Fine. Yes. Colour me shocked. It just doesn't seem very you.' I roll my eyes.

They take a seat on the sofa, shifting Tom over so they can squeeze their butt in. It's so natural, so effortless, that I'm forced to confront the unavoidable truth of it. Dex is here.

Dex is here, in Dadu's house, twice a week, watching these dogs, three times on the second week of the month. They're working and setting down roots and proving every stupid word out of my mouth wrong.

'It's okay. What you said wasn't entirely off base.' Dex smiles at me, but it doesn't quite reach their eyes. 'I'm not saying it was fair in that moment or entirely called for, but you made some points. I heard them. I'm working on it.'

'You're working on it?'

'Being more reliable. Being around more. I kind of like having a routine and a home that doesn't change every two weeks. I've been running for so long that I forgot what it felt like to relax.'

I inadvertently let out a tiny snort.

'Okay, I know that sounds ridiculous because you think I just vacationed for two years, but I am very good at having fun, a little less good at being comfortable in life.'

I feel bad for snorting and have the good graces to lower my eyes in apology. 'I guess I can see that.' We sit with just the quiet panting of the dogs for a minute until I finally break. 'Vacation? Really?'

Dex tips their head back and groans.

'Sodding hell, you're never going to let that go, are you?'

I affect a terrible Valley girl accent. 'Like totally not ever.'

Their answering laugh feels like a reward, and I join them in it. Whatever tension built between us over these last couple of months, the snide comments I've been making under my breath, and the avoidance of each other is left in the past. It's surprisingly simple.

When our laughter petters out, Dex is staring at me with an unreadable expression.

'If neither of us is doing anything, do you think you'd like company tonight?'

The unintended implication of their words thrills me. Logically, I know that Dex wasn't offering to sleep with me. It wasn't some nonchalant come-on. And yet, here I am, recalling the way their pupils blew wide at the sight of me topless or how their moans hummed against my skin.

'It might be nice to have a hand walking the dogs.' I say, pushing aside all inappropriate thoughts.

So that's what we do. A slow, winding amble down narrow streets and across the seafront. The rain has stopped, and we snoop on all the surrounding fireworks, just far enough away not to spook the dogs but to still catch the distant glow of colourful lights from the other side of the city. The stiff sea breeze snags at our edges, and as they wrap their coat firmly around them, I realise what looks different about Dex.

In the months that have passed, the fleeting conversations at family gatherings and otherwise total aversion to one another, they have expanded their wardrobe. It sounds stupid, I know, but when they came home, Dex had about three outfits. In the fortnight I thought they were just visiting, I saw it repeated no less than four times. Shorts, Dickies, one pair of jeans. They had hoodies but no coats. They might have only had one pair of shoes, I wouldn't be surprised. Now, though, it's ever so slightly different. New Chucks on their feet, already worn in with the laces wrapped around their scrawny ankles, a thick Carhartt jacket, gloves. It's all very basic and practical in a way that screams Dexy, but I can't imagine they lugged these things around with them from place to place. They have bought these since moving here. They're accumulating possessions. Starting to lay down roots.

My staring must come off as warmth envy because Dex offers to lend me their hoodie as the night air plummets from nippy to freezing. I accept and can't help the way their scent on it seems to soothe me.

We talk about everything and nothing. I hear about their new job, the business that they're hoping to set up with Hawa and Parker's attempt to woo their friend Mia. I tell them about David's proposal, although they've undoubtedly already been told the story several times by different family members and the theoretical wedding plans Priti keeps texting us in the middle of the night. Despite my talking, I can't shake the strangeness that I have nothing new or exciting in *my* life to share. I can relay other people's news, but in the months that Dex and I have kept our distance from one another, they've made major changes, and I've stayed the same.

It makes me wonder if, maybe, they might have had a few accurate points back in July about the way I live my life.

'There must be something in the air.' Dex shrugs, dragging me back to the wedding conversation.

We have started heading in the direction of Dadu's house again, taking a slightly different route past the pier and curving around the park.

'That made my sister suggest a yellow wedding theme?'

'No, nothing can justify that. I meant that there must be an engagement vibe in the air, something that makes people want to buy big ol' rings.'

'Are you-?' I start asking, despite the thought of them having found someone serious enough to think about engagement with making me queasy.

'Hell, no! Not me. My best friend. She got engaged last month and keeps threatening to make it a destination wedding, have them all traipse out here to celebrate.'

'That's nice.' I say reflexively, relieved, and then, deciding to be honest, add. 'I think it's the age. You hit twenty-seven, start attending at least one wedding a year for the next decade-'

'Then divorce parties at thirty-eight?'

'Yup. Nothing but divorce parties and baby showers after that.'

'Until you hit eighty, of course and then it's funeral central.'

I cackle at their joke, loud enough to make Madogna jump a foot off the ground and smack my hand over my mouth as if that can retract the sound.

The combination of my witch laugh and the pop and whizz of a Roman candle behind us sends Cilla Black-lab sprinting forward. The sheer force and suddenness of it snatches the leash from Dex's hand, and they have no choice but to give chase.

I'm debating running after them, picking Barkbra and Tom up under my arms and helping when I hear someone calling my name. My full name in the dark of the night. Like only a murderer would.

Before I can piece together why it sounds so familiar, Callie jogs into sight with a wave.

'Daena! Hi. I thought that was you, I heard.'

Oh my god. I might have to consider getting a new laugh. That has to be something you can do, right? Train yourself into a new, less noticeable laugh.

'You recognised me by my laugh?' I sound about as pained as I feel by that prospect.

Callie, as always, is infallibly gracious.

'It's a nice laugh. Plus, I thought I recognised Dex next to you.'

252

'Oh.' It's hard to say why, but the thought of Callie seeing me with Dex fills my belly with a sour, guilty sensation.

'How are you guys?'

'We're...great.' I answer, not sure how to encapsulate Dex's life with mine in one sentence. 'How are you?'

'Oh, you know, busy. I got promoted at work, so I had to slow down my PhD classes.'

'I heard. I've missed seeing you in them.' I haven't, but it's the polite thing to say. And then I second-guess that. Why do I have the urge to lie to protect Callie? It's a white lie, but it didn't add much to the conversation. I needn't have bothered. This is exactly what Dex was telling me not to do in France. Shirking hard or real feelings with lies. I don't want to be mean to Callie, but I certainly don't need to lie about my feelings to coddle her.

'That's nice of you to say.' Apparently, she doesn't feel the need to lie and say she's missed me. Fascinating. 'Well, I ought to head back to my girlfriend.'

Girlfriend? I don't mean to, but I say that last part out loud.

'Yeah. Been dating for a couple of months now. She's brilliant.'

'I'm happy for you.' Shockingly, not a lie.

'Thanks. And likewise. It makes sense, you and Dex. I'm glad it worked out for you.'

My frown is screaming, the blush rising in my cheeks a notch louder than my laughter, but Callie doesn't stick around to see it. She bounds away, back to her brilliant girlfriend, leaving me alone with the thought of me and Dex dating.

Chapter Twenty-Seven

Dex

'I can't believe you haven't made a move yet!'

Parker has the gall to look upset by our brother's frankness.

'You can't rush these things.'

'It's fucking Valentine's Day, little brother; there's no better time to seal the deal.' Liam argues, knocking back the last of his can.

Despite the brisk winter night, we are all in the garden of Archer's favourite pub, clinging to our drinks as though they'll keep the frostbite away.

It might seem odd, but I have been reliably informed that this is what birthdays look like as you get older. Just your oldest friends and siblings gathered around a frozen picnic table, chatting shit until one or all of you get too drunk to stand.

The last of Archer's actual, non-blood relative friends bowed gracefully out about an hour ago with an excuse about having to get up early with the kids, but I'm ninety per cent sure it had more to do with us descending in a mumbling, slurred swearing nonsense only decipherable to people who grew up in our house or the Ashraf's.

'She's not a fucking loan,' I protest.

'Dexy agrees with me.' Parker practically glows with pride, and I take great glee in dulling that shine.

'Nah, mate. You live with the girl, it's been five fucking months. Hurry up and ask her out; just don't talk about it like a legally binding document on a deadline.'

'Ack, sod off.' He waves a lackadaisical hand that might have been meant to be a swipe at me, but misses by several inches. Liam and I burst into raucous laughter at his expense. 'Just because you live with a girl doesn't mean you have to marry her.' He pauses, and then it's as though I can see the idea hit him. His eyes blow wide, and he throws his arm around Archer's neck. 'The birthday boy knows what I mean, don't ya? It's been, what, ten years since you asked Poppy to marry you and still haven't made plans to waltz down the aisle.'

'Fourteen.' I correct.

'What?'

'It's been fourteen years.'

'No shit! What's the hold-up, Arch?' Liam turns his ribbing on him, unrelenting even with birthday celebrations.

'Don't bring me into your bollocks.' Archer rubs his hand over his forehead, already exhausted by our antics.

'Hey, isn't this what you brought us here for?' I poke him lightly in the ribs, and he grouses some more.

'Silly me, thinking I'd get to celebrate my birthday without being mocked.'

'Down-right foolish,' I attest.

'Alright, let's change the topic before Archer starts getting lairy.' Liam laughs.

'Thank you.'

255

'I think it's only fair that we pick on Dexy now.' Parker's swaying so much that it might be past time to take him home, but I don't want to spoil the fun.

For years, all I wanted was to be included with my older brothers in things, to belong as one of them. I'm sure as hell not about to turn my back on it now, even if it means getting made fun of.

'Fire away. I'm very hard to mock.' I spread my arms wide as if inviting them to take a physical shot, and it makes them all fall about laughing.

'Yeah, you are pretty good at making yourself look fucking stupid.'

'Thanking you.' I bend at the waist in a grandiose bow.

'We could start with the wedding?'

'Low blow.' I whistle through my teeth.

'No, they're right. All that wasted money. All that fucking time us sweating in suits trying to hunt them down on the street.' Parker smiles as he speaks, and I know it's not malicious. 'It's been done before.'

'By Mum.'

I recollect the painful conversations I had on the phone with my mother nearly three years ago. All the arguments where she tried to guilt me into returning or writing a formal explanation to all the guests, apologising. Maybe I should have gone through with it; perhaps that would have healed my family wounds. Seems unlikely though.

In all honesty, being here, laughed at by my siblings, it all worked out in the end.

'Do we want to talk about the painful yearning?' Liam ruffles my hair.

'Too obvious.' Archer says, his arms still crossed over his

chest, but the slightest hint of a smile in his words.

'What yearning?' I ask. 'I don't yearn.'

'No, you're right. You pine.'

'Do not.' I think all too fleetingly of Dean, of the good night text she sent me over an hour ago, making my insides bubble and fizzy. I remember how hot she looked last weekend working on Hedy, in overalls and with oil streaking her hair, letting me chat her ear off about Hawa and TV and anything I could think of. I'm struck by the want to kiss her. The same want I felt then. The same want I've thought about routinely since we started talking again.

Thankfully, no one pays any attention to me, or else I would probably end up admitting something stupid.

'Or the way they followed Mum around like a guide dog when she had her surgery.'

'Oh, oh!' Parker hops on the balls of his feet, the image of an overexcited child. 'Tell us about your job!'

'The one at the insurance company?' Archer looks as confused as I feel by that request.

'No, not that. That's dull as dishwater. The other one.'

'You have a second job?'

'Apparently so.' I blink, utterly perplexed by the direction this conversation is taking. 'Do you mean dog sitting because I just let Dadu Ashraf pay me in Dr. Pepper and Digestives? It's not exactly going on my resume.'

'No, idiot child. I mean the one you're working on with Hawa.' He smacks me around the back of the head just hard enough to hurt.

'Oi.' I grumble, rubbing the point of contact where his pinky ring clipped my ear.

'Oh, you've been holding out on us.' Liam grins, and it's so similar to Mum's that it's hard to believe they aren't blood-related. 'I knew you couldn't be happy just sorting through a dusty old file cabinet.'

In theory, I probably ought to have been prepared for this. It's not as though it's a secret. With Parker gone, I've taken no pains to hide my plans, currently scattered across the living room carpet back at the flat, but the idea has grown a lot since I first developed it, and giving it voice feels as if it will make it real. If it's real, it can all fall apart, and I'll have to face how much I want it.

I consider lying, claiming that it's nothing, but if I can't be honest with my drunken brothers, when can I? Besides, I really do want it. Pretending that I haven't been working my arse off to make it a reality these last few months wouldn't feel right.

So, mustering up my most sober voice, I unburden myself.

I tell them all about my and Hawa's plan to make the international Skater Girl network an official thing. How it would be a collective focused on connecting minority group skaters across the globe, letting them network and find cheap accommodation. I tell them that Hawa and I plan to run the headquarters remotely, doing double time with our other jobs until it's viable, matching requests up with the right person in the right location, travelling occasionally to make new ones, and building outwards so that no skater has to turn down opportunities based on financial viability. It would be administration and crowdfunding-heavy, but the ultimate goal would be to hold competitions, a chance for people who are usually excluded from the spotlight to shine together.

Maybe I did my brothers a disservice in my imagination because I couldn't ask for a more receptive crowd. They're so on board that it's almost scary, clapping me on the shoulder and saying it's a great idea. Liam knows the old guy who owns the local skate park and offers to put us in touch. Parker says that Mia has friends coming into town next month who might be interested in helping out, and, for one bright moment, I feel as if I might be able to make this happen. As though I might have found a purpose for myself.

It's nice.

And then Archer opens his mouth.

'But you can't call it the Skater Girl Collective. That's naff.'

'Are you technically a girl?' Liam follows up, making Parker snort.

'Well, no, that's just the working name. I guess it was kind of ironic when we called the original group chat that, but that might not translate.'

'It doesn't.'

'It's cringey.'

'Hey!'

'Coming from this old fart that's saying something.'

'Parker!'

'Are you even a millennial? What's the generation before that?'

'Of course, I'm a millennial! We were born in the same generation, you little shit.'

'Same generation but not the same decade.' Parker singsongs, wiggling his body around absurdly.

'Aren't we all millennials?' Liam asks, ignoring the fact that Arch and Parker look ready to go full Bart and Homer.

'Nope. I am a cusper.' I inform him.

'What the bleeding hell is a cusper?'

'They're the ones who are both the oldest of one generation

and kinda the youngest of the other.'

'Jesus, did we need to give that a name?' Archer sounds as if it's the most preposterous thing he's ever heard. 'Just pick one and get on with your life.'

'God, listen to Grandpa here.' Parker teases, causing Liam and I to officially call it a night before Archer throttles him.

We stagger out through the front of the pub, waving goodbye to the bartenders who have worked there longer than I've been alive, and give each other a bunch of sloppy back slaps and overly affectionate bear hugs by way of goodbye.

As I pull away from Archer, he whispers something in my ear, something about fourteen years too late but wonderful nonetheless, and I wonder what exactly is in the air at the moment.

Chapter Twenty-Eight

Dean

One thing about a large family is that gossip spreads like wildfire, and the extended Ashraf-Carpenter-Brown family really puts that to the test.

No sooner has Archer called asking me if I can come work in the shop with Lochlan this Saturday (they're still holding out on hiring a replacement for Parker), than I get a call from my Dad.

'Jaan, I hear you're working in the shop again this weekend.'

'Good afternoon to you, too.' I hold off on unclasping the latch of my tiffin box and turn back to my laptop. No use getting started on lunch if my parents intend to talk through it.

Unbothered by my passive-aggressive greeting, Dad proceeds. 'Is that true?'

'Yes.' I sigh, thinking he's going to scold me for not leaving myself enough time to relax or catch up on my studies.

'Good.'

That was not what I was expecting. 'Good?'

'Yes,' he makes that middle-aged huffing noise that I know is

261

him settling into the low garden chairs he and Mum brought for spring. 'I'm glad you're doing something you enjoy.'

I pause typing up my email, sensing that this conversation is going to require more than half-brain power.

'How did you find out so fast?' What I'm asking is why he cares, but I wouldn't dare to be that upfront about it.

'Serena and your mother are texting.' I hate that parents are mildly tech-savvy these days. There was once a blissful time in my life when neither of my parents knew how to update a Facebook status or how to stalk someone on Instagram. How I long for it back. 'I also hear that Kyle has been trying to offer you a position at the garage. Is that true, Jaan?'

A second term of endearment in as many minutes has me on high alert. Closing my laptop lid and pressing the pads of my fingers against my eyes, I breathe slowly and answer.

'Yes. They want me to take over Parker's position as a full-time mechanic with them.'

'Have you turned them down?'

'No. I've been avoiding them.'

'Ah, Dean, that's not the way you do things. Avoiding people? How long did you think that would work?' He wastes no time whipping out the disappointed dad voice.

'Well, it's May, and Parker officially left at the end of October, so that's seven months. I'd say it's done pretty well so far.' I'm pushing my luck, being snarky, and we both know it, but Dad lets it slide.

'You can't avoid them forever. They need an answer.'

'I don't have one.' This is exactly the awkwardness I wanted to avoid by dodging the issue. I don't want to shoot Archer and Kyle down. Their offer is incredibly nice. But I can't realistically take it. I have a career; I have a term left of my

PhD. That's not how things work.

'Do you not want the job?'

'No. I mean. Yes.' I get caught in his phrasing like a fly in a web. 'I want the job, but I can't make it work.'

'Why not?' he asks, as if it's that simple.

'Because I already have a job, Dad! I crunch numbers and answer emails from nine to five thirty each day, and then I write my thesis and hassle lecturers from six to nine. I can't possibly squeeze another full-time job on top of that.'

'No one is suggesting you work two full-time jobs.' He interjects matter-of-factly. 'You would leave accounting to take this job. That's the offer.'

'But accounting is what I've worked for. All these years. If I finish my degree and an opportunity comes up, I could get promoted. I could make good money.'

'Could is used a lot there.'

'Nothing is certain.'

'And is that what you want to do?'

'Yes, Dad, who doesn't want to make money?'

'No. I mean, is accounting how you want to spend the rest of your life?'

'Oh, um, it's alright.' I'll admit I'm stumped by that question. I wasn't expecting it. 'It's not my dream. It's not as much fun as getting up and working on Hedy, but it pays the bills.'

'Daena Anjali, who is talking about bills right now?' Oh, he's using my middle name. I don't think anyone's first-and-middle-named me since I was sixteen when Dexy and I came home drunk on £3 Lambrini from a party, and I woke the whole house up by losing my key and getting us locked out. 'I'm asking what you want to do with your life.'

'Dad, life is about more than fun.'

He makes a pfft noise. 'But it is about some fun. Kyle pays a living wage. You might not end up with a yacht or buying us a hideous mini-mansion to spend our final days in, but you would be comfortable working at Brown Owl. And importantly, I think you would be happy.'

'I am happy now, Dad.' I chew on my bottom lip, aware that those feeble words wouldn't convince even me.

There's a long pause on the other end, and I can hear my Dad greet the little old lady who lives next door to them over the garden wall before he brings the phone back up to his ear.

'I can't make you change your mind, De. The days when my opinion meant much are long gone, so I will say my piece and then I will leave it alone, okay?'

'Okay.'

'You don't seem happy. You are my daughter, and I want you to be fulfilled in life. Your sisters are chaotic and absolutely bonkers, but I see them, I see them be happy. I don't worry about them the same way I worry about you. You keep following this plan you laid out as a teenager, and I do not think it brings you what you thought it would. I'm not implying that your happiness should look the same as Priti's. I don't know who you would marry if you wanted to, but if you turn Kyle down when he asks you again on Saturday, the offer won't come again. Yeah?'

I nod, feeling as though all the light has been drained from me by this conversation. Despite the unseasonably warm spring day, I have goosebumps on my arms and a slow sinking feeling in my gut.

'I hear you.' My voice is ragged to my own ears as if it's out of practice with honesty.

'Okay.'

CHAPTER TWENTY-EIGHT

'Thank you.' I mutter just loud enough to be picked up by the receiver.

We stay like that for a minute, sitting in our respective locations, letting the heaviness of the conversation roll off of us.

'Why were Mum and Serena talking about that anyway?' I ask, curious how I came up or if my career avoidance is a group topic of conversation among the parents.

'Oh, you know them. Archer is taking the day off for his wedding, and your mother and Serena are conspiring to make sure we all celebrate.'

I choke on my breath, literally gagged by the cavalier tone in which Dad delivers this information. 'Way to bury the lead! Give me two seconds.' I text my sister, demanding she come into my room to overhear this gossip. Now, at least, it's my turn to play a part in the inter-family tea passing.

* * *

For an impromptu elopement party, Serena and my Mum have truly outdone themselves.

We're back at the beach hut, the go-to locale for all budget get-togethers, and by some miracle, the good weather has held out just long enough to make it a pleasant day to spend basking in the sun, day drinking.

There are punch bowls of Pimms, with plump strawberries and fresh orange wedges floating in them, towers of decorated cupcakes and French Fancies, and a full spread of food waiting to be served. The table is lined with serving trays of beguni dal-bhaat, quiches of every variety, and handmade sausage rolls.

Family news has it that Archer and Poppy snuck off to the courthouse at ten yesterday morning, with just Cami and Meggie as their witnesses, and officially tied the knot. They took the girls for a fancy meal before dropping them off with Serena and the other grandkids and having the night to themselves. The few photos they have of it are stunning: Poppy in a cream tea dress and Archer looking crisp in a suit. All four of them smiling unrestrained, the girls beaming with pride.

So the party had to be postponed till today, and, in true Serena fashion, she pulled out all the stops. She's still a little unsteady on her feet after the second hip operation last month, but she's got a good team of minions to do her bidding.

My mum spent all of yesterday posted up in the kitchen with her, decorating cakes and icing elaborate designs onto things currently being crammed in tiny children's mouths. Dexy and Liam reportedly went door to door around all of our pooled neighbours and asked to borrow as many camping and garden chairs as they could find, and Kyle ran around town getting all the food, alcohol, and decorations for her.

The resulting party is unlike anything I've ever seen. Every possible Carpenter-Brown friend and family member who could make it into town appears to be present to offer Archer and Poppy their congratulations. We've expanded across the whole patch of grass, with the generous permission of the other beach hut owners (all of whom have been absorbed into the crowd), and most people surpassed the polite level of drunk a few drinks back.

It's one of those events where you know you'll miss it when it's over. A once-in-a-lifetime sort of high that makes you nostalgic as you commit it to memory.

'I told you, it was something going around,' Dexy returns with my drink and that knee-melting grin of theirs.

'You make it sound like the flu or a tummy bug.'

They shrug. 'Depends how you feel about marriage, I guess.'

'And how do you feel about marriage?'

'Meh. It's strange. I know I've already been engaged and everything, but I feel as though I'd be a child bride... or groom. Does that make any sense?'

'Weirdly, it does. I know my little sister is itching to get hitched and that, in olden times, it was my job to get there first, but I don't think I'm done cooking yet. Not enough to want to take that step anyway.'

'Do you think we will ever feel done cooking, though? Because I'm starting to think that no one knows what they're doing in adulthood. Maybe everyone feels this lost.' Dex's fingers are twisting the ring on their pinky, fidgeting just enough to occupy their excess energy.

'Maybe not. Maybe each new stage of life sets that oven timer back again, but I'm not done enough yet to...taste?' I shake my head, regretting my choice of metaphor, and glare down accusatorily at the glass in my hand. 'Sorry. It might be time to switch to water.'

As if by magic, or more likely just decades of knowing me well, Dex leans over the edge of their chair and picks up a second cup, handing it off to me.

'For you, m'lady.'

'You are incredible.' Without questioning my decision, I tip my face down and kiss their cheek. It's out of rhythm with the flow of our conversation and beyond crossing a line, and yet I can't help myself.

'Dean?'

'Dex?' I think, for an alarming second, that they're about to ask me to kiss them again and a traitorous bubble of hope arises within me.

'Did you take the job at Brown Owl?'

'Oh.' It takes physical effort not to let my disappointment show. This is normal. This is good news. I am thrilled about it, so why am I so let down that they didn't ask about us? 'Yeah. I did. I'm going to work part-time for the next month until I finish my PhD coursework, and then, I'll be a full-time Brown employee.'

They punch me lightly on the bicep and tip their head back, shouting to the sky.

'Finally!'

'Oh, I'm sorry, do you have some secret skin in this game? Did you place a bet with your brothers on the odds?'

'Oh, you know I make a habit of winning bets when it comes to you.' The words are so flawless, their voice a hair-curling purr just loud enough for me to hear. All the blood in my body rushes to my cheeks. The dialogue in my subconscious falls silent, alarm bells ringing, urging me to make the most of this moment.

I seize a passing wave of confidence.

'Can I ask you a question about us?'

Dex's face neutrals out; features open and inviting. I trust them to answer me honestly.

'Why didn't you let me touch you when we were sleeping together?'

They blink rapidly and avert their eyes to see who is nearby. I realise, belatedly, that I wasn't watching my volume, but thankfully, no one around us appears to have overheard. Dadu is talking to Meggie about the dogs, and the only person looking at Dex and me is Pom, her eyes narrowed from the other side of the party.

'Shit, sorry. I never got a chance to explain back in the summer.' I roll my lips inward, not sure I have anything useful to add right now. 'I'm a stone top...sort of. Do you know what I mean by that?'

'Yes, Dexter. I've been a lesbian for a long time now. I know the lingo. Most of the time.'

'Okay, fair enough. I didn't mean to imply that you wouldn't, it's just a touchy subject—poor choice of words.'

Even at their most awkward, stumbling over their words and making grimacing faces, Dex is charming. It's hard to hold back my smile.

'So you don't like being touched in that way ever?'

'That's the complicated part. It's kind of situation-dependent. If things are serious and I like the person I'm with, I sometimes want to let those boundaries down a bit. I have to trust them.'

'You don't trust me?' The hurt makes my voice hoarse.

'What? No, of course I trust you. But I didn't know what we were doing, I thought, we said it was a one-time thing, so—the last person I let touch me was Khloe, if that gives you some indication. Even then, I mostly preferred to give rather than receive. It wasn't about you.'

It's so simple. An easy answer. And just as easily, all the hurt and self-hating questions I've been nurturing since summer disappear. With one little question and a smidge of honesty, I stop myself from overthinking long enough to understand what went wrong with us. That stone I felt lodge inside me back in July, full of sour disappointment and curdling hope, finally passes.

I can hear the hammering of my heart for the first time in months. I can make out what it's saying.

'Dex, can I tell you a secret?'

The anxiety isn't completely gone from their face, but I can see that I've startled them out of it momentarily.

'Interesting take on the game, but sure.'

'Do you remember when you asked when I first knew I was interested in sex, and I said I didn't remember?'

'Yes.'

'Well, I lied. I remember it exactly. The truth is you probably remember it too.' They say nothing, those green-blue eyes shimmering as they watch me. So I paint the picture.

'When I was in year twelve, and you were in year eleven, we both had these crammed mock exam schedules. We were busy all of the time, and I went a bit loopy trying to study as hard as humanly possible. You begged me to take a break, to hang out with you, to study with you, but I couldn't pull myself away.' Their throat bobs, and I know they're conjuring up the memory along with me. 'Then, out of nowhere, it snowed. It wasn't enough that the whole school got a snow day or anything, but just enough that certain kids were stranded, so they cancelled all the mock exams that day. I can't say why, but it sort of felt as if we were set free, out of step with time, and all my responsibilities and worries disappeared.

It sounds stupid now, but I said yes to hanging out with you because there was no more room for guilt. Everyone else had work or school, so I came over to your house and we ate crap and binged TV all day. You lined up all my favourite teen movies to help me relax: Twilight, The Mortal Instruments, and Percy Jackson. At one point, we reached the second Hunger Games movie, which was a weird choice in hindsight, and we went from being all cuddled up and scrolling our phones to you tickling me. You know how I feel about being tickled. And so I hit you with a cushion. Then you hit me back, and one thing led to another until, eventually, I was pinning you down. It was the strange, snowy white sky outside, and the room was just getting dark around us. I remember that I was straddling you, my arm pulled back, ready to absolutely clobber you, and it was like an electric current shooting through me. All I could think about was kissing you.'

'What happened?' they ask, as though they weren't there. 'Why didn't you?'

I chuckle. 'You said *look, it's your loverboy*,' I pitch my voice lower in a poor imitation of them. 'Pointed at Finnick, and hit me with a cushion whilst my back was turned.'

'Oh my god. Yes! You got that nosebleed that got all over the cream sofa.'

'Yup. We spent the next hour trying unsuccessfully to bleach the blood out of it before Serena or Kyle got home, and the whole time, I kept thinking that I had ruined our friendship because, for one second, you said Loverboy and all I saw was you. I didn't think about Finnick or anyone else. I wanted that word to apply to you. I thought that by wanting to kiss you, to love you differently, even for a millisecond, I had changed the way we worked.'

Dex chugs down the end of their plastic cup, wincing as whatever was in it burns on the way down.

'It's my turn to tell you a secret now.' They say matter-of-factly, not responding to my story at all. I feel suspended, unsure whether this is a good or bad sign. 'When I came out, I toyed with the idea of changing my name completely. I didn't

271

know if being butch and trans and having the same name would mean I wasn't trans enough for some people. But I've always been Dex or Dexy, and I wanted to keep that part of me. For a long time, I kept my paperwork in the name December, mostly because it was a hassle, but when I moved back for good last year, I changed it legally.'

'That's fantastic.' I say, meaning it, but underwhelmed.

'To Dexter.'

'What?'

'I changed my name to Dexter.'

'Why?'

'Because I knew that everyone would call me Dex anyway, but also because I didn't want to let go of that part of me, of us. Dexter is what you call me when you're fake mad; you said it that day in the pillow fight. You are the only person who's ever used that name for me, and it felt right. Of course,' they wave their hand between us. 'We weren't talking at the time. So I just didn't tell anyone. The only person who knows is Dadu; she signed off my paperwork. So I promise you, if you ruined our friendship by thinking one non-platonic thought about me, I ruined it a thousand times over.'

'Dex.' Their name comes out as a breathy gasp, as though someone's kissed all the air from my lungs, and, if we weren't surrounded by family, I might take that task on myself.

I want desperately to fist my fingers in their shirt and haul them closer to me. I need to close the distance between us, and I think they do, too. Their eyes are rocketing between mine and my lips, their expression unreadable as they angle their body across the fabric arm of their chair.

A shrill ringing cuts between us, shattering the moment of tension. Reluctantly, Dex, Dexter Carpenter-Brown, drags their eyes away from my lips and pulls out their phone.

One quick glance down is all they need to tell them that they have to answer it.

'I'm sorry. I should get this.' They stand, excusing themself to walk behind the beach huts. I watch them leave, feeling like an exposed nerve, before I decide to follow them.

The very second Dex is done with that call, we need to have a moment alone. I can't bear to face the vulnerability of what we just talked about in front of a crowd, pretending it never happened. I need to kiss them. I should clear things up and then take them home with me to make a mess again.

I follow the sound of their voice, listening to its low whispering rumble, enjoying how the sound of it feels now that I know how they feel about me.

We can make this work. I want to make this work between us. Maybe, and I cannot believe I am saying it, Callie was right. Dex and I make sense.

'I'm not sure, Hawa. They sounded up for investing, but they wanted to speak to one of us in person.'

I wait in the shadows, not wanting to eavesdrop, watching Dex's back as they pace. The person on the other end speaks inaudibly from my distance.

'Yeah, that's what I thought.' There is something off about their resonance; it's off-beat for Dex. Kind of resigned. 'It's not the ideal time for me, but if we need to, I can head out there and— ' they turn, seeing me as they speak. 'hop on a plane tomorrow.'

273

Chapter Twenty-Nine

Dean

I have never thought of myself as particularly dramatically inclined, but I am beginning to develop a flair for making a scene.

I don't stick around long enough to hear more of Dex's conversation. I got enough of it to understand what was happening.

It's exactly as I suspected. They got bored with life here. They're running away again. Ironic, given the speed with which my legs are currently working to get away from them. I'm retracing my route from the potato salad incident of last summer. Away from the pastel-hued beach huts, past the ice cream truck, into the park, across the browning grass where families are picnicking, around the toilet block, across the road, feet slapping against the scorching stone of the promenade, past yet more places to buy ice cream, through the awning of the pier and the arcade, down onto the stony seafront.

Dex called after me for a while, but I lost them back by the swan-shaped pedalos. I get a few minutes of reprieve, just me and the ocean waves roaring before another voice picks up. This voice is like hearing my own on a recording and in absolutely no hurry to catch up. I turn, watching Pom trudge elegantly down the beach, sighing more than yelling my name.

'What are you doing here?' I attempt to sound mad between heaving breaths.

'The question is, what are you doing here? There is a perfectly lovely butch back there, looking adorably confused. Given that you followed them back behind the huts looking like you were about to ravage them on the spot, I'm inclined to agree with their confusion.'

'You know?' I wheeze. 'About us.'

'Oh, please! When will you learn? You may be the eldest daughter, but I run this show. You guys weren't exactly subtle that last day in France, and who do you think arranged for the shared tents or the overlapping dog-sitting shifts?' She looks very smug as she takes the last few steps towards me, not panting or sweating like I am.

In exhaustion, I throw my body onto the pebbles, officially out of fucks to give.

'That was you?'

'Well, most of it. Dadu is also surprisingly meddlesome in her own right.'

'Great! Does everyone know how I feel about Dex?' I want the sea to sweep up and swallow me.

'Uh, no. I think you're radically misinterpreting the text.'

'What?'

'You know, you play a really good game, Dean. You pretend to have it all together, you always have. Sorted and set on your path since we were kids.'

I stare out at the darkened silhouette of the Isle of Wight in

275

the distance, unable to look at my sister and see the inevitable disappointment in her eyes.

'I've watched you shut everyone out for as long as I can remember. Whenever anything was wrong, you would tell Dex, not Mum or Dad. If Dadu asked how you were, you lied. When Dadu needed you, you never cried. You pretend nothing gets past those walls of yours.'

'Maybe it doesn't.' I attempt with half-hearted humour.

She doesn't laugh.

'But you built those walls around Dex. They're already allowed in.' My mind goes back to the drawbridge analogy in France, and I wonder if genetics led my little sister to come up with something so similar or if she just knows me that well. 'The defences don't work with them.'

'Or you, apparently.' My fingers comb through the stones, searching for a pleasing shape.

'I have sister superpowers. It doesn't count. But everyone else is pretty easily fooled. They're not exactly the brightest bunch. You've hidden it well, so it's only Dexy's behaviour that everyone sees.'

'Sees what?'

'De, come on! They're pretty much the gender-neutral monarch of pining. All of it has been directed at you for the last ten months. They watch every door, waiting for you to walk through it. At meals and drinks, they spend most of their time trying to be involved in conversations you're in. They're in love with you. Everyone can see it!'

Picking up a small, oval pebble, I try to steady my breathing before lobbing it into the ocean with a satisfying little *splosh*.

'If they like me so much, then why are they running away?' I ask the horizon.

Pom perches beside me, looking every bit the model she is, with her long legs and effortlessly pretty mini-dress and flats. I'm jealous of the fact that, even on a stone beach, even chasing me down, her hem never once rode or bunched up.

'That's a weird question to ask as someone I've seen flee from no less than two family events involving Dexy.'

I roll my eyes and look ashamed.

'Not my finest moment, but at least when I run away from my feelings, I only make it to the shoreline. They get on a plane and head to a different country's shore.'

'Sick burn,' my sister says sarcastically. I should have known she would be this way. She's too similar to Dad for her own good; unwavering in the ability to hold you hostage until she makes her point. She's less gentle than Dad, her approach has fewer nicknames, and I love yous, but I recognise the playbook. 'Have you been listening when Dex talks lately?'

'Of course I have.' I bristle at the implication that I've sat around daydreaming, staring into their eyes rather than paying attention to them all this time. I'm not a lovestruck schoolgirl.

'Then you know about this thing that they are trying to set up with their friend. I might not pay attention when they talk about the actual nitty-gritty of skateboarding, but I remember them saying it was international. They might have to travel sometimes, not just have to but *want* to.' Oh, crap. 'Just because someone travels doesn't mean they are running away. In the same way that someone, completely stationary in life,' she pokes my thigh, 'doesn't necessarily stay exactly the same.' Double crap. 'Do you get my point?'

It pains me to concede to it.

'When did you get so smart?'

277

'Whenever you got stupid. It's a communal pool of brain cells, only one Ashraf may have them at any one time.'

I pull her in for a hug, planting a kiss on her forehead, and she bats me away. The distaste in her expression is how I know we are returning to normal. The sibling status quo returned.

'Now get out of here. Don't you have a grand gesture or some kind of apology to make?'

She's right, of course. This is exactly the kind of moment that requires a bold declaration of my feelings. In the movies, they make it look so simple. The protagonist always knows what the love interest will need, what will win them back. A guitar in apology, a boombox declaration, catching the next flight to announce their love in an objectionable display that would make it incredibly awkward if they turned them down.

I could try the flight thing; it's certainly the most relevant approach, but I didn't stick around to catch where Dexy was heading tomorrow, let alone what airport or flight. I would need to get several people involved to pull it off, and, frankly, once the word spreads that far, it's almost certain one of them would let it slip to Dex before I got to them.

I debate myself the whole way home. I pass shops and dog walkers, and families, all without processing any of it. My mind is elsewhere, with Dex.

If I attempt to go to the airport, I would need to miss work— wait! I have to quit that job anyway, so that's not a problem. But I would risk spending thousands of pounds just to pull it off. Thousands of pounds that I've spent years saving and hoarding, gone just for the chance to apologise to Dex. On the other hand, if I wait till they get back, I might explode. What if they take my lack of contact as a sign that they shouldn't come

278

back? That wouldn't be enough to keep them away...right?

The walk home flies by, and by the time I pass Hedy in her parking spot, giving her hood an affectionate tap, I've decided that whatever this thing is with Dex is worth the money and the potential humiliation. Right now, I want them far more than I want the cash or my pride.

I'll call Parker when I get in and see if he can keep a secret-

'Hey.'

Dex is sitting on the pavement, their back pressed up against my front door, their feet propped on a bright pink skateboard.

It's a beautiful image. The ultimate Dexy, as they should have always been. There is no avoiding the way their Dickies hug the round curve of their arse or the way their cuffed shirt sleeves cling to those distracting biceps, the tantalising hint of their tattoos creeping up out of sight. Their hair is mussed, as though they've been raking their hands through it. I know it's my fault.

They leap to their feet, kicking the board up to rest in their hand, when I give them a silent wave.

'You didn't come back to the party.'

'I ran away.'

'There's a lot of that going around these days, I hear.' They quip.

Steeling myself to grovel, I straighten my spine.

'I might be a hypocrite.' I lead with, for some unknown reason.

In all my planning to win them over, I got so carried away by the dramatics that I hadn't conjured up the words I wanted to tell them.

'Interesting start.' There's an amused glint in their eye that sets my shoulders at ease.

'Look. I'm sorry. For a whole mess of crap, really. I shouldn't have run away from you. I shouldn't have assumed the worst of you. Today or in July. The things I said then were mean.'

'Some of them were true.' They interject.

'Sure, but you are working on them. I can see it. Everyone can see it. You have a purpose, you're happy. You know when something has to be changed or built upon. I'm proud and a little bit jealous.'

'Of me?'

'Yes. Jealous. You're so good at overhauling your life. Recognising the problems and fixing them, even when it's hard, even when you make a mistake. You ran away from what would have been a terrible marriage. You did that. Sure, it's kind of stupid timing, but it was incredibly brave. You are brave.'

'I couldn't have done that without you.'

'Shut up, this is my apology speech.'

'Sorry!' They wave their hands like white flags.

'I judged you for running away from your problems for a long time, but the truth is, I've been doing the same. At least you went somewhere whilst you did it. I somehow avoided every hard issue I had to face, all from the comfort of my bed. Some of the things you said back in July were accurate. I'm not very good at voicing when I want something. I lie if I'm scared or don't know how it'll be received. I might have been doing it my whole life. But I finally know what I want.'

'Can I speak now?' Dex asks.

'No. If I stop, I'll chicken out of saying this.' They give me a small, huffing laugh, allowing me to continue. 'I want you, Dex. ' I take a step towards them. 'I really want you.'

They meet me, their hands catching mine like a passing magnet. 'You want me?' They bring their palms up, cupping my forearms and my elbows, edging me in closer to them. I think they might kiss me, so I use my last spurt of confidence and jut my head back. It's abrupt, but they take it in their stride.

'But I don't want this to be a fling. If that's alright with you?'

A silence passes, their pupils quavering back and forth, trying to take in all of me. I wait, throat suddenly thick with fear. If I've come this far only to be turned down, I don't know how to recover this friendship. I don't know if I can survive losing them again.

'Dex?' I wait for their usual answer. My name. The call and response we've been doing for as long as we could talk. It doesn't come.

'Is it my turn now?' They say instead.

I steel myself to be hurt. To come away from this the fool. At least I was honest.

'I want to make you happy. Not just now, but for as long as you want me.'

I nod, unable to make any sound come out of my mouth right now and loop my arms around their neck. This kiss is different from the others, needy but less hungry and more of a shared plea for closeness. I flick my tongue against the edge of theirs, and their answering moan makes heat pool between my thighs. Their hands are clamped around my waist as if they plan to pick me up, and although I'm not certain they can manage it, we'd best get inside before I wrap my legs around them and let Dex try.

Pulling away again, I kiss their cheek and grab their hand in mine, ready to drag them over the threshold the second my key pops the lock open.

'I have one more want.' I whisper before unlocking the door.

'Anything.'

Chapter Thirty

Dex

It turns out that giving Dean everything she wants encompasses all of my wants for the evening as well.

We've fucked on almost every surface that it would be considered civilised to. Our clothes are strewn all over the flat, decorating lamps and chairs like modern art. We've had to stop to take multiple refreshment breaks, hopping up to fill glasses of water or feeding each other popcorn on the sofa.

Every time we do, though, we come back together just as enamoured as before. It starts with a kiss. Usually to the cheek or the tip of the nose, and maybe the neck or the earlobe. It's innocent. Gentle. Playful.

Then the other one retaliates in kind, a game builds, marking territory on each other's bodies like a game of noughts and crosses until we're kissing again. My hands caressing her breasts, or her grinding her arse into me in a way that drives me feral. It's always different. We're still learning the ways our bodies fit together, still finding those precious spots that make the other moan unabashedly.

Dean is on her back this time, hands clutching at the metal

frame of her bedpost as I work the length of the strap inside of her. It's the kind of sight I wish I could commit to memory. Late evening sunlight streaming in around her, painting her body like a chiaroscuro still. I consider whether it would be wild to get it tattooed on me, tastefully, of course. Somewhere concealed, that only I could see.

Which is when I realise the permanence of what we're doing. This is it for me, or at least I hope it is. There is no one out there I want to be with more than Dean, no one I would consider spending my life with. For the first time ever, the thought of my future doesn't terrify me.

Dean makes a tender little whimper as I push into the hilt, bringing me back to the present, and her back arches up into me. Instinctively, my hands press against the soft flesh of her hips, guiding us together.

Between her vast toy collection and my multi-function boxers, let's just say it's very convenient that lesbians come prepared for all occasions.

'God, you are gorgeous.' I manage, rolling my hips to pull the strap out an inch before driving back into her.

She moans in response, the sound of her slick cunt welcoming me, and I pick up the pace, enjoying the friction it creates against my clit.

'Faster.' She begs. I oblige.

'You're so good at telling me what you want, princess.' I duck and catch her lips in mine, revelling in the noises I swallow directly from them with each pump of my hips.

'Fuck, yes. Don't stop.'

Another instruction I have no problem following. Dean's legs come up, and I lift her ankles to bracket my shoulders, pressing in deep. This time, it's me groaning, the feeling of her

284

against me so good it can't be hindered by the plastic between us.

It's strangely right to know this kind of closeness with Dean. Almost as if we ought to have reached this moment before. Maybe we would have if we didn't keep standing in our own way.

'Shitshitshit.' Her words bleed together, overlapping with my curses as I near the brink. We've been locked together for hours, making the most of every second and yet I'm still not ready for this to be over.

I brace myself forward on my elbows, Dean rocking into each one of my movements and squeezing against me. It's beautiful and messy and perfectly us. We move as one until we're a tangle of cries and frantic kisses as our bodies crash together.

There's no room for thought in my mind. It's not blank, just peaceful, like that easy limbo between sleep and awake. I'm comfortable, calm, and focused on the burst of pleasure that's trembling through us. I can feel Dean there with me, floating in that same tranquil bubble.

It takes a few minutes for my body to function properly again, limbs shaky and tired from use. A wonderful exhaustion creeping its way up my spine.

I pull out and flop down onto the pillow next to Dean, curling her against me, enjoying the weight of her on my chest. We're back on her bed, plush sheets covered in cartoon peaches ensconcing us. The very last rays of sunlight fading from her ceiling as we watch it, our breathing evening out.

She links her hand through mine.

I couldn't contain my smile if I tried.

'That was-'

'I know.' I confirm.

'I've never-'

'Me either.'

She rolls over, running her finger down the divot between my taped chest. It's sweet, a vulnerable moment that I've never allowed with anyone else. Something I wouldn't imagine enjoying until she does it.

'Really?'

'That was new for me. Coming like that. It's never been like that before. If that's what you're asking.' I lift my arm, drawing her in to lie on my chest. She's soft and pliable as if she's only moments away from dropping off into dreams. I like the domesticity of it, knowing that we could stay like this forever if I wanted. That a new day is coming doesn't have to mean that we're torn apart.

'You call me princess a lot.' She says, trailing that finger back up my stomach. 'I like it.'

'Good.'

'What does that make you, though?'

'I don't know.' I honestly hadn't thought about it as anything more than a name for her. A joke laced with as much affection as lust.

'What's the gender-neutral version of prince? Knight?'

'Suitor?'

Dean's hand ventures up to my hair, playing with the shaved-down edges of it. 'My handsome suitor.'

'It's a little formal.'

'Loverboy.' She says, fingers coming up to cup the curve of my jaw.

We fall into kissing again, slowly and hazy with fatigue. I know that I should get up and get my things before sleep takes me.

I shift my weight, moving my arm to hold Dean closer and the metal bars of the cheap bed frame squeal in protest. My lips give way to a smile, and I feel Dean chuckle into me.

'Remind me to fix that for you when I get back.' I say, falling back against the pillow once again.

'Ooo.' Dean gives me a mischievous look. 'If I knew dating came with free handyman services, I'd have done it sooner.'

'Oh, really?'

'Absolutely. Who doesn't love a big, strong butch doing their dirty work?'

'Dirty work, huh?' I waggle my eyebrows suggestively, and she bats my arm.

'Get your mind out of the gutter.'

I plant a kiss on the top of her head, inhale the sweat and suncream scent of her.

'Whatever you need, Dean, I'll do it for you. For the rest of our lives.'

She doesn't reply. She doesn't need to. The way her fingers trace across the plains of my stomach is enough of an acknowledgement. We're both all in.

This thing that we've started isn't a fling or a bet. It's love. Maybe it took a long time for us to realise it. Twenty-odd years. But we had to grow into this love, develop apart before we could come together.

However, I found her, slow and messy as it was, I have no intention of letting Dean go again.

'Pom will probably be home soon, we shouldn't leave our mess out there for her to see.' Dean says with a sigh.

We both know that our moment of tranquillity is coming to a close.

'And I need to schedule a flight to Amsterdam for tomorrow night. I should probably pack and call Hawa to plan...'

My words fade out. I know I have things to do, but it all feels so far away.

There's a world out there waiting for me. A career I'm supposed to be building. Chores to be done. Bills to be paid. But I don't want to return to the adult world.

I want to stay where I am. I want to build my life here in this bed with my best friend. Or at least order a pizza and eat it beneath the covers.

Leaving now will feel like running away. It doesn't matter that I'll come home again or that it's only for work purposes. I wish I could stay barricaded in our bliss for just one night.

That's when it occurs to me.

I sit up, resting my back against the wall, pulling the duvet around Dean as she joins me.

'What is it? What's wrong?'

I shake my head, keen to elaborate that nothing is wrong before either of us can start overthinking. We've both done enough of that for one day.

Maybe, like falling, my proclivity for running doesn't have to be a bad thing. Maybe there's a way for me to redefine its meaning in my life.

'Come with me.' I say, hoping it comes off as more of a request than a demand.

Dean lets out that amazing cackle of hers, and I instantly see what I've walked myself into.

'I think we did that already.'

'Not that, you heathen. Now, who needs to get their mind out of the gutter? Come with me to Amsterdam.'

'Tomorrow?' Concern screams from the line between her

crinkled brows. I can practically see Dean already trying to run the logistics in her head.

'I have to meet with a few potential sponsors for Skating By, that's what Hawa and I are calling the company, by the way. Skating By. It'll probably be pretty boring that first day, just a bunch of meetings and maybe a couple of photos with local pro-skaters that they want to put me in touch with. But we could stay an extra couple of days, look around the city, make a trip of it.' She pulls the covers in closer around her chest. That beautiful brain of hers whirring away. 'I hear they have good pescatarian food there.'

'How would we pay for it?'

'I can probably only afford to cover my flight,' I admit. Cursing the fact that money makes all romantic gestures more appealing. I don't want that to limit us, though. Love is important; it doesn't have a price tag. I know that she won't stop loving me if I can't pull this off. 'But the accommodation is totally paid for by the sponsors, and I can pack small so you could have the suitcase all to yourself.'

'So I just have to pay for my flight?' Dean nods, an infectious smile splitting her face.

'Is that a yes?'

She's got that look of mischief about her that I adore, and it takes all my effort to hold back from kissing her until she's answered.

'That depends, are you asking me to run away with you, Dexter Carpenter-Brown?'

Setting

When writing this novel, I toyed with creating a picturesque fake English town to set it in, but this is, ultimately, a story about coming home. The further I got into the drafting process, the clearer it became that the city I was writing was my own, so I allowed it to become that.

There is often an urge to homogenise the British identity, but it's not all one thing; it's not even one country. Our accents change every twenty miles, an alarming amount of the population is fighting to heat their homes in winter, and half of us are battling against the last vestiges of the empire.

Moving abroad, I realised that to many people, 'British' only means white Londoners, monarchy, and tea. I don't have a taste for any of those things, so I chose not to write about them.

Romance novels often only show an idealised life. If your protagonist is struggling financially or perpetually unemployed, you can bet that their new partner will have found a way to make that disappear by the end of the book. It is, after all, very easy to imagine falling in love with a millionaire who can erase all your debt or sweep you away at a moment's notice, and much harder to romanticise minimum wage life and the uncertainty that comes with it.

But that is the reality many of us live and fall in love in.

When writing, I wanted to echo that experience, prove that

you can live and love happily without wealth. Dean is anxious about money in a way that only comes from having had none. That pressure can make you feel guilty any time you spend money or enjoy yourself. Dex lives paycheck to paycheck, with no viable plan to end that process any time soon. It's a hard life, but not a bad one, and the reality for many of us in this world.

I am aware that it doesn't make for a comfortable escape from reality when reading, but it's something I needed to see. A happy ending for people like me in a place I love dearly.

For the non-Brits or just the geographically troubled like myself, Portsmouth is very much real.

It is a small island city down at the very bottom of the country, and the second most densely populated city after London. It's a strange, sometimes shitty and often beautiful place with rising poverty rates, a ludicrously distinctive accent, and an incredible cultural identity.

I have replaced independent shop names with fictitious ones and peppered this book with Pompey-isms like squinny and dinlo just to give it that taste of home. Even that doesn't quite do it justice.

If you ever get the chance, I think it's worth a visit, but then again, I am biased.

Play up.

Playlist

Spotify

1. Girls Make Me Wanna Die - The Aces
2. Homesick (with Sam Fender) - Noah Kahan, Sam Fender
3. why did you invite me to your wedding - Kevin Atwater
4. Yes No Okay - Charli xcx
5. Waiting for You - The Aces
6. Bildungsroman - Chase Petra
7. F.E.M.M.E. - Molly Grace
8. Crashed The Wedding - Busted
9. T.M.I - Meet Me @ The Altar
10. When I Come Around - Green Day
11. Therapist's Wet Dream - Amelia Day
12. Eau D'Bedroom Dancing - Le Tigre
13. Soak Up The Sun - Sheryl Crow
14. She's so Lovely - The Butchies

15. Flirting with Her - Sir Babygirl
16. Teenage Dirtbag - Peach PRC
17. Motivation - Normani
18. More! - Nxdia
19. Her Body Is Bible - FLETCHER
20. ur so pretty - Wasia Project
21. Pretty Girls - Renee Rapp
22. Edge of the Earth - The Beaches
23. Hot and Stupid - Beth McCarthy
24. There's A Honey - Pale Waves
25. Somebody I F*cked Once - Zolita
26. Wish You Would - Butch Baby
27. If I'm Honest - Trousdale
28. I'd Do Anything - Simple Plan
29. Clueless - Beach Bunny
30. I Want To Be With You - chloe moriondo
31. Cruel Summer - Taylor Swift
32. Wild Heart - Towa Bird

Acknowledgements

I've been made aware that this isn't common; however, I love to read every word of the acknowledgements. I can't say why, but I like to be reminded that the stories we read are carried on the backs of so many people.

So, without further ado, here are the people without whom his book would not exist.

First and foremost, a special thanks to my wonderful sensitivity reader, Himani, and my fabulous beta readers. Elise, in particular, dealt with a criminal lack of commas in her draft, some dodgy spellings, and reminded me that this was, in fact, a book and not word soup.

Now, a moment for the cover because, well, look at it! Sabira (@sabiralangevin) worked wonders with this thing in less than ideal circumstances, and I cannot thank them enough for all the people who are about to judge my book based on it! I can't say for certain, but, as a self-proclaimed connoisseur of trans-romance, I believe this might be the first time a main character has been displayed with a taped chest on a front cover, and that's pretty fucking special. When I set out to publish this book, I wanted to pay tribute to classic lesbian pulp novels and getting to work with someone who understood that vision so beautifully was a gift.

On a similar note, part of my research involved combing the archives of lesbian pulp fiction both online and in person.

This would not have been possible without the wonderful work of the Lesbian Herstory Archives in Brooklyn, who allowed me to view their shelves. They have a truly phenomenal collection of history curated there, and it's free to access. Please, if you can, visit and support them further!

I came up with the initial nugget of this story floating in the pool of the lovely (and ever so generous) Sam, so it is safe to say that without him and our fellow Voultori, it would not exist.

Likewise, a massive thanks is owed to my bookselling and publishing friends, particularly Bezi, Cam, Haruka and Nat. Every single piece of advice and encouragement you gave kept me (mostly) sane. You reinforced my faith in romance books even when I felt like a cynic.

Now we get to the big boys, the thank yous that I have a hard time summarising into words. To my family, blood and otherwise, the support you have provided me is not quantifiable. You have shaped the person I am, the way I think and my sense of self. There's a lot of you in this story, hints of truths, snapshots of home, and sentences we've said. There will likely be whispers of your influence in everything I write, so prepare yourself for a lifetime of thanks to come.

It will surprise no one who reads this book to find out that I have older brothers. Many of the sibling feelings I wrote down were just sentiments stolen from my real life and transcribed. I'm really not sure how to acknowledge the impact you had on me (and therefore this book) because it's too fucking large.

I should also thank my parents and apologise for the fact that I finally published something you can read, only for it to be riddled with sex scenes. Sorry! You instilled in me a love of reading and storytelling that few others share, and you have dealt with every seemingly erratic, potentially bonkers choice I've made in life. I love you both endlessly.

And finally, Kylie. This is a novel about love, just shy of 80,000 words dedicated to the art of falling and staying in it. You join me in doing that every day, even the hard ones. While writing this book, there were a lot of hard ones, some really, genuinely shitty days, and you held my hand through every single second of it. I couldn't ask for a better partner. I can't wait to wake up and show you I love you for the rest of my days.

About the Author

Westley James is not a real person but rather a combination of two pirates and rejected name suggestions cobbled together to make them harder to Google. They write queer nonsense, only half of which is decipherable, drink a lot of rum, and hate writing bios in the third person. He moved from the British seaside to Brooklyn for love and can currently be found enjoying the delights of second puberty at the hands of testosterone.